# THE GHOST RIDERS

Center Point
Large Print

Also by James J. Griffin and available from
Center Point Large Print:

*Death Stalks the Rangers*
*Death Rides the Rails*
*Ranger's Revenge*
*Texas Jeopardy*
*Blood Ties*
*Renegade Ranger*
*Fight for Freedom*
*Tough Month for a Ranger*

**This Large Print Book carries the
Seal of Approval of N.A.V.H.**

# THE GHOST RIDERS

## A Texas Ranger
## Jim Blawcyzk Story

# James J. Griffin

CENTER POINT LARGE PRINT
THORNDIKE, MAINE

*For All the Western Fictioneers,
and Everyone Who is Keeping
the Western Novel Alive.*

This Center Point Large Print edition is published in
the year 2020 by arrangement with the author.

The text of this Large Print edition is unabridged.
In other aspects, this book may vary
from the original edition.
Printed in the United States of America
on permanent paper.
Set in 16-point Times New Roman type.

ISBN: 978-1-64358-540-6

The Library of Congress has cataloged this record under
Library of Congress Control Number: 2019954743

# 1

"I now pronounce you man and wife. You may kiss the bride."

With these few words during the Mass of their wedding, Father Augustus Clermont of St. Cecelia's Church in San Leanna, Texas united young Texas Ranger Charles Edward Blawcyzk and Mary Jane Jarratt in the Sacrament of Holy Matrimony. Julia Blawcyzk, Charlie's mother, sighed as she thought back on the ceremony, and the reception which followed. Her husband, and Charlie's father, Texas Ranger Lieutenant James Blawcyzk, had warned her while the plans were being made that Polish wedding receptions often ran for three days or longer.

Julia had scoffed at that notion. She'd been proven wrong when, two days after Charlie and Mary Jane left for their wedding trip to Galveston, the party finally wound down. Three days of eating, drinking, and polkaing had left her exhausted, but happy. She hoped her son and his new bride were enjoying their honeymoon. Mary Jane had never seen the Gulf of Mexico. She had seemed almost as excited about that as her first night together with Charlie as man and wife.

Julia was in Charlie's bedroom, looking at his things. Memories came flooding back. She'd long since gotten used to often being alone, what with both Jim and Charlie gone for weeks at a time on assignments for the Rangers. Now, however, with Charlie about to start his new life, a feeling of loneliness swept over her. A tear trickled down her cheek as she held a tintype of Charlie at eight years old, with his first horse, Ted.

Julia's reverie was interrupted by the barking of an approaching dog. She hurried onto the porch to see Jim, and Charlie's collie, Pal, heading toward the house. Jim was shirtless and drenched with sweat, his chaps slapping against his legs as he walked. Sweat stained his Stetson, and soaked the bandanna hanging limply around his neck. He was scratching the old saber scar which ran across his stomach. Pal bounded alongside him, barking furiously at something Jim held in his right hand.

A delicious warmth suffused Julia as she watched her husband approach. Even after all these years of marriage, the sight of his body still filled her with desire. True, as was inevitable, Jim had aged some over the years. His face was bronzed and wrinkled from constant exposure to the harsh Texas sun and wind, and traces of gray were showing in the hair at his temples and around his ears. Still, that blond hair was as thick and unruly as it ever was, and Jim's eyes were still a deep crystalline blue. He hadn't gained much weight with the passage of time, either. His belly was still flat, his waist and hips still slim.

"Jim? Where's your shirt?" she asked, when Jim reached the porch.

"Ask your son's dang dog," Jim answered. He opened his hand to reveal a scrap of cloth. "This is what's left of it. G'wan Pal, get on outta here!"

He tossed the scrap into the yard. Pal grabbed it in his teeth and ran off, shaking the cloth and growling furiously.

"I took off my shirt and tossed it over a branch while I was standin' up a couple of fence posts that went down in the last storm," Jim said. "Next thing I knew Pal had grabbed it and run off. By the time he was through runnin' the brush and scrub, that shirt was torn to shreds. It was my favorite, too."

"You need some new ones anyway," Julia answered. "You're back earlier than I expected. It's not quite suppertime yet. Why don't you take a bath? By the time you're finished, I'll have everything on the table."

"Soon as I care for the horses," Jim said. He gave Julia a quick kiss on the cheek, then headed for the corral. Pal came running back and followed Julia into the kitchen. She opened the oven, cut a piece off the roast, and gave it to him.

"Thank you, Pal," she said. "I never thought I'd be able to get Jim to toss out that raggedy old shirt." Julia had tried several times to discard the faded, worn, stained, and much-patched garment, but somehow Jim always knew when she threw it in the trash, and retrieved it. He never gave her the opportunity to get rid of the shirt while he was away from home, either. Every time he left on an assignment, that old shirt was either on his back or tucked in his saddlebags. At long last, thanks to Charlie's rambunctious collie, the shirt had met its demise.

After feeding Sam, Sizzle, Ted, Splash, and Ben and Jerry, the draft horses, and making sure they had plenty of water for the night, Jim fed and watered the rest of the animals, the paint horses he and Julia raised and sold on their small ranch, the milk cow, and the chickens. The chores done, he headed for the house.

*Jim had come home from a Ranger patrol several months previously to find an addition built onto the back of his small ranch house. He pulled Sizzle to a halt as he stared at the new room. Behind him, Sam looked at the addition and snorted.*

*"What the devil is that, boys?" he exclaimed to his horses. It didn't take long for him to find out. Before his feet were even out of the stirrups, Julia was on the porch and pleading with him to*

*hurry inside. She made him close his eyes until they were in the new room.*

*"Now, Jim," she said.*

*Jim opened his eyes to see a full-sized clawfoot bathtub in the addition. Even more amazing, water was piped directly to the tub. A hole in the bottom was apparently a drain.*

*"What?" was all he could say.*

*"Isn't it wonderful?" Julia said. "I've wanted something like this ever since our trip to Kansas City, and our hotel had tubs like this. I've saved every dime I could, until I had enough money to pay for it. There's even a boiler outside which heats the water, so I don't have to boil kettles on the stove, then haul them in here to fill the tub. And it drains, too. No more dumping water from a heavy tub. Do you like it? I wanted to surprise you."*

*"Well, you sure did," Jim said.*

*"You're not mad, are you?"*

*"Of course not," Jim said. "It's just a bit of a shock, seein' somethin' this fancy in my own house."*

*"But do you like it?"*

*"I'll have to try it first."*

*Jim did try the tub, and had to admit it was as luxurious as any tub he'd ever bathed in at a big city hotel. It didn't take him long to wonder how he'd ever managed without one. Thanks to Julia's wish and determination, the Blawcyzk house now had something most residences in Texas, even many of the finest, didn't have . . . a full bathtub with hot and cold running water. Jim looked forward to soaking in it every time he returned home.*

When Jim reached the house, he headed straight for the bathroom. Julia had already drawn his bath. The tub was filled to the brim with steaming hot water and bubbles . . . and wife.

"I thought this was gonna be my bath," he said. "And hot water? In this summer heat? I was thinkin' of a cool bath."

"It is," Julia answered. "There's plenty of room in here for the both of us . . . as if you didn't already know that." She lifted her hand from under the suds and languorously patted the edge of the tub, then draped one leg over the side. "C'mon in and join me, cowboy. The water's absolutely perfect. I promise you, it's not too hot at all."

After several weeks on the trail, followed by Charlie and Mary Jane's wedding, then days of working around the ranch, Jim didn't need a second invitation. He practically ripped off his clothes to join Julia. He settled deep into the water, lying back against her.

"Ahh . . . this is heaven," he said, as Julia began to massage his neck. "Soakin' in a nice, hot bath with an angel. Sure beats tryin' to wash up in some cold, muddy creek."

Julia's hands drifted lower. When she tickled his ribs, Jim laughed uncontrollably. That was one of the big, rugged Ranger's few weaknesses. He was extremely ticklish along his ribs. Once Julia started in on those, Jim soon was completely helpless.

"Stop, Julia, please," he pleaded.

"And if I don't?"

"I'll just have to do this."

Jim rolled onto his stomach, wrapped his arms around Julia, and together they both sank deeper into the tub. Jim crushed his lips to hers.

"Oh, Jim!" she gasped, as they disappeared under the bubbles.

# 2

Charlie Blawcyzk was lying in his bed, in the suite he and his new bride, Mary Jane, had taken at the beachfront Galveston Island Hotel. Mary Jane was in the sitting room, composing a letter to her parents. When Charlie had pointed out to her they would most likely arrive back home before the letter even got there, she told him she wanted to describe the coast for her parents while she was right on the spot, not from memories several weeks old. It didn't matter to her which got to San Leanna first.

Charlie locked his hands behind his head and propped himself up on his pillow. He smiled to himself as he thought back on their arrival in Galveston, and the last few days. They'd left their wedding reception long before it was over, in order to catch their afternoon train from Austin to Galveston. By the time they reached their hotel, it was close to midnight.

"Well, Charlie, here we are," Mary Jane said, once the bellboy had deposited their luggage and left. "What do you think we should do next?"

"I'm thinkin' some shut-eye would feel good right about now," Charlie answered. "It's been

13

a real long day, and I'm plumb tuckered out."

"What was that?" Mary Jane flashed him a look that could kill.

"I'm only kiddin', Mary Jane. I guess mebbe I should give you a kiss."

"That's more like it. Here." Mary Jane kissed him on the cheek, then the lips. "How's that?"

"It's a start. But, where do we go from here?"

"You mean you don't know, Charlie?"

"Well, I've got the general idea, but I've never actually done this before."

"You can't be serious."

"I'm deadly serious, Mary Jane. I've never been with a woman before."

"Even with all the saloons and gambling halls you've visited while riding for the Rangers? All the women you must have met in those places? And you never took a woman to bed, not even once?"

"Nope. I can't say I wasn't tempted, more'n once, but I was raised to wait until I was married. My pa didn't lay with a woman until he married my ma, and he taught me his values. Well, that and the Commandments. 'Thou Shalt Not Commit Adultery', says the Lord. Then, once we were engaged, I never would have thought of bein' unfaithful to you. You know that. So, I reckon this is new territory for both of us. But it should be a lotta fun figurin' this out."

"I was hoping more along the lines of exciting," Mary Jane said.

"Should be that too." Charlie wrapped his arms around her and kissed her, hard on the lips. He kept kissing, moving his lips down her neck, to her cleavage. Mary Jane responded by slipping her hand inside his shirt, to rub his chest, then his belly. She slipped her hand lower, feeling a response in his groin.

"Um, Charlie," she said. She pulled her hand from inside his pants.

"Yes?" He nibbled at her left ear.

"I think we should stop."

Charlie pulled back. "Huh?"

Mary Jane laughed at the expression on his face, a combination of shock, disappointment, and frustration.

"No, I don't mean it that way, silly. Just for a minute. I believe this will work better if we take our clothes off."

"Y'know, I believe you're right," Charlie hastily stripped off his clothes. He sat on the edge of the bed, waiting in anticipation. Mary Jane deliberately took longer, peeling off one article at a time, until she finally stood before Charlie, completely undressed.

"Now I'm ready, Charlie."

"Wait just a bit, Mary Jane. Now it's my turn to say hold on a minute. I just want to look at you, for a little while."

Charlie ran his gaze over his wife. He'd seen paintings of nude females, of course, but this was the first time he'd seen an actual, flesh and blood woman standing in front of him, completely naked. He took in the shape of her body, the light brown hair lying softly on her shoulders and falling to her full, round breasts, the curve of her hips, her long, shapely legs. For her part, Mary Jane looked him up and down, his broad chest, with its thin covering of blond hair, his flat belly and slim hips, and the obvious signs in his groin that he was ready to make love to her, to take her, fully and completely, as his wife.

"That's long enough, Charlie." She pushed him gently back on the mattress, lay on top of him, and molded her body to his.

"Mary Jane, how long are you gonna be writin' that letter?" Charlie called. His reflections on their wedding night had him ready to make love again.

"I won't be much longer, Charlie. Just a few more pages."

Charlie sighed. His mind drifted once more. The last few days, of course, hadn't been all one session of lovemaking after another. Mary Jane had insisted on shopping, naturally. She had been thrilled at her first glimpse of the Gulf of Mexico. They'd gone for several longs walks on the sand, just holding hands, not kissing in public, of course. Even for a newlywed husband and wife, that would be improper. Charlie was amused by the bathing suits worn by visitors to the beach. The women were completely covered, except for their feet. Their outfits had voluminous skirts, and even their heads were covered with large, wide-brimmed hats. The men were also completely covered, except for their lower arms, and their legs halfway below the knees.

"Dunno how they can swim at all, all wrapped up like that," Charlie said. "I'd sink like a rock if I tried swimmin' in one of those get-ups."

"Especially if you were wearing one of the ladies' suits," Mary Jane said, with a giggle. "You'd look pretty funny, too. And it would be pretty hard to explain to your Ranger partners."

"You know what I mean, Mary Jane," Charlie answered. "Heck, back home all we do is strip off all our clothes and jump in the creek."

"Charlie!" Mary Jane said, pretending to be shocked.

"Hey, don't play the innocent young thing with me," Charlie said. "I know some of you gals do the same, when us men aren't around."

"And sometimes when you are, too!"

"Mary Jane!" Now it was Charlie's turn to be shocked.

"Well, when we get back home you and I can go swimming together, if you'd like, Charlie."

"What do you mean, if I'd like?"

"I thought that was what you'd say. But if you really want to take a swim here in Galveston, I understand there are beaches, separated for men and boys, women and girls. You could find one of those and go there. From what I have heard, just like at home, you don't need to wear anything at all."

"You really think I want to leave you and spend an afternoon on the beach with a bunch of men, rather'n with you, Mary Jane? Forget it. In fact, let's head back to our room."

"Charlie! It's the middle of the afternoon."

"I know." Charlie grinned wickedly. "There's no law says we have to wait until after dark to make love."


Charlie's reverie was interrupted when Mary Jane returned to the bedroom.

"I've finished my letter, Charlie," she said. "We can mail it in the morning."

"About time," Charlie grumbled. "I've been waitin' for you."

"I can see that," Mary Jane said. "Do you ever intend to put your clothes back on?"

"Not as long as I'm in this bed, and you're here with me." He sat up, took her by the wrist, and pulled her to him.


After their lovemaking session, they lay side by side.

"Charlie," Mary Jane said. "What's going to happen when we get back home?"

"We'll probably make love a lot," Charlie answered. "At least, I sure hope we will."

"Charlie, I'm being serious. How soon do you think you'll have to leave?"

"With the Rangers, you can never be certain," Charlie answered. He shrugged. "But it'll most likely be pretty quick. Not long after we're back in San Leanna."

"So you'll be on the trail, heading to who knows where, chasing outlaws, and I'll be back at work in my family's store, worried about you."

"You know what I do, Mary Jane. We had this talk before we got married. I'm a Texas Ranger, and always will be."

"I know, and I can accept that. But I'm a woman, and always will be. You can't stop me from worrying when you're gone."

"I know. All I ask is don't fret too much. Don't worry yourself sick. Besides, now that I have you, I've got a powerful reason to come home without any bullets in me," Charlie said.

"You're not helping, Charlie."

"Then perhaps this will." Charlie rolled onto his side, took Mary Jane in his arms, and kissed her, once again.

# 3

While Jim and Julia made love in the tub, nearly one hundred and fifty miles to the west of their home, in the little settlement of Menardville, seat of sparsely populated Menard County, an entirely different scene was taking place. Under the cover of a vicious west Texas dust storm, a group of twenty raiders, dressed in white robes, with white, wide-brimmed hats on their heads and white bandannas pulled up over their faces, all mounted on white or gray horses, was attacking the town.

"Down every last one of 'em you can," the leader ordered, as he gunned down the general store's owner. "Fewer we leave alive, the fewer there are to follow us . . . or be witnesses. Jones, Martin, get in that store, clean out the cash drawer and whatever you can carry."

A bullet fired from the two story county courthouse steps split the air just over his head. He ripped his horse around, fired twice, and Sheriff Tyler Dwight was slammed against the courthouse wall, with two bullets in his chest. Another of the raiders put a bullet through the belly of Deputy Mike Conrad. Conrad doubled over and somersaulted to the road. The only remaining deputy, Bill Hogan, managed to clip one of the raiders, hitting him high in his left arm, then return fire from the raiders left him riddled with bullets. He slumped over a hitch rail, bent double, blood flowing from his bullet-torn body running down his arms and fingers, off his head, and dripping to the road.

Methodically, the raiders looted the town, shooting everyone they came across, emptying the bank's vault, taking every bottle of liquor from the saloon, stealing all the horses from the livery stable, even taking the dresses from the dressmaker's shop and the hats from the milliner's. When they had grabbed everything they could carry, they galloped off and disappeared into the dust storm, leaving most of Menardville in flames. Except for a few citizens who had reached safety in the courthouse, six or seven who managed to find hiding places elsewhere, and two who survived by playing dead, the raiders had wiped out almost the entire population of the town.

# 4

Two days later, in the dead of a cloudy night with a new moon, the raiders hit some thirty miles east of Menardville. This time, their target was the hamlet of Brady, which had just been chosen as the McCulloch County seat. Brady was so small it hadn't yet hired a town marshal and deputy, instead relying on the county sheriff to provide deputies to protect the town.

The raiders started the attack by throwing a lit coal-oil lamp through the front window of the sheriff's office. Two deputies, young Dave Kenedy, who had been appointed to his post only six weeks previously, and veteran Hugh Murphey, were on duty, but, at this time of night, once they had made their rounds of the town both were sleeping in bunks in the back room. County Sheriff Dale McIlroy allowed his deputies that privilege, as long as they slept fully dressed, with their boots on, and their gunbelts around their waists, in case of trouble. Of course, in the six years McIlroy had been sheriff, once the saloons closed down there had never been so much as a store broken into, let alone real trouble.

The lamp shattered when it hit the floor, the oil spreading and quickly taking flame. Kenedy and

Murphey rolled out of their beds at the sound of gunfire, the crackling of flames, and the yells of the outlaws.

"We gotta get outta here, Dave, before we roast," Murphey yelled. Already, both men were choking on the thick, black smoke filling the office.

"Listen to the gunfire out there, Hugh," Kenedy shouted back. "We'll be shot down soon as we hit the door. We ain't got a chance, no matter what we do."

"Take this! Mebbe we can blast our way outta this furnace." Murphey pulled two shotguns off the gun rack and tossed one to Kenedy. "On the count of three, I'm gonna yank open the door. We'll go out runnin'. Stay low, and blast the first gunmen you see. Once you've emptied both barrels of that scattergun, pull out your six-gun and keep shootin'. With any luck, we'll get a few of 'em, and surprise those raiders enough we'll scare 'em off."

"It's more likely we're gonna get ourselves shot fulla holes," Kenedy answered.

"I hate to admit it, but you're probably right," Murphey admitted. "Still, I'd rather die from a bullet in my guts than burnin' to death. You goin' with me, or you gonna stay here and fry?"

"Well, since you put it that way . . . let's go."

"All right. One . . . two . . . three!" Murphey pulled open the door, and both deputies burst outside.

Kenedy got off one barrel of his shotgun before at least half-a-dozen bullets ripped into him. Somehow, he remained on his feet, and managed to pull the trigger of the second barrel. The buckshot didn't have a chance to spread before it hit one of the raiders, the close-bunched shot raking across his back. The raider let loose a high-pitched screech, slumped over his horse's neck, and rolled to the street. Kenedy dropped to his knees. Several more slugs hit him, slamming him back, dead.

Murphey's first shot tore two raiders out of their saddles. A third galloped his horse up to the deputy, leveled his pistol, and put two quick bullets into Murphey's belly. Murphey pulled the second trigger of his shotgun as he jackknifed. The buckshot plowed into the dirt at his feet, then Murphey followed it, pitching to his face in the small crater the shot had dug out.

"Couple of you pick up the three of our men those blasted lawmen gunned down," the apparent leader of the group ordered. "We can't chance anyone identifyin' 'em. Gotta take 'em with us, and get rid of 'em later. Hack, Mayberry, follow me. The rest of you, start cleanin' out this town."

The leader and the two men he'd chosen galloped to a small, white-painted house at the far end of the main street. Sheriff Dale McIlroy was inside, along with his wife and two teenage sons. Roused from his sleep by the initial gunfire,

McIlroy had thrown on his boots and gunbelt, and attempted to rush to the aid of his town. However, the raiders had stationed four men outside his house, and as soon as McIlroy opened the door a fusillade of lead drove him back inside. Now, he and his two sons, Chuck and Eddie, were exchanging shots with the outlaws.

"Get ready to pull back, men," the leader ordered, as he rode up to the house. "We've wasted enough time on this small-town lawman already. Keep me covered."

He reached inside the white robe he wore, and pulled out a stick of dynamite and a bundle of lucifers. He snapped off one of the matches from the bundle, scratched it to life on his saddlehorn, and touched it to the dynamite's fuse. He waited to make sure the fuse took, and, once it spluttered to life, tossed the dynamite through the sheriff's living room window.

"Let's git, men!" The raiders turned their horses and raced for safety. A moment later, the sheriff's house exploded with a tremendous roar.

"They'll be pickin' up pieces of that lawman all over half of Texas," one of the raiders said, laughing.

"Never mind that," the leader said. "Time to finish what we started, and get on outta here."

Twenty minutes later, the raiders raced out of town, leaving behind a ruin of burning buildings, looted businesses, and death.

# 5

Julia had been searching everywhere for Jim, to no avail. He'd seemed especially restless the past few days, even more so than usual when he'd been home for too long, rather than out riding the trails for the Rangers. She was used to him getting antsy after he'd been home for a while. However, this time he seemed particularly troubled. The faraway look in his blue eyes when she'd tried to talk to him at breakfast told her she might as well have been talking to one of his horses, for all the response she got. In fact, she had told Jim she was indeed going outside to talk to Sam, his old paint. Jim's reply had been a "That's nice, dear," followed by an unintelligible mumble.

Julia gave up attempting to make conversation with him, and did head to the corrals. Like Jim, it always soothed her to just watch the horses as they nibbled at hay, chased each other around, or dozed in the sun. However, she didn't have the almost mystical connection to horses he did. She'd never seen another person who could communicate with the equine species as well as her husband. Charlie came close, but even he didn't have quite the ability with horses his father did.

When Julia came back inside, Jim was nowhere to be found.

"Jim?" There was no answer. Julia had searched through the house, finding no sign of him. There was not a sign he'd been in the bathtub he'd grown to enjoy even more than she did. She then looked through the pastures, corrals, and barn. Sizzle and Sam were still in the main pasture, so she knew Jim couldn't have gone far. No horseman, cowboy, or Ranger ever walked if he could ride his horse. She tried the swimming hole in the creek, thinking perhaps he had decided to cool off with a swim, but he wasn't there, either. Frustrated and a bit angry, Julia returned to the house. If Jim wanted to disappear, so be it. She got along just fine without him for weeks on end anyway, thank you very much. But he'd better not expect any supper tonight, either. She wasn't about to sit across the table from a man whose thoughts were a million miles away.

Pal was waiting on the porch for her. He thumped his tail when she climbed the stairs, then followed her inside. He ran down the hall, whining, and went into Charlie's bedroom.

"Pal, Charlie's not here," Julia called after him. "He'll be home in a few days. Get back here, boy."

When Pal didn't respond, Julia followed him. She stepped into Charlie's room, and found Jim, sitting on the edge of their son's bed. He held the same tintype of Charlie and his horse that she'd been crying over just a few days earlier. Lying in his lap was the rusty old Colt which had been Charlie's toy gun as a youngster. Jim's eyes were moist. It was obvious he also had been crying. Pal was sitting at his feet, licking his hand.

"Jim, I've been looking all over for you. Where have you been?"

"Just took a wander around the place, then came back here, to Charlie's room," he answered.

"You miss him, don't you? Perhaps even more than I do. I can see you've been crying, at least a bit," Julia said. She sat alongside him and placed a hand on his shoulder.

"Of course I miss him," Jim said. "He grew up so quick. It just seems like yesterday I was teachin' him how to ride and shoot. Now he's all grown up, and married. Pretty soon he and Mary Jane'll be havin' kids of their own."

"If he's ever home long enough to manage that," Julia answered. "After all, it takes two people to make a child."

"Hey, we got Charlie, didn't we?" Jim said.

"Of course. And I don't blame your being away so much for us not having additional children," Julia said. "If it was in God's plans, we would have had more."

"Well, at least we got a good one," Jim said, with a sigh.

"We certainly did," Julia answered. "Listen,

you've been moping around this place long enough. Why don't you ride over to the McCues', find Smoky, then head into town? Smoky can have a few beers, you can have your sarsaparillas, and you can play some cards. Get supper while you're there. That will give me a night off from cooking. A change of scenery might be just what you need."

"I get plenty of those ridin' for the Rangers," Jim said.

"You know what I mean, Jim. Since you haven't gotten any orders, and it's been almost three weeks at home now, you're starting to act like a caged bear. So go get Smoky and have some fun. In fact, I think I'll ride over to Smoky and Cindy's with you. I'll visit with Cindy while you and Smoky are in town. I haven't seen her since Charlie and Mary Jane's wedding, so it will give us the chance to catch up on some gossip. What do you say?"

"I say it couldn't hurt," Jim answered. "Let's go saddle the horses."

Forty minutes later, they rode up to the small ranch owned by Jim's long-time Ranger partner, Sergeant Smoky McCue, and his wife, Cindy. They were on the front porch when Jim and Julia came into the yard.

"Jim, Julia! Howdy," Smoky yelled out. "What brings you by? Jim, don't tell me you've heard from Cap'n Storm, and we've got orders."

"No, it's nothin' like that, Smoke," Jim answered. "Julia decided she was tired of havin' me underfoot. She thought perhaps a night in town, playin' cards and havin' a few drinks, would help me settle down a mite. I have to admit, I've been pacin' around the house like a cornered mountain lion."

"So I said we'd come over here, and I could visit with Cindy while you two headed into town," Julia added.

"Julia, that's the best idea I've heard in weeks," Cindy said. "Smoky's been gettin' pretty restless too. And it's been far too long since you and I have had a nice, long visit, just the two of us. In fact, my darling husband, why don't you and Jim just spend the night in town? That will give me and Julia a night to ourselves, also. And Jim, don't worry about your stock. Julia can spend the night here, then I'll ride over to your place with her in the morning, and help her tend to the animals. Is that all right with you, Julia?"

"It sounds like the perfect plan," Julia answered.

"So as long as you two are agreeable, everything is set," Cindy said.

"Boy howdy, you won't have to ask me twice," Smoky said. "I'll saddle Midnight and be ready to ride in a jiffy."

Jim whistled as he rode along, while Smoky, as always, had a cigarette dangling from his lips. The two Rangers couldn't have been more opposite in appearance. Jim was tall, lean, and fair, not handsome but ruggedly good-looking, with unruly blond hair under the tan Stetson he wore, and clear blue eyes. His face usually wore an easy smile, and his eyes were almost always sunny. However, his face grew hard, and those blue eyes could glitter like chips of ice, whenever he faced a lawbreaker. He was also left-handed, so the heavy Colt Peacemaker he carried hung at his left hip. Unlike many of the Rangers, he didn't wear a second six-gun for a spare, but preferred to reload in the middle of a gun battle if necessary. His predilection for brightly colored shirts was well known, and the subject of much teasing from his fellow Rangers.

Smoky, his long-time riding partner, was a bit shorter than average, with a wiry build. He was dark-complected, and had eyes of such a deep brown hue they almost appeared black. He sported a pencil-thin moustache, of which he was inordinately proud. However, his most distinctive feature was his hair. It was jet black, but through some freak of genetics had gone prematurely gray not at the roots, but at the tips. This gave it an appearance of a puff of smoke, which had supplied Smoky his nickname. His given name was known only to a very few. His wife Cindy, and Jim, were two of those. Even after all these years, Jim, sworn to secrecy, had not revealed that name to anyone else, not even Julia. In contrast to Jim's fondness for bright shirts and plain old blue denims, Smoky always dressed mainly in black, except for a bright red neckerchief looped around his neck. One of the few men who wore two guns, and who could shoot equally well with either hand, his twin Colts rested in black holsters, attached to a black gunbelt around his waist. And unlike Jim, who never smoke, cursed, or drank anything stronger than sarsaparilla, Smoky enjoyed his tobacco and liquor, and had been known on more than one occasion to let out a violent string of cuss words. While Jim had always been a one-woman man, loyal only to his wife, Julia, Smoky, until he met Cindy Lou, had been a ladies' man, ever ready to spend a night with a woman. The only things the two had in common were their love of cards, particularly poker, and their determination as Texas Rangers to bring outlaws to justice. That, and their unquenchable friendship.

Even their horses were different. For years, Jim had ridden Sam, a one-man animal, a palomino and white splotched tobiano paint with a vicious temper. After Sam had been crippled by outlaws during a raid on Jim's ranch, Jim continued to use him as a pack horse, and another paint, Sizzle, an overo with sorrel and white patches, became his riding horse. Sizzle was as gentle and sweet-natured as Sam was vicious. However, like Sam, he was also a one-man horse, allowing no one to ride him but Jim. Smoky favored dark horses, the first being his steeldust gray, Charcoal. Once Charcoal got too old to carry Smoky for weeks on end, he was put out to pasture, and replaced with Midnight, the jet-black gelding Smoky was now riding.

However, as different as they were in appearance and personality, both men were exactly alike when it came to dealing with outlaws: Tough as bulldogs, and tenacious as terriers. Once they were on the trail of desperadoes, they never quit until their quarry was brought to justice . . . or dead, with Jim's or Smoky's bullets, or both, in them. It didn't matter how much they were out-numbered, or how great the odds against them. The only way Jim and Smoky would ever return without the men they were after would be in coffins, riddled by the renegades' bullets. So far, that hadn't happened, although both had been severely wounded more than once in the course of their Ranger careers. Their commanding officer, Captain Earl Storm, usually saved his toughest cases for them.

"Where do you want to have supper, Jim?" Smoky asked, once they reached the edge of town.

"I'm thinkin' we'll head over to O'Malley's

place," Jim answered. "I'm ready for a nice, thick steak, smothered in onions, with some of Don's fried potatoes on the side. And Ellen's pecan pie to finish up."

"That sounds like a good choice to me," Smoky answered. "Then the Shenandoah for drinks and cards?"

"Yep. Beau serves up a lot better drink than Stan over at the Silver Horse."

"How would you know that?" Smoky asked. "You never drink anythin' but pop or milk."

"Because the pop's always colder at Beau's place. And just as a connoisseur of wine can tell the difference from one to another, I can tell one sarsaparilla from another."

Smoky merely snorted, and shook his head. Sizzle did the same.

"Horse, when I want your opinion, I'll ask for it," Jim told him. "Move on up there. My belly's complainin' it ain't been filled for far too long now." He kicked Sizzle into a lope.

A few moments later, the pair allowed their horses a short drink from the trough in the town plaza, then crossed the square and reined up in front of O'Malley's Restaurant. They dismounted and looped their horses' reins over the hitch rail, Jim as always giving Sizzle a peppermint, then headed inside. The restaurant was bustling, with almost every table filled. Folks came from miles around for the food and atmosphere. O'Malley's was known for its steaks, and especially for Don O'Malley's fried potatoes. He seasoned them with a blend of spices of his own creation, a secret recipe he divulged to no one, not even his wife or six kids. He had a copy written down, sealed, and locked in his safe, with instructions it was only to be opened in the event of his death.

Ellen O'Malley's touch was evident in the restaurant's décor, which was far more genteel than most frontier eateries. White lace curtains hung at the window, and white linen tablecloths covered each table. Wall shelves held her collection of blue-willow patterned plates, and a vase on each table held a single fresh flower. The waitresses wore red or blue gingham dresses, and white aprons. Ellen insisted on keeping the place immaculately clean. Even the ashtrays were emptied regularly.

"Smoky! Jim!" Ellen, who with her husband Don owned the restaurant, called when she spotted them. "C'mon over here. We've got one table left."

Jim and Smoky crossed the crowded dining room to the table Ellen had indicated, in the far back corner, on the opposite wall from the kitchen door.

"Howdy, Ellen," Jim said. "Real busy in here tonight."

"It certainly is," she answered. "It's been this way all day. You boys want coffee?"

"Now Ellen, what kind of a silly question is that?" Smoky said, chuckling.

"I guess it was a pretty useless one," Ellen answered, with a laugh of her own. "I'll be right back with a full pot."

Jim and Smoky exchanged greetings with several of the other customers. San Leanna was a small town, so they were acquainted with just about everyone who lived there. Smoky rolled and lit a cigarette while he waited for Ellen to return with their coffee.

"This was a fine idea Julia had, Jim," he said. "I need a night on the town."

"I reckon I do too, Smoke, even though I didn't realize it," Jim answered. "Matter of fact, after we eat we should stop at Jarratt's on our way to the saloon, and pick up a little something for our wives, just to surprise 'em."

"That's a good thought," Smoky agreed. "Women always like unexpected gifts. Ah, here comes Ellen with our coffee."

"You waitin' tables tonight, Ellen?" Jim asked, as she put two mugs and a full coffee pot in front of them.

"I've got no choice. Two of our girls are out with the grippe, and Ellie Scott asked for the night off. You know Jud Baker's been courtin' her. I think tonight's the night he's finally gonna ask her to marry him."

"Ellie could do far worse," Smoky said. "Jud's

a real hard worker. He took that patch of ground no one thought was worth anythin' and turned it into a nice little farm."

"I think he'll make her very happy," Ellen said. "Speaking of wives, how are Julia and Cindy? And have you heard from Charlie or Mary Jane, Jim?"

"Julia's doin' fine," Jim said. "She's just a bit tired of havin' me underfoot, so she sent me out for a night in town. Said it would do me some good. And save her from havin' to cook supper. Far as the youngsters, no. I'd imagine they're too busy to take the time to write home. I'd bet a hat we don't hear from 'em until they get back home."

"Cindy's fine too," Smoky added. "Julia's visitin' her while Jim and I are outta their hair."

"Well, give them both my love. And since you're after supper, how about it? Are you boys ready to order?"

"I sure am," Jim answered.

"Jim's always ready to eat. You should know that by now, Ellen," Smoky said. "Especially when it comes to sweets."

"Hey, you don't do so bad yourself, Smoke," Jim retorted. "Now, if you'll stop interruptin'. Ellen, I'll have the biggest steak you have back in the kitchen, a double order of Don's spuds, and whatever vegetable's on the menu tonight."

"That would be pinto beans."

"Good. Plenty of those, and you know how I want my steak cooked."

"I certainly do. Until it's just about burned black as charcoal. All right, Jim. How about you, Smoky?"

"I'll have the same, only my steak's gotta be so rare it's almost still mooin'," Smoky answered.

"You've got it. And I'm imagining you'll both want dessert?"

"Ellen, that's an even sillier question than askin' if we wanted coffee," Jim answered. "If you don't save me an extra large slice of your pecan pie, I'll have to arrest you."

"Oh, really? On what charges?" Ellen asked.

"Fraud, for promising pecan pie you don't have. You can't torture a man by promisin' him pecan pie, then not deliverin'."

"Jim, you know, sometimes we do run out. You're not the only person around here who likes pecan pie," Ellen answered. "But don't worry. I baked several today, so we have plenty. Let me put your orders in. Don'll have your food ready quick as he can. Of course, it does take a bit longer to burn your steak, Jim. I'll bring some bread and butter to hold you over."

"Thanks, Ellen."

"You're welcome."

Smoky and Jim engaged in small talk while waiting for their meal.

39

"There's a few strangers in here tonight, Smoke," Jim observed.

"Seem to be," Smoky agreed. "They don't seem to be lookin' for trouble, though. They appear downright peaceable."

"San Leanna's not the kind of town that attracts troublemakers," Jim said. "There's not much reason for people to come here, unless they're visitin' friends or family, or conductin' business. It's not like we're a big cattle, mining, or railroad town. Men lookin' for excitement'll generally head to a bigger place, where there's more saloons, gamblin' parlors, and sportin' houses. Plus don't forget, Tom Colburn and his deputies do a good job of keepin' everyone in line."

Tom Colburn was the San Leanna town marshal.

"And let's hope the town stays this way," Smoky said. "Ah, here comes our supper now."

Ellen carried a tray laden with food, and placed it on their table.

"Here you go," she said, as she set their plates in front of them. "One burnt to cinders steak for you, Jim, and one still on the hoof for Smoky. Lots of spuds, and plenty of beans. Just don't light any matches for awhile after you eat them beans. I've also brought some more bread and butter, and a fresh pot of coffee."

"Boy howdy, Ellen, that steak you gave Jim

is the biggest one I've ever seen," Smoky said. "Looks like an entire heifer."

"Well, he asked for the biggest one we had, and that's what he got," Ellen answered. "And I'm not worried. We both know Jim. He could eat that steak, another one the same size, and still polish off an entire pie for dessert."

"Hey, don't exaggerate," Jim protested. "I might have to leave a few beans on my plate to be able to do that."

"I'm not so certain about that," Ellen said, with a laugh. "Well, enjoy your meal. I'll be back to check and see when you're ready for dessert."

"I'm certain we will. We always do," Jim said. "Thanks, Ellen."

Usually having to eat in a hurry when on the trail, Jim and Smoky lingered over their supper. They took more than an hour to savor the tasty dishes Don had prepared.

"You boys about ready for your pie?" Ellen asked, when she noticed they were just about done eating, only a few scraps left on their plates. Smoky had rolled and lit another quirly.

"Just about," Jim said. "Ellen, you mind askin' Don to come out here for just a minute, if he has the time? Smoke'n I'd like to tell him personally how much we enjoyed our supper."

"I'm sure he can visit with you for just couple of minutes. I'll get him," Ellen answered.

Jim and Smoky drained what was left of their

coffee while they waited for Ellen to return with her husband. When the kitchen door opened, three men, in cowboy gear, rose from their table and pulled out their six-guns. They spread out to cover the room.

"Don't anybody dare move. We'll plug the first one who tries anythin'," the evident leader ordered. Jim and Smoky started for their guns, but thought better of it. With the restaurant being so crowded, they couldn't take a chance on trying for the apparent robbers. Their bullets might well hit an innocent bystander, instead of one of the outlaws. They would just have to bide their time, and wait for an opportunity to stop the holdup.

Don and Ellen had come out of the kitchen, and stopped short when the leader leveled his pistol at them.

"You two, get over here," he ordered. "We want all the money from your cash box. Get it, and quick. If you don't, we'll start pluggin' your customers, one at a time."

"All right. All right, Mister," Don answered. "I don't want to see anyone get hurt. I'll get you the money. It's right over here, under the counter."

"Get a sack, and put it in there," the leader ordered.

"Sure. Sure," Don said. "Just please, I'm askin' again, don't harm any of my customers."

The leader shoved Don behind the counter,

following him closely. Don reached under it, pulled out the cash box . . . and a large meat fork. He spun, and drove the fork into the outlaw's belly. Don was a big, powerful man, a former track layer for the Texas and Pacific Railroad. He put that fork into the outlaw's gut with all the strength he had, shoving it deep into his intestines. The outlaw howled, dropped his gun, grabbed his belly, doubled over, and fell to the floor.

Reacting instantly, before the other two men could recover from their surprise at seeing their leader go down, Jim and Smoky leapt from their chairs, pulled their pistols, and shot. Each hit his target squarely in the chest. Smoky's man was slammed back into the wall by the impact of the bullet. He slid slowly to the floor, then toppled onto his side. Jim's spun a half-circle, then pitched to his face.

"Don't anyone run. Everything's all right," Jim said, as people, beginning to panic, started to rise from their seats to flee the restaurant. "Everybody stay right where you are, until we check these men. We don't want anyone gettin' hurt by bein' trampled. Don, are you okay?"

"I'm fine, Jim. Just a bit shaken up, that's all."

"What about you, Ellen?"

"I'll be all right, after my nerves settle," she said.

"Good. Smoke, let's make certain these

hombres don't have any fight left in 'em. Don, if that sidewinder tries to move, you stick him again," Jim said. The outlaw Don had stabbed was lying curled up on his side, whimpering with pain, his hands wrapped around the fork still stuck in his gut.

"I don't think he's goin' anywhere, but I'll keep an eye on him," Don assured him.

"Bueno." Jim and Smoky examined the men they had shot, finding them already dead. They headed across the room, to where Don stood over the one he had downed.

"You took an awful chance there, Don," Jim said.

"I realize that. But he was gonna kill me, no matter whether I gave him the cash or not," Don answered. "I could see it in his eyes, and he'd already thumbed back the hammer of his gun. His finger was twitchin' on the trigger."

"Don't matter none, things worked out all right," Smoky said. He looked at the wounded outlaw.

"Mister, your pards are dead. If you pull through, you're facin' a long time in Huntsville. Texas Ranger. You're under arrest."

"You're . . . you're a . . . Ranger?" the man choked out. "Don't see . . . any . . . badge."

"Both of us are," Smoky replied, nodding at Jim. "We were both off duty, so we weren't wearin' our badges. Came into town for a nice, relaxin' evenin', startin' with a good supper. You and your pards sure ruined our plans."

"Besides, lots of Rangers don't even wear badges," Jim added. He and Smoky were two of the few who did, silver star on silver circle badges hand-carved from Mexican cinco peso coins. He turned to face the door when it flew open, and San Leanna Town Marshal Tom Colburn raced in. He carried a double-barreled Greener, with both hammers cocked.

"What in blue blazes is goin' on here?" he demanded. "Drop those guns, both of you."

"Hey, easy, Tom," Jim said. "You don't want to plug me or Smoke, do you?"

"No, I sure don't," Tom answered, with a sheepish grin. "Yelled orders before I recognized you two. What the devil happened?"

"Well, first, you might want to lower that scattergun, and uncock those hammers, Tom, before it goes off," Jim answered. "We've got everythin' under control." He nodded at the three men sprawled on the restaurant's floor. "These three tried to rob the place. Might've gotten away with it, too, except Don put a fork through one's guts. That gave me'n Smoke the chance to down the other two."

"I'm surprised you let 'em get the drop on you," Tom answered, as he lowered the Greener and eased down the hammers.

"Our fault," Smoky said, shaking his head in

45

disgust. "We were a bit too relaxed. You know how it is, Tom. We were home, and San Leanna hardly ever has any trouble, so we weren't lookin' for any. Boy howdy, I'd reckon we won't make that mistake again."

"You can bet your hat on it," Jim added.

"How about these three? What kinda shape are they in?" Tom asked.

"The two we nailed are dead," Jim answered. "The other one's in bad shape, I'd imagine."

"Anyone go for Doc Watson?"

"I sent my dishwasher, Pedro, for him," Don answered. "He should be here in a few minutes."

"All right," Tom said. He turned at the sound of hard-ridden horses coming to a sliding stop out front. A moment later, two of his deputies, Joe Fleming and Bob Fairbanks, rushed into the restaurant.

"Sorry, Tom," Joe said. "We were clear on the other side of town, when we found out about the ruckus. Got here as soon as we heard. You still need us?"

"That's all right. The excitement's all over," Tom answered. "Jim Blawcyzk and Smoky McCue happened to be havin' supper here when three hombres tried to hold up the place. Two of 'em are done for, and we're waitin' for the doc to see how bad the other one's hurt. Don stuck a meat fork right in his brisket. But, as long as you two are here, you mind takin' those bodies down to Stevenson's? I'd imagine they're ruinin' folks' appetites."

"Sure, we'll handle that chore," Joe said. "C'mon, Bob, let's drag these sorry carcasses out of here and load 'em on our horses."

"All right," Bob agreed. Each man lifted a body under its shoulders and dragged it outside. They had no sooner removed them when Dr. Collin Watson hurried in, carrying his medical bag. Right behind him was Pedro Gonzalez, the dishwasher, who was gasping for breath, after his desperate run to the physician's office.

"I understand you had a bit of shooting trouble here, Don," he said. Watson was young, slightly shorter than average, with close-cropped dark, wavy hair, and spectacles framing his dark eyes. He was considered one of San Leanna's most eligible bachelors.

"We certainly did, Doc," Don answered. "Three men tried to rob the place. Jim and Smoky got two of 'em. The third one's lyin' right over here."

Watson crossed the room and knelt beside the badly wounded man.

He *tsked* softly.

"I didn't know the Texas Rangers were using forks for weapons now," he said.

"We aren't," Jim answered. He and Smoky were now alongside the doctor. "Don did that, and if he hadn't, you probably would've had a lot more wounded to treat . . . and most likely some folks to pronounce dead."

"Indeed." Watson lifted an eyebrow. "Well, at least you didn't pull the fork out of this one's abdomen," he said. "That would have caused even more damage, and more rapid bleeding. As it is, I doubt I'll be able to save him. It appears the damage to his intestines is too severe. I'll know better once I have him in my office, where I can examine him more thoroughly."

"It don't matter whether . . . or not I live . . . or . . . die," the wounded outlaw gasped. "You'll pay for this. This . . . entire town's gonna . . . pay . . . for what . . . y'all . . . did."

"I've heard that kind of talk plenty of times before, Mister," Jim answered. "It doesn't mean anythin'. Only one you might want to talk with is your Maker, in case you do cash in your chips."

"Go ahead and scoff . . . Ranger. Mark . . . my words. This town's gonna . . . be sorry it . . . ever crossed us."

"Tom, if I'm to have any chance at all of saving this man's life, we need to get him to my office, and I mean right now," Watson said.

"All right." The marshal chose two men. "Hank, Murray, give me a hand gettin' this jasper to the doc's. The rest of you, go on about your business. If you still have appetites after what happened here tonight, finish your suppers. If not, go on home. I might need statements from everyone

48

who was a witness, but I doubt it. If I do, I'll let you know. Don, Jim, Smoky, what happened seems pretty clear cut. I reckon you can wait until mornin' to give me your statements. Might as well hold off until we see if Doc can pull this hombre through. Is there anythin' I should know before I leave, though?"

"There is just one thing, Tom," Jim answered. "Actually, now that I think of it, there are two."

"What's that, Jim?"

"First, that skunk and his pards interrupted our supper. We never did get our pecan pie. There's gotta be some kinda law against that."

"I dunno, Jim." Tom shook his head. "I can't think of one. What's the second thing?"

"I can't answer that one. Only Don can. Don, you're the one who stuck the fork in that renegade. So tell me, was he still rare, medium, or well done?"

Don picked up a dishrag from the counter and threw it at him. The wet rag caught Jim squarely in the face.

"You still expectin' pie after a crack like that?" he asked.

"I sure am," Jim answered. "The day I let an outlaw keep me from my dessert is the day I shoot myself. Soon as your nerves are settled, you can bring me and Smoke our pie, and more coffee."

"I should've known." Don shook his head.

Muttering, he went back into the kitchen, along with Ellen. The wounded man was picked up and carried outside, to be brought to Doctor Watson's. A few minutes later, Ellen returned, with two huge slabs of pecan pie, and another pot of coffee.

"Here you go, boys. And thanks for helping out. I have no doubt those men would have killed Don, and probably just about everyone in here, if you hadn't taken a hand. And who knows what they might have done to me? Your meals are on the house tonight."

"We were just doin' our jobs," Jim answered. "So there's no need to thank us."

"And especially not to give us a free supper," Smoky added.

"Pish tosh," Ellen retorted. "You're eating for free, and that's that. I won't even be bringing you a bill, and if you try'n leave any money on the table I'll make certain it gets back to you. Mercy sakes, even I could be lyin' dead on the floor, or perhaps kidnapped and being . . . being . . . well, you know, if it hadn't been for you two. So there will be no more arguin' about it. Or do you want me to have Don stick a fork in your bellies, too?"

"Ouch." Jim winced. "I reckon she's got us there, Smoke."

"She sure does," Smoky agreed. "All right, Ellen. You win. We won't try'n pay for our supper."

"That means you won't try and pay for the pies I'm sending home for Julia and Cindy, either. Right?"

"You're gonna have leftover pies?" Jim asked.

"Take a look around," Ellen answered. "Those men scared just about everyone out of here." Indeed, besides Jim and Smoky, there were only four customers left.

"I guess they did," Smoky said.

"So I might as well send pies to Julia and Cindy, rather than just throw them out," Ellen said. "You boys take your time. Just let me know when you're ready to leave."

"All right," Jim answered. He and Smoky did just that. They lingered over their pie and coffee for nearly forty-five minutes, before finally getting up to go.

"G'night, Ellen. G'night, Don," Jim said.

"G'night," Smoky added.

"The same to you two," Don answered. "And thanks again."

"Hey, if you hadn't started the ball rollin', we couldn't have done a thing," Jim answered. "Not with so many customers in here, who might have taken a slug meant for one of those renegades. You gave us the break we needed."

"But you had the fast guns," Don answered.

"And accurate ones," Ellen added. She handed a boxed pie each to Jim and Smoky. "Now you make sure those pies get to your wives. Don't eat them on the way home, yourselves. And Jim, don't you dare give any of that pie to your horse, either."

"Hey, if you think takin' on those three outlaws was tough, that'd be nothin' compared to what would happen if Julia and Cindy discovered we ate their pies," Jim said, laughing. "C'mon, Smoke, let's get outta here. I'm certain Don and Ellen want to lock up and go home."

"All right, Jim. Don, Ellen, as usual, supper was delicious," Smoky said. "Next time, though, we could do without the entertainment."

"I've gotta agree with you there," Don answered. "Thanks again."

"Yes, thank you. You two be careful," Ellen added.

"We always are," Jim said.

"And pigs fly," Don retorted, with a chuckle. "Yes, sir, pigs fly."

By the time Jim and Smoky finished their meal, Jarratt's Store had long been closed, so they headed straight for their next stop.

"Well, I'll be jiggered. Jim Blawcyzk and Smoky McCue," Beauregard Stanton, owner of the Shenandoah Saloon, exclaimed, in his soft Virginia drawl, when the two Rangers walked through the door. "I'd just about given up hope of ever seein' either one of you in my place again. What brings y'all by?"

Stanton was the scion of a wealthy Lexington, Virginia plantation family, the oldest of nine children, five boys and four girls. He had grown up in a life of luxury and leisure, accustomed to a lavish lifestyle, with his every need cared for, his every whim catered to. However, as had happened to so many other Southern families during, and after, the War, the Stantons had lost everything. What the War itself hadn't taken the Yankee carpetbaggers and the Southern scalawags had. Three of Beau's brothers died fighting for the Confederacy, and two of his sisters died from consumption before the treaty at Appomattox had finally ended the conflict. His other siblings had drifted off while the fighting was still going on. Beau's father died shortly after the War ended, and his mother wasted away after his passing, dying only three months later. With nothing left in Virginia, Beau, as did so many other Southerners, drifted west, to Texas. He found the only job he could, as a swamper in a Waco saloon, and soon discovered he had a talent for saloon keeping. He worked his way up to assistant bartender, then chief. He saved every dime of his meager earnings he could, and after a few years had enough money to buy a place of his own. Wanting to settle in a small town, he left Waco, wandered into San Leanna, and found an empty building for sale. He purchased that, and through hard work converted it into the

Shenandoah Saloon, named after his beloved home in Virginia's Shenandoah Valley. Affable and easy going, Beau was quick to make friends, so was ideally suited to his chosen new life as a saloon keeper.

Another reason his place was so successful was its décor. The lighting was brighter than in other places, and the paintings on the walls were not the usual garish pictures of women in various stages of undress, or depictions of gunfights and cattle drives. Instead, the paintings were bucolic scenes of Beau's former home, the Shenandoah Valley and Blue Ridge Mountains. The piano was kept well-tuned, and Bailey Thornton, its player, knew an extensive repertoire of dance, traditional, and classical tunes. And unlike most Texas saloons, which usually stank of spilled liquor, tobacco smoke, and sweat, Beau's mainly smelled of the cedar sawdust he spread thickly on the floor. He kept the place as spotlessly clean as possible for a frontier barroom. Even the cuspidors were regularly emptied and polished. In addition, while he had the usual female entertainers, they were not "soiled doves", but were employed strictly to dance with the patrons, and perhaps entice them to drink or gamble a bit more than they'd planned, but nothing else. There were no upstairs rooms, and any man desiring to bed one of Beau's girls was quickly, and firmly, invited to leave the premises. However, Beau harbored no illusions about what his girls might do after hours. He was well aware they often made arrangements to meet a customer, as soon as they were through work for the night. But, he had no control over them once their work for the evening was done, and if any of the girls wanted to make a few extra dollars whoring, that was none of his affair.

"Howdy, Beau," Jim answered. "We've been without orders so long just about every chore on our places is done, so we decided to take it easy for a night, come into town, and have a little fun."

"In other words, your wives got plumb tired of lookin' at your ugly faces, and threw you both out of the house," Beau replied, laughing.

"You've got it pretty much pegged, Beau," Smoky admitted, when he and Jim bellied up to the bar. "Only it was mainly Julia's idea. But Cindy was right quick to go along with it."

"Well, you're certainly welcome here," Beau said. "I assume you want your usual?"

"That's right, Beau," Smoky answered. "Sarsaparilla for Jim, Old Grand-Dad for me."

"Comin' right up." Beau rummaged under the bar, and came up with several bottles of pop. He opened one, and poured the contents into a mug he set in front of Jim. That done, he took an almost full bottle of Old Grand-Dad from the top back bar shelf, then set it and a glass in front of Smoky.

"Do you want me to pour you a glass, or just leave the bottle, Smoky?" he asked.

"Now, Beauregard Stanton, that's one of the doggone most obvious questions I've ever been asked in my entire life," Smoky replied. "Almost as senseless as askin' Jim which he likes more, horses or people. Everyone knows Jim prefers the company of his horses. Of course, just leave the bottle."

"All right," Beau said. "I hear you boys got into a bit of a shootin' scrape over at O'Malley's."

"Boy howdy, it didn't take long for the news to spread," Jim said.

"I don't need to remind you San Leanna's a small town, and this is a saloon you're standin' in," Beau pointed out. "Anything that happens around here, I get word of it, real fast. So, what happened? I got most of the story, but I'd rather get it from you boys, first hand."

"There's not much to tell." Jim shrugged. "Three men tried to hold up the place. There wasn't a whole lot Smoky and I could do to stop 'em, not with the restaurant packed jam-full of customers. If we'd started shootin', it's most likely some innocent bystanders would have taken slugs. Luckily, Don happened to have a meat fork handy. He shoved it into one hombre's gut, which gave me and Smoke the chance to take care of the other two. They're both dead, and the one Don stabbed probably won't make it, either, accordin' to Doc Watson. Everyone else is all right."

"Sounds like Don gave that scoundrel a real bellyful," Beau said, with a chuckle.

"Not you too, Beau," Smoky said, groaning. "It's bad enough I have to put up with Jim's awful jokes. Listen, that's enough talk about what happened at O'Malley's. Jim and I came into town to relax and have fun, and we intend to do just that. We're gonna have a few drinks, in fact, I plan on gettin' good and drunk, and also play some poker, if there's a game we can sit in on."

"There's always room at my table for you and Jim, Smoky. You know that," Jackson Briggs, the Shenandoah's house gambler, called from his seat at a back corner card table. Standing behind him was his favorite of Beau's girls, Lucy Monroe, a buxom blonde, who this night was wearing a tight fitting, daringly low cut blue satin gown, which did little to hide the curves of her figure, nor the full breasts threatening to escape their confinement at any moment. A blue, cut-glass pendant nestled in her cleavage. At the table with Briggs were two other men, Bob Ferguson, who owned the feed store, and Sam McGuire, a cowboy from the Circle T Ranch. "Just carry your drinks right over here and you can get in on the next hand."

"Thanks, Jackson," Smoky answered. "Beau, there you have it. You just keep the drinks flowin', and we'll all have a good time. C'mon, Jim."

He picked up his glass and bottle, Jim took his sarsaparillas, and they went over to Briggs' table. After howdies were exchanged, they took seats.

"Those two of Ellen's pies you have there?" Briggs asked.

"They sure are," Jim answered.

"You want to play for those?"

Jim shook his head.

"Not a chance, Jackson. Ellen sent those pies along for our wives. I like livin' too much to chance losin' 'em in a card game. Bet your fancy hat on it."

"Oh, well, it was worth asking." Briggs shuffled the cards. "Five card stud all right with you two? That's what we've been playin'."

"It's fine with me," Jim said.

"Same here," Smoky agreed.

"Then let's play." Briggs began dealing the cards.

Since Jim never had taken up smoking, nor drank anything stronger than sarsaparilla, had never been heard to issue a cuss word, nor had ever been with a woman except Julia, his wife, folks meeting him for the first time tended to think of him as some kind of choir boy, or perhaps a plaster saint. However, while slow to

58

anger, when riled Jim had a temper which could explode without warning. One thing which was guaranteed to set that temper off was anyone attempting to harm any of his horses. In addition, Jim had one other major vice, poker. He loved to play the game, and was nearly as good at it as most professional card sharks. Therefore, two hours later, either he or Briggs had won most of the pots.

"You about ready to call it a night, Jim?" Smoky asked. His voice was slurred, for he'd consumed the first bottle of Old Grand-Dad Beau had provided, as well as more than half of another.

"I'd like to play a bit more, but mebbe we should quit," Jim answered. "You seem a bit the worse for wear, Smoke."

"That . . . that's just . . . nonsense," Smoky answered, adding a curse for good measure. "I ain't had all that much to drink."

He put the loosely rolled quirly he'd managed to build, despite his shaking hands, between his lips, pulled a lucifer from his vest pocket and thumbed it to life on his belt buckle, then attempted to touch it to the end of his cigarette. Instead, he missed. The lit match singed his upper lip and moustache.

"Ow!" Smoky yelped, and let out a string of oaths.

"Smoky, some of the gals around here said you

had hot lips for 'em, until you got married and settled down," Briggs said, dryly. "Until now, I didn't know they meant that literally."

"Briggs, you can go . . ."

"Easy, Smoke." Jim didn't let him finish. "I reckon mebbe callin' it a night isn't such a bad idea after all. Let's get the horses to the stable and get ourselves a room at the Duncan."

"No hotel, no sir," Smoky retorted. "I wanna go home and make love to my wife."

"That ain't gonna happen, at least not tonight, Smoke," Jim said. "We promised our wives we'd stay in town overnight, so they could have some time to themselves, to catch up on gossip and do whatever else it is women do when there ain't any menfolks around. Besides, there's no way you'd be able to stay in the saddle. You try ridin' Midnight and you'll fall flat on your face before we make a mile."

"I can outride you any day of the week, Jim Blawcyzk, drunk or sober," Smoky answered. "In fact, let's prove it, right now."

He attempted to stand up. When he did, his boot heel caught in a chair rung. Smoky fell to his face.

"Jim, I was gonna bet you Smoky *could* ride a mile," Bob Ferguson said. "I'm sure glad I didn't get the chance. I would've lost."

"A mile? Heck, he couldn't even get five feet," Sam McGuire said, laughing.

Smoky rolled onto his back, and lay there, cursing.

"Soon as I get up I'll show the both of you," he grumbled.

Lucy came from behind Briggs, placed her right foot on Smoky's belly, just above his belt buckle, and pushed down hard, her shoe's high heel jabbing into his gut. Smoky burped loudly, so loudly it echoed through the saloon.

"I think you'd better just lie there a little, until you get at least some of your senses back, Ranger," she said.

Four young cowboys, who had been standing at the bar for most of the night, nursing whiskies, turned to look at the commotion.

"Show the both of 'em what?" one of them said, laughing. "Heck, you can't even get that little ol' gal's foot outta your gut, and you're gonna give those hombres what for? I hardly think so."

"This ain't none of your affair, cowboy," Jim said. "So why don't you just turn around, get back to your drinkin', and keep your nose out of other folks' business, before you get it broken for stickin' it where it don't belong?"

"Why don't you try and make me?" the cowboy challenged.

"Because I'm not lookin' to start any trouble," Jim answered. "I might suggest you do the same."

"He's givin' you good advice, Mack," Josh Miles, another cowboy standing at the bar, added. "I know you boys are new to these parts, but those two men are Texas Rangers. You don't want to tangle with 'em."

"Those two old geezers, Rangers?" Mack answered, with a sneer. "I can't believe that. Besides, Rangers ain't as tough as everyone claims. They're just a bunch of troublemakers, hidin' behind a badge. We're not scared of a couple of broken-down, drunken old fools playin' lawdogs, are we, fellers?"

His companions murmured in assent.

"Now you've done it," Miles said, as Smoky came to his feet, suddenly almost sober. "Don't say I didn't warn you." To Jim and Smoky he continued, "Jim, Smoke, these here young'ns just hired on with the Double M. I reckon they're lookin' to learn the hard way about not buttin' in where they're not wanted. Try'n take it easy on 'em, will you? Don't hurt 'em too bad."

"And try not to bust up my place too much, all right?" Beau added.

"I'm not makin' any promises, Josh," Jim said. "Neither is Smoky. Beau, we'll try'n make this quick and clean." To Mack he said, "Mister, you might have been able to get away with callin' me old, mebbe even a fool. But I'm not a drunk, never have been, never will be. In case you hadn't noticed, this here is sarsaparilla I'm drinkin'. As far as my pardner here, neither's he, but just like you fellers, once in a while he likes to go on a tear. Now, I believe you said you're not afraid of a couple of broken-down old geezers. You gonna back up those words, or are you and your pards gonna crawl out of here on your bellies?"

"Why, you . . ." With a curse, Mack and his three partners charged Jim and Smoky. The first to reach them swung at Jim's chin. Jim ducked the punch, drove his head into the man's middle, then flipped him over his shoulders. The cowboy landed on his back on Briggs' card table, smashing it flat. He lay groaning, tried to get up, then fell back, out cold. Jim was rocked by a punch to his jaw from another cowboy. He staggered back, took two hard blows in his belly, and another to his ribs, before he could recover. He parried the next punch aimed at his stomach, then slammed three quick rights and lefts to the cowboy's gut, which folded him into a finishing punch to the point of his chin. The blow knocked the man backwards into the bar. He hung there for a moment, his eyes glazing, then slid to the floor.

Mack and the remaining Double M hand had backed Smoky into a corner. He absorbed several blows to his face and body, but now his powerful left smashed directly into Mack's nose, flattening it. Mack howled in pain, and grabbed his busted nose with both hands. Smoky punched him twice in the gut, then when Mack folded, kneed him in the chin. Mack dropped like a rock.

The last Double M man standing kicked Smoky in the crotch. Smoky moaned, but fought off the intense pain to land a solid punch of his own to the cowboy's left eye, which immediately swelled shut. Showing no mercy, Smoky moved in for the kill. He dropped the man with a combination of lefts and rights, the final one a vicious blow to the groin. The Double M cowboy dropped to his knees, then pitched to his face. He lay unmoving.

"You'll be feelin' that last punch for quite a while, Mister," Smoky muttered to the unconscious cowboy. "That'll sure teach you not to kick a man in the . . ."

"Smoke, you all right?" Jim broke in.

"Yeah. I'm okay," Smoky said. "How about you?"

"I'm fine," Jim answered. Both of them stood hunched over, their chests heaving.

"Beau, I reckon I owe you for a card table," Jim said. He rubbed the lump rising on his jaw.

"Don't worry about it," Beau answered. "It was worth losin' one table to watch that fight, and to see those young blowhards get their comeuppance."

"Boy howdy, that sure didn't take long," Sam said. "The fight was over almost before it started."

"I knew it'd be quick. I tried to warn those boys they weren't any match for Jim and Smoke, but they wouldn't listen," Josh said. He took his mug of beer, walked over to where Mack lay senseless, and poured it over his head. Mack came to, spluttered, and rolled onto his back.

"What . . . what happened?"

"You and your pards got your butts whupped by a couple of broken-down old geezers, that's what happened," Josh said. "Now, I suggest you take your friends and get outta here, before you start any more trouble you can't finish."

"Smoke, I think it's time we called it a night too," Jim said. "I'll collect my winnings and we'll get outta here. Unless you need us to stick around and talk to the marshal, Beau."

"No, you go on," Beau said. "There wasn't any real damage done, and I think these boys have learned their lessons. They won't be lookin' for any more trouble."

"In fact, I'd wager they won't be lookin' to do anything for a few days except lick their hurts," Briggs added. He handed Jim his proceeds from the night's play, as well as the pies.

"You're probably right about that, Jackson," Josh said.

"Okay, then we'll head out," Jim said. "C'mon, Smoke. Buenas noches, everybody."

By the time they got outside, the liquor Smoky had consumed, along with the punches he'd absorbed, finally showed its full effect. He doubled over.

"Jim, I think I'm gonna be sick," he moaned.

"Somehow, I'm not surprised," Jim answered. "And it *is* your own dang fault. Well, go ahead. Don't let me stop you."

"All . . . urk." Smoky emptied the contents of his stomach into the street.

"Lemme know when you're finished, pard," Jim said, as Smoky continued to vomit. It took several minutes before Smoky's stomach was emptied and he finally felt well enough to climb into the saddle.

"Let's go, Jim, before I puke again," he said.

"Okay."

Jim and Smoky got their horses settled in Munson's livery stable, then went to the Duncan Hotel, where they obtained the last available room. By now, Smoky was once again feeling ill, his legs so shaky Jim had to help him up the stairs and into their room. Smoky toppled face down on the bed, and immediately passed out.

"I don't care how sick you are, pard, you ain't hoggin' the whole bed," Jim muttered. He pulled off Smoky's boots and removed his gunbelt, then shoved him aside. That done, Jim knelt down and said his evening prayers. He undressed, and slid under the sheets. Smoky began snoring, so loudly the noise seemed to shake the walls. Jim shook his head.

"And this was supposed to be a nice, relaxin' night in town," he murmured. "It sure didn't turn out that way. Well, let's just see what tomorrow brings."

He reached over and turned down the light, then rolled onto his stomach. After covering his head with his pillow to drown out at least some of the racket Smoky was making, he soon drifted off to sleep.

As usual, Jim was awake with the sun the next morning. Smoky was still sprawled across his side of the bed, dead to the world. Jim said his morning prayers, then climbed out of bed. He winced when pain shot through his ribs and gut.

"I guess that hombre tagged me a mite harder than I figured," he muttered. "Better try'n do somethin' about that." He pulled on his shirt, denims, socks, and boots, then headed outside to use the privy. Once he was done, he obtained a pitcher of hot water and a bar of Pear's Soap from the desk clerk, then headed back to his room. He found Smoky still sleeping, so he placed the pitcher on the washstand, unwrapped the soap and put it alongside the basin, then stripped out of his clothes, poured the hot water into the basin and began washing. He ducked his head in the water to soak his face and thatch of unruly blond hair, then allowed the water to run down his shoulders, back, and neck. He soaked a washcloth and pressed that against the bruise on his left side, then practically jumped out of his skin when Smoky let loose a blood-curdling scream.

"Smoke! What the devil's wrong with you?" Jim asked, turning to stare at his partner. "You scared me outta ten years of my life. And it's high time you finally woke up."

"I . . . I forgot where I was for a minute," Smoky stuttered. "I thought I was at home, and expected to wake up with Cindy next to me. Instead, I opened my eyes to see your naked, hairy butt. Believe me, that's a sight no man should have to see first thing in the mornin'. Ow."

Smoky shook his head, then yelped at the pain.

"You ain't exactly a sight for sore eyes either, pardner," Jim retorted. "You gonna get up, or are you just gonna lie in that bed all day?"

"I reckon I'd best get up," Smoky said. He rolled onto his back, waited a moment for the room to stop spinning, then attempted to sit up. He groaned, and fell back on the mattress.

"Mebbe I will just stay here all day instead," he said. "My poor head."

"Oh no, you won't," Jim answered. "We've gotta get back home, and we still need to stop by Jarratt's first. So get your sorry butt outta that bed before I drag it out. You might want to clean up some, too. You don't exactly smell like roses and lilacs. I left you enough water."

"All right, all right. Soon as you're through

washin' up, I'll pull myself upright . . . I hope," Smoky answered.

"That's more like it. I'll be done in a jiffy."

Jim finished washing, toweled himself off, then redressed. Once he was finished, Smoky, with a moan, sat up and swung his legs over the edge of the mattress. He remained there for a few minutes, head hanging, then forced himself to stand upright. He removed his gunbelt, undressed, stumbled over to the washstand, and gave himself a rudimentary washing.

"There. You satisfied now, Jim?" he asked, as he dried off.

"I will be once you've gotten your duds back on, so we can get outta here and get some breakfast," Jim answered.

"Don't even mention food," Smoky pleaded. "My stomach's in no shape to hold anythin' down."

"Your stomach's condition don't make no never mind to me," Jim said. "Mine's tellin' me it's plumb empty. I'm starved. We're goin' down to the dinin' room, where I'm gonna get me a double order of bacon, ham, and eggs, with lots of fried spuds, and plenty of biscuits. And an entire pot of coffee. You could use some of that, I'd bet my hat on it."

"I guess you're right," Smoky conceded. "I'll at least try'n force some coffee down."

After Smoky finished redressing, he and Jim

tossed their saddlebags over their shoulders and headed downstairs.

"Good mornin', boys," Ezekiel Duncan, owner of the hotel which bore his name, greeted them, from behind the front desk. "Sleep well?"

"Mornin', Zeke," Jim answered. "Smoky sure did. He slept like a baby . . . a baby with the croup. His snorin' was enough to wake the dead. Although I should point out he was more passed out from drinkin' a couple bottles of red-eye than actually sleepin'."

"I surmised as much, just from his appearance," Duncan said. "Also heard you had a bit of trouble last night. Hard to believe somethin' like that robbery happened here in San Leanna."

"Those hombres probably figured they had easy pickin's, in a town this small," Smoky said. "I reckon they found out different."

"Indeed. Well, I'm glad you got a good night's sleep, anyway. Say hello to Cindy and Julia for me."

Duncan turned his attention to another guest. Jim and Smoky went into the crowded dining room, and found an empty table in the back corner. Dora, the head waitress, came over, carrying a pot of coffee and two mugs.

"Good morning, Jim, Smoky," she said. "I've got your coffee here. I don't mean to rush you, but are you ready to order? We're real busy this mornin'."

Dora had been with the Duncan since it opened. She was in her late fifties, with iron-gray hair and sparkling blue eyes. Her motherly manner made everyone feel welcome.

"I sure am," Jim said. "Double order of bacon, ham, and eggs, lots of spuds, and plenty of biscuits."

"How about you, Smoky?"

"Just coffee for me, Dora. Thanks."

"Ah, yes, I heard about your escapade in the Shenandoah last night. Really, Smoky. A man your age should know better."

"I know, I know. Reckon I made a plumb fool of myself. A man has to do that once in a while."

"I suppose. And after what happened at O'Malley's, I can't really blame you. I'm certainly grateful no one got hurt, except the robbers. I'll put your order in now. It may take a bit longer, since we're so crowded, but I'll tell Burt to hurry it along."

"We appreciate that, Dora," Jim said.

Smoky rolled and lit a cigarette. He and Jim drank several cups of coffee while waiting for their meal. When the food arrived, Jim dug into his platter, while Smoky merely tried to keep his stomach from churning. Halfway through their meal, Marshal Colburn came in.

"Mornin', boys. Mind if I join you?" he asked.

"Not at all, Tom," Jim answered. "Pull up a chair."

"Gracias."

Dora hustled over to greet the town lawman. She placed a coffee cup in front of him.

"Good morning, Marshal. Your usual?"

"Sure, Dora. Hotcakes and sausage."

"I'll bring it along with Smoky and Jim's meals."

"That'll be fine. Thank you."

Colburn poured himself a cup of coffee, took a swallow, rolled and lit a cigarette, then took a long drag on it.

"I've got good news for you two. There won't be an inquest. The third robber died durin' the night. He never said a word before he went to Hell, except for babblin' some nonsense, Doc says. He couldn't make heads nor tails out of whatever he was tryin' to say. Since it's plain what happened, there's no need for an inquiry. Doc Watson'll write up a report statin' those hombres died durin' the course of committin' a crime, and Josiah Stevenson'll plant 'em later this mornin'."

"They have any identification on them, Tom?" Jim asked.

Colburn shook his head.

"Not a thing. Nothin' in their saddlebags, neither. And their horses weren't anythin' special. Three or four brands on all of 'em, which means trackin' down whoever they got 'em from would be more trouble than it's worth. No, I'm just gonna close the books on this one. Those hombres are shakin' hands with the devil right about now, and Texas is better off without 'em."

"Then that's that," Smoky said. "Here comes Dora with our breakfast."

After having their meal, Jim and Smoky's next stop was Jarratt's General Store. Like most frontier establishments, Jarratt's opened early, at seven a.m., to serve the ranchers and farmers who were its main clientele. Mike Jarratt was sweeping off the front walk when they approached.

"Jim! Smoky! Howdy. Bethea and I hoped we'd see you two before you left town," he said. "We heard about the ruckus at O'Malley's last night. Good work, and good riddance to the likes of those hombres."

"Howdy yourself, Mike," Jim answered. "Yeah, our nice, relaxin' night in town didn't turn out quite the way we expected. Is Bethea inside? We both want to pick up a little somethin' for our wives. Neither one of us is much good at pickin' out female stuff, so we'd like her to help us."

"She sure is," Mike answered. "C'mon in. Bethea, Jim and Smoky are here," he yelled, through the open front door.

Bethea Jarratt came from behind the counter, where she was stocking a shelf with tinned peaches.

"Good morning, Jim, Smoky."

"Mornin' yourself, Bethea," Jim answered.

"Same from me, Bethea," Smoky added.

"What brings you by?" Bethea asked. "Have you heard from Charlie? We just got a nice letter from Mary Jane. She says they're having a wonderful time in Galveston, and to say hello to you and Julia. I can hardly wait to see them again."

"No, I haven't," Jim said. "I don't imagine I will, until he and Mary Jane get back home. It won't be long now. They'll be here next week. Charlie's leave is up then, so he'll have to get back to work."

"Besides, I'd imagine Charlie has his mind on other things instead of writin' letters," Mike said, chuckling. He winked at his wife. "Things mebbe you and I should be thinkin' about doin' tonight, Bethea."

"Why, Michael Jarratt!" Bethea blushed. "You shouldn't talk like that where people can hear. It's just not decent."

"Neither is what I'm thinkin' about."

"Michael!" Bethea blushed even redder. "You're incorrigible. Enough of that kind of talk. Smoky, Jim, may I help you with something?"

"You sure can," Jim answered. "It was our wives' idea for us to take a night in town. We want to get 'em a thank you present. Nothin' too fancy, just a little somethin'."

74

"Every woman wants something fancy," Bethea said. "She may say she doesn't, but she does. I believe I have just the thing. Step over here and take a look at these."

They followed Bethea to a side counter, from which she removed a white blouse, trimmed in lace. Embroidered flowers highlighted its bodice.

"I just got these in from St. Louis. They're the latest fashion, perfect for going to socials, perhaps a church dance, or even a dinner party. I'm certain Julia and Cindy will be taken with them. What do you think?"

"I dunno," Jim said. "I like it, but I'm not certain Julia will."

"Of course she will," Bethea replied. "Smoky?"

"I'm certain Cindy would really appreciate one of those, but what about her and Julia having the exact same blouse?" Smoky said. "That might be a problem."

"Nonsense. It needn't be one at all. This one with the blue flowers will complement Cindy's complexion very nicely. And the one with the yellow will pick up the brown in Julia's eyes, so it will be very flattering. They'll have the same blouse, but different. Take my word for it, your wives will love these. And don't worry about getting the right size. I know men don't know about such things, but I've been selling clothes to the womenfolk in this town for years, so I know just about everyone's size. I think these would be the perfect gift."

"Bethea's right, boys," Mike added.

"You've convinced me," Jim said. "I'll take one with the yellow flowers."

"And I'll take the one with the blue," Smoky said.

"Wonderful," Bethea said. "I'll wrap them right up. Is that all you'll need today?"

"That's everything I need," Jim said. "Well, except some more peppermints for my horses."

"And I need some more Bull Durham and cigarette papers," Smoky said.

"I'll get those while Bethea wraps the blouses," Mike offered.

The purchases were made and paid for. After saying goodbye and taking their leave of the store, Jim and Smoky went to the livery stable, to retrieve their horses for the ride home. Hal Munson was sitting on a barrel outside the front door. He got up at their approach.

"I figured you boys'd be along any time now," he said. "Got your horses fed, watered, and brushed for you. All you've gotta do is saddle up and you can be on your way. Sure is a lot easier dealin' with Sizzle than that Sam hoss of yours, Jim," he said.

"I've gotta give you that, Hal," Jim answered, with a laugh. He headed inside the barn. Sizzle gave a loud whinny as soon as he saw him. When

Jim entered his stall, he buried his muzzle in Jim's belly, then nosed his pocket.

"Of course I've got your candy," Jim said. He gave the big paint a peppermint, then rubbed his shoulder. "Ready to head home?"

Sizzle nickered.

"All right, then. I'll get your gear."

Sizzle and Midnight were quickly saddled and bridled, the packages from Jarratt's and the pies from O'Malley's hung from their saddlehorns. Smoky, still feeling the effects of the previous night's drinking, swayed a bit when he mounted, but the fresh air and coffee had taken most of the edge off his pounding headache, and his stomach was starting to settle down.

"See you boys later," Hal said. "Although I doubt you'll be around much longer. It's about time the Rangers sent you back out."

"It sure is," Jim agreed. "Adios, Hal."

"See you, Hal," Smoky added. He and Jim put their horses into a walk. They would keep them at that pace for half-a-mile, until they warmed up, then put them into a lope. They rode easily in the saddle, enjoying the warmth of the morning air, the sun on their backs. They had gone a little more than two miles when the hoof beats of a hard-ridden horse came to their ears.

"Someone comin' fast, Smoke," Jim said. "We'd better see who it is."

They turned to face the oncoming rider,

loosened their Colts in their holsters, and waited with their hands on the guns' butts. A minute later, Bobby Taylor, the young Western Union telegrapher, came into view. He rode up to them and pulled his horse to a sliding stop.

"You're in an awful hurry, Bobby," Jim said.

"Boy howdy, that's for certain. I'm sure glad I caught up with you two," Bobby answered. "This came in just after you left. Seemed too important to wait until I got off this afternoon, so I closed the office and chased after you."

He handed Jim a yellow Western Union flimsy.

"Urgent need you in Austin now ES" was all it said. Jim passed it to Smoky, who quickly scanned it.

"Seems like we've got orders, Jim," he said.

"We've got orders."

# 6

Jim and Smoky made the rest of the trip home at a hard gallop. They stopped at Smoky's house first. As they expected, Cindy and Julia were not there.

"They must've already gone over to my place, Smoke," Jim said. "We'll catch up to 'em there."

"It'll only take me a few minutes to gather up my gear, then we'll be on our way again," Smoky answered. He dismounted, headed into the house, and grabbed a spare shirt, socks, and underwear, as well as extra ammunition for his guns, along with a good supply of beef jerky. He stuffed everything in his saddlebags, then remounted. Fifteen minutes after arriving at Smoky's, they were on the trail again. A short while after that, keeping their horses at a walk, so as not to startle their wives, they rode into Jim's yard. Julia and Cindy were on the porch, working on a needlepoint sampler.

"We're home," Jim called out.

"I can see that," Julia answered. "I can also see you must have done more than just relax last night. What happened to your face?"

Jim's jaw was swollen, and black and blue, from where the Double M cowboy's fist had connected. Smoky's was in even worse shape.

"We got into a bit of a scrape in town," he answered.

"It looks like it was more than just a bit of a scrape," Cindy said, looking at Smoky's battered face. "Just what did happen?"

"Like Jim says, there was a bit of trouble," Smoky replied.

"Yeah. Let's just say the next time we get the notion to relax with a night in town, just shoot us," Jim said, with a chuckle. "It'd be more merciful. Suffice it to say we did everything but."

"Meaning what, exactly?" Julia demanded.

"Meanin' three hombres tried to rob O'Malley's restaurant while we were eatin' supper," Smoky said. "They were bent on killin' some folks, too, seems like. Don stopped one by stickin' a meat fork in his gut, then me'n Jim had to take care of the other two. They won't be botherin' anyone else."

Julia and Cindy had been married to the lawmen long enough to know what Smoky meant. They didn't need to ask the fate of the three would-be robbers.

"That still doesn't explain the bruises on your face, Smoky," Cindy said. "You didn't get drunk and start a fight, did you?"

"Just a little. But no, I didn't start that fight," Smoky said.

"But we sure did finish it," Jim continued.

"We went over to the Shenandoah to get a few drinks and play some poker. Four new cowboys, young'ns who just hired on at the Double M, from what Josh Miles told us, decided they wanted to try'n prove they were tougher than us. They found out different."

"Why am I not surprised?" Julia said. "Was anyone else hurt?"

"You mean durin' the holdup? No," Jim answered. "And those Double M boys ain't hurt all that bad. They'll be nursin' some bruises for awhile, that's all. More importantly, we got a wire from Headquarters. We've got orders. We have to leave, right now."

"Right now?" Julia said. "I'd hoped you'd be home when Charlie and Mary Jane returned."

"So had I," Jim said, "But the message said Cap'n Storm needs us right quick, so whatever the trouble is, it's gotta be somethin' major. We'll be ridin' out soon as I can get my gear together. Oh, and after giving you these."

He dismounted, as did Smoky, then untied the packages from their saddlehorns. Jim handed one to Julia, Smoky one to Cindy.

"Those are pecan pies from Ellen. They had some left over, so she sent you and Cindy each one," he said. "Along with her love."

"Well, these are certainly a welcome treat," Cindy said. "Ellen makes the best pecan pies in the county."

"We also got both of you a little somethin', for comin' up with the idea for me'n Jim to spend the night in town, havin' fun, even though it didn't quite work out the way we'd planned," Smoky said. He gave Cindy the package containing her blouse. "Bethea Jarratt said you'd like these. I hope she was right."

Cindy ripped open the wrapping, and unfolded the blouse.

"Smoky, it's beautiful. Thank you." She wrapped her arms around him and gave him a big kiss.

"This one's yours, Julia," Jim said, as he handed her his package. Julia exclaimed with delight when she opened it and saw the contents.

"This is perfect, Jim. It's just wonderful."

"Bethea said it was the latest fashion from St. Louis," Jim explained.

"Well, it certainly is lovely. And the colors are perfect. But be honest. You two didn't pick these out."

"No, we sure didn't," Jim confessed. "Bethea did."

"She chose well," Cindy said. "I can hardly wait to try mine on. But as far as wearing it, that will have to wait until you two get back from wherever you're headed."

"Speaking of which, we'd better get movin'," Jim said. "Julia, I'm sorry to have to leave on such short notice, but there's no choice."

"I understand, Jim. It's not the first time this has happened, and it surely won't be the last," Julia answered. "All I can say is, like always, be careful."

"The same goes for you, Smoky," Cindy added.

"We'll do our best," Smoky promised. He and the ladies waited in the yard while Jim got his supplies together. Jim lingered in the corral for awhile, talking to Sam and giving him several peppermints. The aged paint, Jim's longtime trail partner and friend, was finally content to remain behind when Jim headed out. He whickered, and nuzzled Jim's chest, then lay down and stretched out on his side in the sun.

"That's right, ol' pard, just take it easy," Jim said. "You've earned it." He went back to where the others were waiting, put his spare clothes and supplies in his saddlebags, then took Julia into his arms for a long, lingering kiss. Smoky did the same with Cindy, like Jim and Julia reluctant to end their embrace. At last, they released their wives, and climbed into their saddles. With final goodbyes, they put their horses into a lope, and headed for Austin. Julia and Cindy watched them until they rode out of sight.

Two hours later, Jim and Smoky reined up in front of Ranger Headquarters. They dismounted, looped their horses' reins around the tooth-marked hitch rail, Jim as always giving Sizzle a peppermint, then went inside. They walked down a long corridor, to Captain Earl Storm's office. Storm heard them coming, and called to them before they even reached his door.

"Jim, Smoky, get on in here. I've been waitin' on you. I was beginnin' to think you'd never get here."

They stepped inside Storm's office.

"Howdy, Cap'n," Jim said.

"Never mind that. We don't even have time for howdies," Storm answered. The captain had a build like a bulldog, was barrel-chested and lantern-jawed. A beat-up light Stetson covered thick, brown hair. His dark eyes glittered with anger. "Grab coffee if you want, then take a seat. I need you both on the trail, today."

"There's that much trouble, eh, Cap'n?" Jim said.

"There surely is," Storm answered. He waited for his two Rangers to pour coffee, and take chairs, before he said more. While Smoky rolled and lit a quirly, Storm filled his pipe with tobacco, lit it, and took a long puff.

"What's this all about, Cap'n?" Smoky asked. "I've never seen you so all-fired worked up, like you seem to be now."

"Murderers. Raiders, committin' mass killings, and wanton thievery and lootin'. Not to mention burnin' every town they hit down to the ground, that's what's stickin' in my craw," Storm answered. "And we've got hardly any idea where to start searchin' for those renegades. Here, take a look at these."

Storm took several papers from the folder on his battered desk, and passed copies of each to Jim and Smoky. Their expressions grew darker as they read the reports. Jim gave a sharp whistle when he passed his papers back to Storm.

"I see what you mean, Cap'n."

"That's right. There's a gang of raiders raisin' Cain all over west Texas," Storm said. "They only hit at night, or when the weather is bad. As you just read, they wear white robes, masks, and hats, and ride white or gray broncs. A couple of 'em have been shot durin' their raids, mebbe killed, but no one knows for certain. They pick up their dead or wounded and take 'em with 'em when they ride out, after destroyin' a town."

"So no one can identify the shot hombres, and mebbe get a clue as to who some of the others are," Smoky said.

"That's right," Storm agreed. "Folks have taken to callin' those sidewinders the Ghost Riders. I hear tell some even believe they really are ghosts, and that no bullets can stop 'em. Well, I'm here to tell you they ain't no ghosts, and they'll find out lead sure can stop 'em . . . Ranger lead."

"You have any idea where we should start searchin' for 'em, Cap'n?" Jim asked.

"Just somewhere in west Texas," Storm

answered. "I know, that's a whole lotta territory. But that's about all I can come up with. So far, those so-called Ghost Riders have destroyed Menardville, Brady, and a couple of small settlements that weren't even on the map, Hazard and Frawley. Those last two they completely wiped out. They've also hit several ranches, killed every last man on 'em, and burned them down too."

Storm paused when more footsteps sounded in the hallway. A minute later, Jim Huggins stepped into the office. Like Jim Blawcyzk, Huggins had also been a lieutenant in the Rangers. His son Daniel had followed in his footsteps. Huggins and Jim had ridden together many times in the past. However, Huggins had retired to a professorship at Baylor University in Waco. Despite his new, mainly sedentary life, he was still tall and lean, his hair now more gray than brown. Since joining the faculty at Baylor, he had grown a neatly trimmed goatee.

"Howdy, Cap'n. Jim, Smoky. Good to see y'all again." He nodded at each man. "Sorry I'm late. My train from Waco was delayed by a bent rail."

"I'm surprised to see you here, J.R.," Jim said. "I thought you settled down to the nice, peaceful life of a college professor."

"I thought I had," J.R. answered. "However, truthfully, I was gettin' kinda bored. That, and classes are out for the summer. So, when Cap'n Storm got in contact with me, and asked for my help, I said why not? I'm back, at least for this one job."

"That's all right, you're bein' a bit late, J.R.," Storm said. For years, whenever Huggins and Blawcyzk rode together, their same first names had led to some confusion, until it was finally decided that Huggins would go by his initials, J.R.

"J.R.," Storm continued, "take a quick look at those papers on my desk. Jim and Smoky can fill you in more as you ride." To Jim and Smoky he said, "Like J.R. said, I talked him into comin' out of retirement, and back to ridin' for the Rangers. That's how dire this situation is. Those Ghost Riders, whoever they may be, are wreakin' havoc all over west Texas. I want them found, and stopped, before they can strike again. Any questions?"

"I've got none," Jim said.

"Me neither," Smoky added.

"None from me, either," J.R. said. He looked at the map on the wall, behind Storm's desk. Pins marked the locations where the raiders had struck. "Seems to me that outfit's makin' a circle. They started in Menardville, hit Brady, then doubled back to attack Hazard and Frawley. I figure if we head west, from where they hit last, Frawley, we'll come across some sign of 'em. An outfit that large can't just disappear without a trace."

"That's why I talked you into comin' back to the Rangers, J.R.," Storm said. "That logical mind of yours. Jim here's, the best tracker in the outfit, and Smoke's close behind. Jim's also the best rider we've got, and we're sure gonna need his, and his horse's, stamina when it comes to chasin' down that bunch. However, J.R., you can think ahead, mebbe figure out the gang's next move. And there isn't any question the three of you are among the best fighters I've got. I figure if y'all can't find and stop the Ghost Riders, no one can."

"It's just like playin' chess," J.R. said. "A matter of odds, and moves. We'll find those men, Cap'n."

"We sure will," Jim added. "Bet your hat on it. But I think we'd also better stop in Brady and Menardville on our way, just to see if we can come up with more information. Mebbe by now someone'll recollect somethin' about one or more of those riders."

"I certainly hope so," Storm said. "Both about the information, and runnin' down that outfit. But this is probably the toughest assignment you've ever been handed. I wish I could give you more to go on, but I just don't have anythin' else. All I can say is good luck, and may the Good Lord ride with you."

"We appreciate that," Jim said. "Smoke, J.R., let's hit our saddles. Adios, Cap'n. We'll get in touch with you as soon as we have anythin' at all, as to those Ghost Riders' whereabouts."

"Ghost Riders!" Storm snorted in disgust. "They sure ain't no ghosts. They're flesh and blood riders, real bad hombres who need a dose of lead to stop 'em. I'm countin' on you three to do just that. Vaya con Dios."

Jim, Smoky, and J.R. left the captain's office, went outside, untied their horses, and mounted. J.R.'s mount was a blocky, blaze-faced, dark chestnut gelding.

"Nice lookin' cayuse, J.R.," Jim said. "Appears he's a study bronc, and has plenty of bottom."

"His name's Monte, and he'll do," J.R. answered.

"Good. Now let's ride."

Jim swung Sizzle away from the rail, and put him into a trot, with Smoky and J.R. just behind. Twenty minutes later, they passed the Austin city limits, and pointed their horses westward.

# 7

Three days of steady riding later, Jim, Smoky, and J.R. were nearing their first destination, Brady. Dusk found them still a little more than twenty miles from town, so they made camp for the night alongside a nameless creek, which fed into the San Saba River. They cared for their horses, then picketed them for the night on a patch of bunch grass, except for Sizzle, who would never wander far from Jim. By the time that was done, full dark had fallen.

"You gonna cook supper again tonight, Jim?" Smoky asked.

"Don't I always?" Jim answered.

"Yeah, I reckon you do. That's because outta the three of us, you're the only one who can come up with somethin' that's almost edible," Smoky said. "Me'n J.R. can't even boil coffee without burnin' it, let alone cook up a mess of vittles."

"That's the Gospel truth," J.R. added. "Why, if I hadn't married Cora, I'd have plumb starved to death years ago. She tried to teach me how to cook, but it just didn't take. So, like usual, me'n Smoke will gather up the firewood while you get things ready."

"Too bad it's gonna be bacon, biscuits, and

beans again," Smoky said. "I'd sure have liked to bring down one of those pronghorns we spotted this afternoon, but I couldn't chance a rifle shot. That might've brought us some unwanted attention."

"Well, if it's any comfort, when we get to Brady tomorrow, we'll have ourselves a good supper in one of the restaurants," Jim answered.

"If there are still any left," J.R. said. "Don't forget, the town was pretty much destroyed. We'll be lucky if any of the eatin' places were spared."

"If not, I'm fairly certain we'll find someplace where we can round up some grub," Jim said. "Meantime, the sooner you boys gather up some firewood, the sooner we'll eat."

A fitful breeze sprang up while the three Rangers ate their supper. Scudding clouds would reveal, then obscure, the waxing gibbous moon. After last cups of coffee, and a final cigarette for Smoky, they pulled off their boots, hats, and gun-belts, then slid under their blankets and pillowed their heads on their saddles. With their six-guns near at hand, in case of any unwanted visitors in the middle of the night, they prepared to sleep, since dawn would find them once again on the trail.

Jim, as usual, said his evening prayers. Ordinarily, by the time he was done, Smoky and

J.R. would be fast asleep, snoring softly. However, when Jim rolled onto his side, he noticed Smoky had lit another cigarette, while J.R. had pushed his Stetson back from over his eyes and was staring at the sky.

*Oh well, I guess mebbe none of us are as tired as we figured we were,* Jim thought. He rolled onto his belly and nestled his face in the crook of his elbow. Even as a kid, he'd never been able to sleep on his back.

Most nights, once Jim's face was buried in his pillow, or on his saddle when sleeping under the stars, he quickly fell asleep. However, blissful slumber wouldn't claim him this night. His mind was restless, his muscles tense, his stomach knotted. He tossed and turned, then pulled his Stetson down tighter over his head, all to no avail. He could not shake off the sense of foreboding keeping him awake. He sat up and grabbed his Peacemaker when an unfamiliar horse whinnied nervously. He looked over at their horses, and when Monte neighed again, he realized the whinny had come from J.R.'s new mount. Not only Monte, but Smoky's black, Midnight, was also nickering worriedly, and pulling back on his picket line. Most upsetting to Jim, his own horse, the normally unflappable Sizzle, was also trotting back and forth anxiously. He'd stop for a few moments, standing as still as a statue, neck arched and ears pricked sharply forward while he stared across the prairie, searching for something which had apparently upset him, then give an anxious neigh and resume pacing.

"Somethin's wrong," Jim muttered. He tossed off his blankets, pulled on his boots and grabbed his gun, then headed over to Sizzle, who was once again gazing at the horizon. When Jim reached him and patted him on the shoulder, the big paint jumped, and whickered his fear.

"What's the matter, Siz?" Jim asked. "Somethin's really gotten under your hide, that's for dang sure." Sizzle nudged his shoulder. Jim turned at a slight sound behind him.

"It's only me comin' up behind you, Jim," Smoky called. "Don't plug me, will you?"

"I've thought about doin' just that, many times. But I reckon it can wait for another night, Smoke," Jim answered, with a slight chuckle. When Smoky, who also held his gun at the ready, reached his side, he continued, "It's a good thing you shouted that warnin'. Jumpy as I am, it's plumb likely I just might have drilled you. Bet a hat on it."

"So you're feelin' it too, huh?" Smoky said. "And what's gotten into your horse? I've never seen Sizzle act like he is."

"I dunno," Jim admitted. "Where's J.R.?"

"He's takin' a look-see around the other side of our camp," Smoky answered. "Whatever it is that's got us and the horses spooked has also gotten under J.R.'s skin. Mebbe you'd better stay with these broncs while I take a look around, too. We sure don't want to lose them."

"That's a good idea, Smoke," Jim agreed. "Be careful."

"I aim to be," Smoky answered. "You just try and calm down these animals, because if you can't, there sure ain't anyone else who can. Which would mean there really is somethin' bad out there in the dark." He disappeared into the night.

Jim's nerves became even more taut once Smoky was out of sight. Sizzle seemed to pick up on his rider's tension, for he became even more anxious, tossing his head and shoving Jim in the back.

"Siz," Jim finally said. "I hate to do this, but I'm gonna picket you along with Monte and Midnight. You seem scared enough you might run off, and I can't chance that." He picked up Sizzle's halter from the ground where he had left it, placed it on the horse, then led him back to his saddle. He removed his lariat, along with a picket pin and hammer from his saddlebags, then tied the rope to Sizzle's halter. He led the paint back to where the other two horses were picketed, tied the other end of his rope to the pin, and drove that into the ground.

"That'll hold you, just in case," he said. He patted the horse's shoulder. "It'll be all right.

We'll figure out what's got us all spooked, and take care of it."

Jim kept his gun in his hand and kept peering into the dark, straining to see whatever was out there. He soothed the horses, as best he could, with a soft, calming voice, stroking their muzzles. The minutes ticked by slowly while he waited for Smoky to return. Finally, his partner's voice called out.

"Me and J.R. are comin' in, Jim. Ease off that trigger."

Jim gave a sigh of relief, as he removed his thumb from the hammer of his Colt and eased the gun back into its holster.

"You find anythin'?" he asked, when both men materialized out of the gloom.

"Not a thing," Smoky said.

"Me neither," J.R. added. "Doesn't seem to be any reason at all for us to be so jumpy, but boy howdy, I'm really on edge."

"Same goes for me," Smoky added. "Now, sometimes humans'll get all het up for no reason, but why're the horses so upset, too?"

"I dunno," Jim answered. "A lotta horses spook real easy, but not Sizzle. Your Midnight, either, for that matter."

"Monte's pretty steady too," J.R. said.

"Well, whatever it is, we'll just have to hope it's nothin' we should be worried about. Mebbe it's just the wind, or some smell we can't quite put our fingers on, but the horses have picked up."

"That'd be our noses, not our fingers, Smoke," Jim said, with a laugh. "Guess there's nothin' to be done about whatever it is. Tell you what. You two try'n get some sleep. There's no point in all of us losin' a night's shut-eye. I'll stay with the horses, and keep 'em calmed down."

"That sounds like a good idea," J.R. said. "Guess I don't have to remind you to stay alert."

"I reckon not," Jim said. "G'wan, get outta here. Good night."

" 'Night, Jim," Smoky said.

"Yeah. Good night," J.R. added.

With Jim on watch, Smoky and J.R. did manage to snatch some sleep, although neither man slept very well. When the sun topped the eastern horizon, gilding it in brilliant shades of yellow and gold, they rolled out of their blankets, still bleary-eyed.

" 'Mornin', Jim," Smoky shouted. "I take it everythin's all right."

"Everythin's just fine, Smoke," Jim called back. "Guess we were all lookin' for ghosts that weren't there. Get the fire goin' and I'll start the coffee boilin'."

"All right."

The three men ate a hasty breakfast, then, still tired, saddled and bridled their horses and swung onto their backs.

"I don't know what it was back there," J.R. said, as they heeled the mounts into a walk. "But whatever it was, I'm sure glad to leave it behind."

Jim and Smoky nodded silent agreement.

# 8

Jim, Smoky, and J.R. kept their horses at a steady, ground-eating lope for most of the next day, a gait which covered plenty of ground, yet still was not excessively hard on the mounts. They arrived at Brady just around two in the afternoon. When they reached the edge of town, two young men, on horseback, materialized from the brush on either side of the trail. They each held rifles, which they leveled at the Rangers' chests.

"Don't make a move, hombres," the nearer, and younger, of the pair ordered. "Don't even twitch, or we'll put bullets in you. Just keep your hands away from your guns and raise 'em."

"How can we raise our guns if we have to keep our hands away from 'em?" Jim asked.

"Oh, a smart mouth," the nearer man said. "You want me to shut it permanent-like, by puttin' a bullet through your teeth? Now, do what I said, and get your hands up. Pronto!"

"Better do what he says, Jim," J.R. advised. "These boys mean business."

"All right," Jim answered. "We ain't lookin' for trouble." He raised his hands shoulder-high. As soon as he did, the unmistakable clicks of a pair of Colts' hammers being thumbed back sounded from behind the two cowboys.

"I'd recommend *you two* drop those rifles and reach, unless *you* want bullets in *your* backs, instead of you pluggin' my pardners," Smoky ordered. He'd circled around the two sentries, while Jim and J.R. rode straight into town. "And don't even think about pullin' those triggers, hopin' you'll be faster'n me. I can drop you both before either of you gets off a shot."

The cowboy closest to Smoky uttered a curse.

"Better do what he says, Eddie. He's got us pinned."

Both men let their rifles fall to the dirt, then lifted their hands over their heads. Jim and J.R. lowered their hands, pulled their own pistols from their holsters, and aimed them at the two young men.

"Next time you try to get the drop on some-one, you might want to make certain of how many pardners he's got travelin' with him," Jim advised. "We spotted your little trap from a ways back, so we set up one of our own . . . one which you neatly rode right into, thank you very much. And if you boys had made the mistake of killin' us, you'd have let yourself in for real trouble. We're Texas Rangers. Now that you know that, one of you mind tellin' us what's got the pair of you so all-fired on the prod?"

"You're Rangers?" the cowboy called Eddie said.

"Sure enough are," Jim answered. "On the trail of the renegades who attacked this town. Got our badges in our shirt pockets and our papers in our billfolds, if you're of a mind to see 'em. However, I'm the one askin' the questions, and I ain't heard an answer yet."

Eddie shrugged.

"Reckon we might as well tell 'em, Chuck," he said, "seein' as they're Rangers and all."

"Not to mention they've got their guns aimed right at our briskets . . . and backs," the cowboy named Chuck said. "All right. If you're Rangers, on the trail of the men who just about destroyed this town, like you claim, we've got no quarrel with you. My name's Chuck McIlroy. My kid brother here is Eddie. Our pa was Dale McIlroy, the McCulloch County sheriff. When those hombres raided Brady, some of 'em surrounded our house. We tried to fight 'em off, us and our pa. Even our ma, her name was Eleanor, threw a few bullets at 'em. We didn't have much luck, but neither did they. When they figured out it would take more time than they wanted to gun us down, they blew up the house. That's what's left of it, just over yonder." He indicated the splintered remnants of a blown-down picket fence, behind which sat a few burnt, shattered timbers. "The dynamite must've landed right at pa's feet, because we never found anythin' left of him, at all. Not even his boots, or his belt buckle. There wasn't much left of ma, either, just enough to give her a decent burial. Me'n Eddie still ain't certain how we survived. Both of us recollect the explosion, but nothin' after that, except a couple of neighbors pullin' us from under the rubble. Since that day, we've been watchin' day and night in case those raiders decided to return and finish the job. We stop every stranger who comes into town, just to make certain he's not one of the outfit come back to scout things out again."

"We're sure sorry about what happened to your folks, all of us," Jim said. "And we're gonna make certain the men responsible pay. You can bet your hat on it. But that still doesn't give you any call to draw down on everyone passin' by. Now, we came here to see if we could get any more information that might possibly lead us to that gang. You reckon you might give us a hand with that?"

"We'd be glad to, Ranger," Chuck answered. "You mind if we get our guns back now?"

"Go ahead," Jim answered.

"Much obliged." The two brothers lowered their hands, dismounted, and retrieved their Winchesters. Once the rifles were shoved back in the saddle boots and the boys were back on their horses, Jim, Smoky, and J.R. put up their own guns.

"Where do you want to start, Rangers?" Chuck asked.

"We've been ridin' long and hard the past several days," Jim answered. "We'd like to take care of our horses, get some chuck, and mebbe a room for the night. Once all that's arranged, we'd like to talk with anyone who was here the night of the raid."

"We can show you where to do all that," Eddie said. "The folks around here are pretty tough. They ain't gonna let that raid destroy Brady. The Hotel Dixie's already been rebuilt. Same with Grandma Hussey's Café. And the Brady Saloon, of course. That was the first place to go back up. We don't have a store yet, since Mack Dunn was killed in the raid, so we're waitin' on someone to move into town and open a new place. For now, we're buyin' stuff from San Saba, and havin' it freighted over. The livery barn ain't been started yet, but Luke Jessup's got the corrals back together. He'll take good care of your broncs. Me and Chuck'll help get you settled, and we'll also spread the word you're in town, and want to talk with folks. They'll sure be happy to know the Rangers are after those hombres. Of course, most everyone's bound to notice you anyway. They'll probably look at you a little suspiciously, so you might want to pin on your badges."

"That's not a bad idea," J.R. said. He pulled his

badge from his shirt pocket and pinned it to his vest. Jim and Smoky did likewise.

"Good. We're all set. Let's go." Jim lifted Sizzle's reins and heeled him into a walk. He and his partners followed the brothers down Brady's Main Street. As Eddie had said, the citizens of the town had wasted no time in beginning the resurrection of their community. Most of the debris and rubble had been carted away. Several new structures had already been completed, their siding either still unpainted raw wood, or freshly whitewashed. Still others were in various stages of construction. As Eddie had also said, most of the passersby stared at the trio of badge-wearing newcomers accompanying the brothers into town. He and Chuck led them two blocks past the hotel, then left down an alleyway. At its end was a pile of blackened timbers, all that remained of a large stable, as well as a new shed and two newly re-fenced corrals. One of those held several horses. A shed behind one held feed and tack. A small tent was alongside the other one, with a middle-aged, moon-faced man sitting on a small barrel in front of it.

"Howdy, Luke," Chuck called. "Got a couple of customers for you."

"Looks more like three," Luke answered, as he rose from the barrel and went to meet the newcomers. "Don't matter none, I'll take all the business I can get. Men, I'm sorry the accommodations for your horses won't be up to my usual standards, but I'll take care of 'em real good. Won't have my barn rebuilt for a spell, but at least none of the horses in my care got burned to death. Seven got stolen, though. Rangers, huh? Sure glad to see you boys. I reckon you're here about those renegades who plumb near destroyed this town. Sure hope you catch 'em. When you do, bring 'em back here and I'll put the ropes around their necks my ownself. Although plenty of other folks would like that chance, too."

"Luke," Chuck broke in, when the hostler finally paused for breath, "just take care of their horses, will you? Rangers, me'n Eddie forgot to tell you Luke don't ever shut up once he gets wound up . . . and he's always wound up."

"Yeah," Eddie added. "I'm kinda surprised 'ol Luke didn't talk those raiders to death. Rangers, now that I can get a word in, this here's Luke Jessup, the livery owner. Luke, Rangers . . . you know, you hombres never did give us your names."

"Lieutenant Jim Blawcyzk, that's BLUH-zhick," Jim answered. "It's Polish, and most folks can't pronounce it. Can't wrap their tongues around it, and end up gettin' 'em all tangled up. Easier to just call me Jim, or Ranger. My pards are Lieutenant Jim Huggins, better known as J.R., and Sergeant Smoky McCue."

"Well, don't just set there," Luke answered.

"Swing offa them broncs and turn 'em into the first corral, that's the empty one. You can stow your gear in the shed yonder. No one'll touch it, I guarantee you. Your horses, neither. I sleep with one eye open and a shotgun alongside me. Only reason those raiders got seven of my horses is there were too doggone many of 'em for me to plug. They pinned me down, then cornered me in the barn when they set it afire. I reckon the only reason they didn't fill me fulla lead is they figured I'd already been shot, and my body'd be eaten up by the flames. Lucky thing for me they didn't wait to make certain. I was able to bust out a few boards in the back wall and get out before the whole shebang collapsed. It was darn close, though."

"Like Eddie said, Luke, if you'd tried talkin' 'em to death, instead of attemptin' to shoot those raiders, they'd all be six feet under right now," Chuck said. "Just open the gate for us, will you?"

"All right, all right," Luke answered. He slid open the gate's bars, and the five men rode in, then dismounted.

"I'll get some feed ready for your horses," Luke said, as he slid the bars back in place.

"Just a minute before you do," Jim said. "I'd like to ask you a couple of questions about those raiders, if you don't mind. And when you answer, give me the short version."

"Not at all, Ranger," Luke agreed. "Go ahead."

"All right. They're pretty simple," Jim answered. "Did you happen to get a look at any of those men?"

"No, I sure didn't," Luke answered. "They all had on white robes, with white pillowcases or some such over their heads to mask their faces. White or light-colored hats over those. Couldn't even catch a glimpse of their boots."

"How about their horses? Any marks, anything which might be recognizable?"

"Nope." Luke shook his head. "All whites or grays. Some white markings on a couple of the grays, blazes or stars, mebbe one or two had white stockings, but nothing you wouldn't see on a thousand other broncs. No brands, neither, at least none that I could see."

"What about the horses they stole from you?" J.R. asked. "Any unusual markings on them, or any brands?"

"Four of 'em weren't mine. They belonged to men boardin' their horses in my stable, which of course I don't have any more, leastwise until I get it built back up," Luke said. "And all four of those boys are dead, so I reckon they don't need those broncs anymore. Still, it's a shame they got stole . . ."

"Luke," Chuck said.

"Huh?"

"Shorten it up, or these here Rangers will die of old age before they even get back on those raiders' trail. The raiders, too, for that matter."

"I'm just now gettin' to the point," Luke protested.

"Shortest way is the direct way," Chuck retorted. "Just tell the Rangers what they want to know, not one of your infernal, all-fired windies."

"All right," Luke said, frowning. "Far as my horses, they wore my brand. Nothin' fancy, just a plain ol' LJ on their left hips. All of mine had several old brands, too. Nothin' which would stand out, like a paint, or bald-faced palomino, or anythin' like that in the whole bunch. Only bays, chestnuts, and one sorrel."

"Well, at least those LJ brands will help identify 'em, if we happen to come across any of your horses," J.R. said.

"Luke, did you happen to hear any of those men say anythin', mebbe call out a name or somethin'?" Jim asked.

"Nary a word. They just kept shootin' and shootin', then shootin' some more. Kept me pinned down while they fired the barn and ran off my stock. Now, if you don't have any more questions, let me start grainin' your horses."

"Sure, Luke, and much obliged," Jim said.

"Ranger, two or three folks in town heard those men shout a couple of names," Eddie said. "Soon as you're settled in the hotel we'll round 'em up for you. Tell you what. After you get your room, why don't you take the time to clean up, have some grub at Grandma Hussey's place, then meet us at the saloon, say around five thirty?"

"That sounds like a good plan to me, Jim," Smoky said. "You agreeable?"

"Don't see why not," Jim said, with a shrug. "I'm about ready for some decent chuck, instead of bacon and beans."

"Good," Eddie said. "Soon as you finish takin' care of your horses, we'll bring you to the hotel."

While their horses ate, the Rangers groomed them thoroughly, removing several days' worth of trail dust and grime from their coats. As always, Jim left Sizzle with a peppermint, and a promise to check on him later. Satisfied their horses were in good care under Luke's capable hands, unless of course the hostler talked the animals' ears off, they shouldered their saddlebags and followed the McIlroy brothers to the newly rebuilt Hotel Dixie. Except for the sign over the front door, the building was still unpainted, and cracks showed between the raw planks which had been used for the outside walls, and which had shrunk under the relentless Texas sun, but at least Jim and his partners wouldn't be sleeping on the hard ground for this night, and would have a real roof over their heads.

"Jock, got some lawmen here who need rooms for the night," Chuck called, when they entered the lobby. "Rangers, this here is Jock MacDougal, owner of the Dixie."

"Sure, and it's a pleasure to make your acquaintances, gentlemen. Come in, come in. I apologize the accommodations are a bit Spartan, but the new furnishings I ordered haven't arrived." He waved his hand around the lobby, which was sparsely furnished with a few ladder-back chairs, a scorched desk, a linen chest, and a smoke-blackened sideboard, on which sat several pitchers of water. An old door perched on two empty whiskey barrels served as the front desk. There were no pigeonholes for the room keys and guests' messages. Instead, there were merely nails driven into the wall behind the desk, only one of which had a key hanging from it.

"We'll take three rooms if you've got them," Jim said, "Either that, or one with two beds. We'll share if we have to."

"I wish I could grant ye that request, but I've only got one room, with one bed. All the others are full up, with folks who haven't rebuilt yet. However, ye all are welcome to that room, and it'll only be a dollar for the night." MacDougal spoke in an unusual accent, a combination of Scots Highland brogue and Deep South, most likely, Jim would guess, from southern Mississippi.

"We've had worse," Jim answered. "The price is a bit steep, but we'll take it. It will be a nice change from rollin' our blankets out on the hard ground."

"Fine, fine," MacDougal said. "If ye will just sign the register." He turned the book to Jim, dipped a quill pen in an inkwell, and handed that to him. Jim signed in his nearly illegible scrawl, then dug a silver dollar out of his pocket and gave it to the clerk.

"Well, I can't read your signature, but as long as I've got your money, I guess that will be all right," MacDougal said. He bit the coin to make certain it was genuine, then gave Jim the key to Room 8.

"I'd be Jim, and my pardners are Smoky and J.R.," Jim answered.

"Rangers, seein' as you're all set for now, me'n Eddie'll wander on outta here, and start roundin' up folks," Chuck said. "The saloon's across the street, and up a block. We'll meet you there at five thirty."

"We'll see you then," Jim answered. "Adios for now."

"Adios."

"Rangers, I don't have a saloon or café in my hotel," MacDougal said, once the brothers had left. "No women, either, although sometimes a man'll bring a girl from the saloon here to take advantage of the facilities, if you know what I mean. I don't want the bother. However, I do keep a stock of something extra-special on hand,

111

for those whose throats are dry, and might want a wee drop of spirits. Have any of you ever sampled *The Glenlivet*?"

"I sure haven't," Smoky answered. "Never even heard of it, for that matter."

"Same here," J.R. said.

"And I don't drink anythin' stronger than sarsaparilla, so I haven't," Jim said. "But I appreciate the offer. Just a glass of water would be fine."

"How about you other two gentlemen?" MacDougal said. "I'm offering ye a chance to taste the ambrosia of the gods, the finest single malt whiskey ever to come out of bonnie Scotland. Ye all will most likely not taste the like of it again, once you leave Brady."

"I'll try some, sure," Smoky said.

"I might," J.R. said. "First, just how much will this 'ambrosia of the gods' cost us?"

"A mere dollar, for the closest sample to heaven you'll ever find on this Earth," MacDougal said. "It's a miracle my precious hoard survived. I keep it in a special cellar, deep under the building. The heat from the fire dinna shatter the bottles. In fact, the labels dinna even get scorched, and the corks weren't even singed."

"A dollar?" J.R. echoed. "That's not 'mere'. I can buy an entire bottle of decent whiskey for that price, in almost any saloon."

"Aye, 'tis a bit dear, the cost," MacDougal answered. "However, I'm offering ye the chance to sample nectar so sweet, t'will make a young lady's kiss seem bitter by comparison. A drink which will sooth your throat like a woman's caress, go down smooth as silk, and warm your belly with the passion of a lover. All that, for just one dollar. And ye'll not find any rotgut whiskey in any saloon which compares to *The Glenlivet*, at any price."

"He's convinced me, J.R.," Smoky said. "How about you?"

"I can't say no, not after a spiel like that," J.R. said. "Mr. MacDougal, seems to me you could outtalk a medicine show man."

"Aye, that could be. But ye won't regret your choice. Many men in Scotland say they'd rather have a dram of *The Glenlivet* than make love to a beautiful woman . . . or their wives. Which might explain why there are so few babies bein' born back in my home country."

MacDougal laughed at his own joke, one he'd clearly told many times before. He opened the left door of the sideboard, then removed a bottle and four glasses. He set the bottle on top of the sideboard, uncorked it, and poured three glasses half-full of the amber liquid. The fourth he filled three-quarters full with water.

"That will be a nickel for the water, and a dollar each for the whiskey," he said.

"You charge for water?" Jim said, disbelieving.

"Aye, that I must," MacDougal answered. "It

cost me dearly to dig my well, and of course I had to buy rope, a pulley, and a bucket so I can draw water. It all adds up to considerable expense."

"If you say so. My mouth's dry as cotton, so I reckon I've got no choice," Jim answered. Reluctantly, he dug in his pocket, pulled out a nickel, and handed it to the hotel owner. Only then did MacDougal pass him the glass of water. Smoky and J.R. each gave MacDougal a silver dollar, then he handed them their drinks.

"Gentlemen, I propose a toast," he said, raising his glass. "To your success in finding those men who destroyed Brady."

"And to them not puttin' bullets in our guts when we do," Smoky added. He took a sip of his drink.

"Well?" MacDougal asked.

"You're right, Mr. MacDougal," Smoky answered. "This is, without a doubt, the finest red-eye I've ever tasted."

"Red-eye!" MacDougal was indignant. "Ye can't call *The Glenlivet* 'red-eye'. Ye haven't sampled anything so sweet since your mother suckled you at her breast. Haven't ye any appreciation for the finer things in life, mon?"

"I apologize if I've offended you," Smoky answered. "Force of habit. This is indeed the best liquor that's ever tickled my taste buds."

"Ah, that's what I wanted to hear," MacDougal said. "J.R.?"

"I have to agree with my pardner. This is the smoothest, mellowest drink I've ever had the pleasure to sip," J.R. answered.

"And your water, Jim?" MacDougal asked.

"It cut the dust from my throat," Jim said.

"Splendid. Will ye be liking another?"

Jim shook his head. "I can't afford it. Reckon I'll just go back to the stable for my canteen, after a bit."

"How about you two gentlemen? Will ye be liking another drop?"

"Uh-uh," Smoky said. "I'd like to savor just this one glass."

"And I never take more'n one or two drinks at a time," J.R. added. "Besides, we've got to clean up and get supper before we meet the McIlroy boys over at the saloon. Reckon we'd best get a move on."

"You're lookin' to wash up? Then ye'll be needin' towels, soap, and water," MacDougal said. "I'll get ye some."

"Wait," Jim said. "First, how much?"

"Jim, ye cut my heart to the quick," MacDougal replied. "I'll not take advantage of poor way-farers, in need of lodging for the night."

"How much?" Jim repeated.

"Fifteen cents for a pitcher of water. A quarter for the soap, and ten cents each for the towels," MacDougal answered.

"Any chance of gettin' that water heated?"

"Certainly, for another twenty-five cents."

"Never mind. I'll use it cold. Far as the soap I've got my own, right here in my saddlebags," Jim said. "Got a towel, too, but I'll pay the ten cents so I won't have to use mine, then hope it dries before we leave, and I have to stuff it back in my saddlebags. The three of us'll share the one towel, and the water. And I'm sure glad you don't 'take advantage' of folks. I'd hate to think what it would cost us if you did."

"I assure you, I barely get by," MacDougal said.

"Of course you do," Jim answered. "Before we head upstairs, we just need to know if you saw any of those raiders, or heard a name. Anythin' which might help us."

"No, I did not," MacDougal answered. "As soon as the shooting started, I dove behind the front counter. I'm afraid I'm not a very brave man. I dinna emerge from hiding until those men were gone, and the entire town was ablaze. I'm sorry I can't help ye."

"It doesn't matter," Jim said. "So far, it appears no one has seen any of those men's faces, nor anythin' they might recognize about 'em." He handed MacDougal a quarter. "I'll take that water and towel now."

MacDougal bit the coin, then shoved it in his pocket. He opened the linen chest, rummaged around in it, and came up with a tattered, once white but now dingy gray, towel. He handed that and one of the pitchers off the sideboard to Jim.

"Here ye go. Room 8 is up the stairs and down the hall to the right. I hope ye'all will be comfortable."

"I'm certain we will be," Jim said. "C'mon, Smoke, J.R. Let's go."

The three lawmen tromped up the bare-wood stairs, then down an uncarpeted, dimly lit corridor to their room. Jim turned the key in the lock, opened the door, and stepped inside, with Smoky and J.R. close behind.

"What the . . .?" Smoky exclaimed. "Even by out here in the middle of nowhere west Texas standards, this has got to be one of the worst furnished, and built, places I've ever seen."

The room's furnishings were one double bed, with only one sheet and a thin blanket for covers, one chair, three hooks for clothes, and a wash stand with basin. There wasn't even a chamber pot under the bed. Thin curtains fluttered at a partially open window. The walls were plank, and unpainted or papered. As had the wood used on the exterior of the hotel, those planks had shrunk, leaving large cracks between them, so that you could hear everything from the adjoining rooms, and even spy on your neighbors, were you so inclined.

"Boy howdy, you said a mouthful, Smoke," J.R. agreed. He slung his saddlebags over the chair, pulled off his gunbelt and hung it from a hook, then stretched out on the bed.

"How's the mattress?" Smoky asked, as he sat on the edge of the bed.

"Think it's stuffed with nails, if it's stuffed with anythin' at all," J.R. answered. "I know the McIlroys said MacDougal rebuilt this place in a hurry, but he sure didn't spend a whole lotta cash on it."

"He's definitely Scotch, all right," Jim said, glancing at one of the spaces in the wall, catching a bit of movement from the next room's occupant. "Given the chance, MacDougal would probably bleed this town just as dry as those outlaws we're after. Well, we're only gonna be here for one night, so let's make the best of it." He placed the pitcher and towel on the washstand, then took off his Stetson, bandanna, shirt, and gunbelt, and hung those on a hook. He dug in his saddlebags and came up with a washcloth, and a half-used bar of Pears' Soap. He had discovered that brand some months back. Unlike the harsh soaps so prevalent, Pears' was a much milder product, of a translucent amber color. With the beating a man's skin took from the harsh, unforgiving Texas sun and wind, he didn't need the additional punishment of a harsh, alkaline soap. Jim poured some water from the pitcher into the basin, ducked his head into it, then wet the washcloth and soap and worked up a lather. He scrubbed his face and upper torso, then took the towel to dry off. He winced as he ran the towel over his face, then his chest and belly.

"How's that towel, Jim? A mite scratchy?" Smoky asked.

"A mite? I'd've been better off towelin' myself dry with prickly pear pads," Jim answered. "I've taken Comanche arrows that didn't leave scratches as deep as this towel has."

"Well, mebbe at least you softened it up a bit for me'n Smoke," J.R. said. "You gonna shave, Jim, or are you just about done?"

"Nah, I'm not gonna bother with shavin'," Jim answered. "Soap and water are yours, whenever you want it."

"Great," J.R. said. He got off the bed. "Dunno about you two boys, but I'm plumb starved. Let's hope the chuck in this town is better'n the hotel."

J.R. quickly washed and redressed, followed by Smoky. They once again belted their guns and holsters around their waists, then headed for supper.

Unlike the Hotel Dixie, Grandma Hussey's Café had been rebuilt to look almost exactly as it had appeared before the raid on Brady. And its proprietor, "Grandma", resembled anything but her name. The Rangers were taken aback by the petite woman who boomed a greeting when they walked into the café. At this hour, before the usual suppertime, they were the only customers.

"Howdy, boys," she shouted. "Been expectin' you. I'm Grandma. Chuck and Eddie McIlroy told me you'd be stoppin' by for some vittles. Plop yourselves down at that back corner table while I bring the coffee. I'll only be a minute." She disappeared into the kitchen, while Jim and his partners took their seats.

"She don't look like any grandma I've ever seen," Smoky said, as he pulled the makings from his vest pocket and began to roll a cigarette.

"Yeah, and this place don't look like any restaurant I've ever been in, either," J.R. added. Indeed, the café had red velvet curtains at the windows, red cloth napkins on the tables, and risqué paintings of scantily clad women hanging on the walls. In one corner, discreetly half-hidden by white lace curtains, trimmed with red velvet bows, were an oak table and four chairs. Above that table hung several paintings of open shirted or bare-chested, Stetson hatted, gun-toting young cowboys.

"Long as the food's good, and there's plenty of it, I don't care what the place looks like," Jim said. "I'm about ready to eat an entire steer, hooves, horns, and all."

"I heard that. And you Rangers won't go away from my place hungry, you can bet your hat on that." Grandma had returned, brandishing a steaming hot pot of coffee and three mugs.

"Jim. You've been here before," J.R. said.

"Nope." Jim shook his head. "This is my first time in Brady. Never before been here in my life."

"Then where'd this nice lady pick up 'bet a hat'? You're the only hombre I've ever heard use that expression," J.R. retorted.

"I started sayin' it after a cowboy wearin' that nice, fancy sombrero nailed to the wall over the counter bet me that hat against my dress he could eat six of my steak dinners in an hour," Grandma said, as she started pouring their coffee. "He lost. I don't suppose any of you would care to bet one of those silver star in silver circle badges y'all are wearin'? I'd be plumb tickled to have one of those."

"No, we sure ain't interested in doin' any gamblin'," Smoky said. "Just want some supper, even if it is a mite early. We've got a lot to do before we pull out in the mornin'."

"What'll you boys have?" Grandma asked. "I've got a special on pork chops today. Three of 'em in an order, nice and juicy. Those come with plenty of fried spuds, pork gravy, black-eyed peas, biscuits with butter and honey, and all the coffee you can drink. Got a nice, homemade apple crisp for dessert, if you ain't filled up by then."

"That sounds good to me," Smoky said.

"Same here," J.R. added.

"Fine with me, but make mine a double order of everything, especially the apple crisp," Jim said.

Grandma shot him a look of incredulity.

"Are you certain about that, Ranger? That's an awful lot of food, and lookin' at how skinny you are, you don't seem to have enough of a belly to hold it all." She patted Jim's stomach. He blushed.

"He'll eat all of that, and then some," Smoky said. "Count on it."

"I guess then it's a good thing you didn't take me up on that bet, Ranger," Grandma said to Jim. "It appears you would've won . . . and I'd have plumb hated to hand over my blouse to you."

She glanced down at her bosom. Jim blushed even redder, while Grandma and his partners laughed.

"I'll go start makin' your supper now," she continued. "It'll be ready right quick. You need anything else at the moment?"

"I just have to ask you this," Smoky said. "You sure don't look like my grandmas did, or any grandma I've ever seen, for that matter. You don't exactly dress like one, neither."

Grandma Hussey was at least eighty years old, her face, although covered with fine wrinkles, still attractive. Her hair, which she wore loose to her shoulders, had long since turned to silver. She was tiny, no more than five foot two. However, her sizable breasts were still round and firm, her figure slim, with a trim waist and hips. Her blue eyes sparkled with life. She was dressed in a low cut blue silk blouse, trimmed with silver spangles, and a flowing red, white, and purple striped skirt. Large silver hoops dangled from her ears, and her lips were painted bright red. Rouge emphasized her high cheekbones.

"You mean this silly old thing?" she answered. "It's just something I threw on this mornin'."

"Well, it sure fell in all the right places. And there's got to be more to it than that," Smoky insisted.

"All right, Ranger, I'll confess, there is. But you'll have to squeeze it outta me," she retorted, then sat on his lap. "Are you ready to question me?"

This time, it was Smoky's turn to blush.

"I'd purely love to, but I'm a married man," Smoky answered. "All of us are, for that matter."

"Didn't realize that made a difference," Grandma said, pouting. She stood back up, and smoothed her skirt.

"It does to us," Smoky said.

"Just my luck. Three good-lookin' lawmen wander into my place, and they're all married. Oh well, you can't blame a gal for tryin'. I'll tell you the story behind this here café."

"I'm listenin'," Smoky said.

"All right. Seventeen years back, my husband

up and died on me. Left me penniless. We had three kids, two boys and a girl, but one of the boys got himself killed in a stupid knife fight, over a woman, and the other boy and girl are grown and moved to California. They've both got a passel of kids, which means I couldn't ask them for help. So, I took the only job I could find, waitin' tables in this place. Scraped and saved until I had enough to buy it from old Mort Tucker, who owned it. Problem is, business was okay enough, but I was still strugglin'. Then, one day, Sam Peavey, who owns the Diamond SP Ranch about five miles west of town, was in having supper. I was complainin' about how slow business was, so he told me, laughin' about it, that I should change the name from Sandra's Place to Hussey's, which just happens to be my real last name. Sam said men would just flock in here to see the 'hussies', even though my name has an 'e' in it. Sam was jokin', but I just looked him dead in the eye and said 'Why not?' So I fixed up the place like a French whorehouse, or at least what I think a French whorehouse looks like, renamed it 'Grandma Hussey's', figurin' most men don't know how to spell anyway, so they wouldn't notice the difference, fancied up my dress, and business went through the roof. Sure, some folks are laughin' at me behind my back, but thanks to Sam's idea, for which he gets free meals for life, I'm laughin' all the way to the bank. Leastwise I

124

was, until those raiders hit it. But unlike a lot of folks, I didn't have all my money in the bank, so I had enough left to rebuild. I always keep a good chunk hidden away in my little house, out back. It's behind a thick prickly pear hedge, so those hombres missed it. Me, too, since I was holed up back there. And because they struck after I was closed, no one was in the building to get hurt when those men attacked, and burned it to the ground."

"What about that table in the corner?" J.R. asked. "The one behind the curtains?"

"Oh, you mean the one with the handsome cowpunchers' pictures on the walls," Grandma answered. Her blue eyes lit up, mischievously. "That's for the ladies. You men shouldn't have all the fun. Of course, a lot of the women in town claim to be scandalized by those paintings, but most of them seem to wander in here, on a regular basis. And I painted those pictures myself. It wasn't too hard to persuade some of the young cowboys around here to take off their shirts and make a few extra dollars. Especially for a harmless old lady. Ah, if I were only sixty years younger."

"I'd imagine you could still give some of those cowboys a run for their money, even now," Smoky said.

"Darn straight I could, if I were that kind of woman. You too, for that matter," Grandma answered. "But I'm not, at all. This place is just for good, clean fun, a spot where folks can relax and have a good meal at a fair price, and maybe let their imaginations run a little bit wild, thinkin' of what they might be doin' in here, besides just eatin'. I've got two young waitresses, Debbie and Dahlia, who will be comin' in shortly, pretty young things. Debbie's a cute, blue-eyed blonde, while Dahlia's a fine-lookin' colored gal. And a good-lookin' feller, name of Joe, as a waiter. The gals dress like I do, and the feller like one of those cowboys in the pictures, leavin' his shirt half-unbuttoned. But nothin' happens. Folks know they can look, but not touch. I keep a shotgun under the counter in case anyone gets an idea to start trouble, and Joe wears a gun on his hip. I know how to use that shotgun, and Joe's real quick with his pistol. No one's gotten out of line in my place yet."

"Sounds like you're doin' quite well," Jim said. "I've gotta admit, you have a clever concept here."

"I'm doin' just fine," Grandma answered. "I serve good food, at reasonable prices, with a bit of entertainment thrown in. But, as I said, it's all just good, innocent fun. That's why I'm not bothered, at least not by most folks. Even Reverend Hutton, the circuit riding Methodist preacher, stops by for a meal when he's in town. As far as those who don't like what I'm doin', they can just darn well stay away . . . which they do. Now, enough about me. I'd imagine you boys are real hungry, so let me get started on your supper."

"Mrs. Hussey . . ." Jim began.

"Grandma. You want something else?"

"Yeah . . . Grandma. I've got just one quick question, if you don't mind," Jim said.

"Go ahead. Shoot."

"You said you were in your house when those raiders attacked the town. I don't suppose you heard any of 'em say anythin' which might help us track 'em down, or mebbe catch a glimpse of one of 'em."

"I wish I could say I had, Ranger, but I'd be lyin' to you. All I heard was a whole lot of shoutin' and shootin', and all I saw was a bunch of flames and smoke. Sorry I can't be of more help."

"You wouldn't have been any help if you'd gotten yourself killed," Jim answered. "Don't fret yourself about not seein' those renegades. If you had, you'd most likely be dead."

"Well, *that's* a comforting thought," Grandma retorted. "Now, you boys just relax and enjoy your coffee while I get your supper."

"That's the feistiest ol' gal I've ever run across," J.R. said, once Grandma was in the kitchen, out of earshot. "Those renegades would have bit off more than they could chew if they tangled with her, I'm guessin'."

"Boy howdy, you said a mouthful," Smoky answered. "She'd have given 'em what for, then tied 'em in knots and turned 'em inside out." He stubbed out the butt of his cigarette in the ashtray at the center of the table, then rolled and lit another smoke.

Jim took a swallow of his coffee. "If the food's as good as this coffee, we'll be eatin' real well tonight," he said. "This is one fine brew."

The three men relaxed over their coffee, Smoky enjoying his cigarette, until Grandma returned, carrying plates piled high with food.

"Dig in, boys," she ordered, as she placed their meals in front of them. "I'll be right back with your bread, butter, and molasses. Your second helpin', too, Ranger," she added to Jim. "Let me know if anythin' ain't right."

"I'm sure everything will be just fine," Jim assured her.

"Well, you just let me know if it isn't."

The bell attached to the door jingled as another customer entered. Grandma hurried off to welcome him.

"Don't hardly know where to start, there's so much food here," Smoky said. He and his partners started working on their meals.

"I'm plumb full," Jim said, as he pushed back from the table an hour later. "Can't squeeze in another bite. My belly's about to bust."

"J.R., we're seein' history bein' made, right in front of our very eyes," Smoky said. "Mark this date down. The day Jim Blawcyzk finally admitted he wasn't hungry. It's never happened before, and most likely never will again."

"Yeah, I have to admit, I never thought I'd live to see the day when Jim said he couldn't eat some more," J.R. answered. "This is a first, all right."

Grandma came hurrying over.

"I see you boys are just about done," she said. "Can I get you anything else?"

"Just our bill," Jim said. "Everything was plumb tasty. Best meal I've had in a month of Sundays."

He had downed not only his double order, but an entire pan of apple crisp.

"Same goes for me," Smoky added. "The meal was wonderful."

"I'll second that," J.R. agreed. "You're a fine cook, Grandma."

"Why, thank you, Rangers. You'll turn a gal's head, with talk like that."

"Wouldn't have said it if we didn't mean it," Jim answered.

"And here I thought folks came in just for my good looks," Grandma said, with a laugh.

"Those are merely an added bonus," Jim said. "And as much as we'd like to stay for some more coffee, if we could fit it under our belts, we've got to meet the McIlroys over at the saloon.

We're already a bit late, so we really do have to get movin'."

"I understand," Grandma said. "I'll have your bill ready in a jiffy. And make certain to stop by for breakfast."

"We'll do just that," Jim assured her.

A few minutes later, the bill was paid. Jim and his partners left the café for the short walk to the Brady Saloon.

"Rangers! Over here!" Chuck called, when they pushed through the batwings and stepped into the bar. He and his brother were seated at a table in a back corner, along with several other men.

"Sorry we're a few minutes late," Jim apologized, when he, Smoky, and J.R. reached the group. "The food was so good at Grandma Hussey's place we just couldn't tear ourselves away."

"Jim means he couldn't tear himself away," Smoky corrected.

"That's right," J.R. added. "Besides a double order of everything, Jim also polished off an entire apple crisp, all by himself . . . as well as two pots of coffee."

"I reckon that's so," Jim conceded.

"Well, pull yourselves up chairs and we'll palaver a spell," Chuck said. "These men here are Mike Sutton, owner of the saddle shop, Sven Jorgenson, the blacksmith, and Jesse Holms, who runs the feed store. Men, Rangers Blaw . . . Blah . . ."

"BLUH-zhick," Jim helped, as he settled into a chair. "Told you it's easier to just call me Jim."

"And you're dang right about that," Chuck agreed, with a laugh. "Rangers Jim, Smoky McCue, and J.R. Huggins," Chuck concluded.

Handshakes were exchanged all around.

"Glad to see Austin's finally tryin' to do somethin' about those Ghost Riders," Holms said. "I hear tell they've been raisin' Hell all over half the state."

"Yeah, but even you Rangers can't do anythin' about them, although we appreciate your tryin'," Sutton said. "Those riders just come outta nowhere, strike, then disappear into thin air, seems like. You'll never catch 'em."

"Oh, we will catch up to 'em, you can bet your hat on that," Jim said. "It might take a while, but we will run them to ground."

"And when we do, they'll be sorry for ever startin' up trouble, and causin' so much death and destruction," Smoky added.

"You mean you're gonna gun them down, rather'n takin' the chance of bringin' 'em in for trial, and them mebbe gettin' away with what they've done?" Jorgenson asked. "That's a fine idea, although even that's more'n they deserve."

"Smoky didn't say that," J.R. answered. "It depends on what those men do when we finally find 'em. We're duty bound to bring 'em in alive, if we can. But, if they try'n fight, rather than surrender, well . . ."

"Enough said, Ranger," Eddie said. "You men want a drink?"

"I can stand a beer," J.R. said.

"Same here," Smoky answered.

"Sarsaparilla for me, or water if this place doesn't have that," Jim said.

"We'll have Marty bring your drinks right over," Chuck said. He turned and signaled to the bartender, who hurried over to their table, wiping his hands on his apron.

"I see the Rangers have arrived," he said. "Glad to have you in Brady, gentlemen, at least what little bit those Ghost Riders left of it. I'm Marty Halloran. This is my place. What can I get for you?"

"Jim Blawcyzk. Sarsaparilla," Jim requested.

"Nothin' stronger?" Halloran asked.

"Nope," Jim replied. "I don't begrudge any man his liquor, but I never touch the stuff. Just never developed a taste for it."

"All right, one sarsaparilla," Halloran said. "What about you two?"

"Beer for me," J.R. said.

"Same here," Smoky added.

"Comin' right up."

"And when you come back with those drinks, Marty, plan on stayin' with us for a couple of minutes," Chuck said. "The Rangers are lookin' for any information which might help lead 'em to those Ghost Riders. I know there's a thing or two you can tell 'em."

"Glad to do anything I can do to help," Halloran answered. "Be right back with those drinks. And they're on the house. No arguments," he said, when Jim started to object. "Your runnin' down the men who destroyed this town is more'n enough payment. Not that I think you'll be able to. I figure, even if you do catch up with the Ghost Riders, they'll cut you down before you ever have a chance to get off a shot. And I hate takin' money from dead men." Shaking his head, he headed for the bar.

"Nice to see he has so much confidence in us," Smoky muttered.

"It's not that, so much," Sutton said. "We've all seen firsthand what those men can do, while you haven't. I know how tough you Rangers are, and if anyone can bring those men to justice, it's you boys. But you're buckin' mighty long odds . . . mighty long."

"We've bucked those before," Jim said. "Ain't lost so far . . . although we've been roughed up a mite. But that hasn't stopped us yet, and these Ghost Riders, whoever they are, ain't gonna stop us either. We'll get 'em, one way or the other."

"I hope you're right, Ranger," Sutton said. "Well, here's Marty with your drinks."

133

Halloran placed mugs of beer in front of Smoky and J.R., and a bottle of pop, along with an empty glass, in front of Jim. He pulled a chair from under the next table, reversed it and straddled it.

"Enjoy the drinks, men, and there's plenty more if you want," he said. "Now, I've got to get back to my other customers, so ask your questions and let me return to work."

"Of course," Jim said. "There's really only one. Did you hear or see anythin' which might help us identify any of those men?"

"Just this," Halloran said. "The man who appeared to be leadin' the outfit had a kind of unusual voice. It was sort of thin and reedy-soundin'. But it was also a voice that you'd listen to, when it gave an order."

"Marty's right," Sutton agreed. "The leader had a distinctive voice, all right. Kinda like mebbe his vocal cords had been damaged or somethin'. There was a bit of a wheeze to it. He rode kind of funny, too. Sat a bit twisted in the saddle, kinda like he was hurt, or mebbe crippled up a bit, in his right side. Of course, I could be wrong. Mebbe it was just the way the robe he was wearin' was bunched up, or blowin' in the wind. But it seemed to me he definitely had a problem of some sort, perhaps a broken bone or cracked ribs that didn't heal quite right."

"Well, that'll help," Jim said. "Marty, unless

you've got somethin' else to add, I'm finished questionin' you."

"Wish I could give you more, Ranger, but that's all I can say," Halloran answered. "I'd better get back to the bar. A couple of hands from the Double D just came in, and they look mighty thirsty."

"Go ahead, and we're obliged," Jim answered.

"Glad to help," Halloran said.

"Ranger, I've got somethin' which also might help," Holms said. "I heard the hombre leadin' the bunch call out a couple of names. One was Hack. The other was Mayberry."

"Now we're startin' to get somewhere," Jim said. "We have a voice, a man who might be partially crippled, and now two names."

"Yeah, but that's nowhere near enough to go on," Smoky said. He took a drag on his quirly. "Hack's probably a nickname, and Mayberry's a real common name in Texas. All over the South, for that matter. And we don't have any real description of any of those Ghost Riders. We don't know how tall any of 'em are, what they weigh, hair or eyes color, bearded or clean-shaven, none of that. Far as the leader's voice, and him mebbe bein' crippled up, there's lots of men who could fit that description, thanks to the War."

"It's still more than what we had, Smoke," J.R. answered. "I'll take any clue we can get."

"Well, I've got a couple for you," Jorgenson said. "First, I couldn't get to my gun, but I did take a red hot pair of tongs and throw them at one of those men. It hit him on the left cheek. He howled with pain, so I know I got him pretty good. He's most likely got a real nasty scar on his face."

"Thanks. That's another good lead," Jim said.

"I've got another one," Jorgenson said. "Me'n Pop Warner tried to follow those hombres, but just couldn't trail 'em very far. Pop was a town marshal over to San Saba some years back, and he was real old. He caught a bullet in his shoulder from one of the raiders, but still took after 'em. The slug must've hit an artery, because he bled out while we were on their trail. I had to give up, and bring Pop back. Not that only the two of us could've done much anyway, if we had caught up to 'em. But I did notice one thing. One of their horses throws out his left front foot. Leaves a real obvious track. If you find that horse's hoof prints, it just might lead you to the Ghost Riders. I know, a lot of horses have an oddity in their gaits. But this one is more noticeable than most."

"Well, that might just be the best lead of all," Smoky said. "My pardner Jim, here's, real good with horses. He can tell two black horses apart in the complete dark, on a cloudy night with no moon. I guarantee if we get anywhere near the trail of those renegades, Jim'll pick up that horse's tracks."

"Any of you have anything else you can tell us?" J.R. asked. "If not, we'll finish our drinks and head back to the hotel. We'll be ridin' out at sunup, so want to get some shut-eye before then."

"No, I reckon not," Jorgenson said. "We all just want to wish you the best of luck findin' those Ghost Riders. Wish we could come along, but that's just not possible."

"Gracias," Jim said. "If any of you do happen to think of anythin' else, get a message to Captain Storm at Ranger Headquarters. He'll make sure it gets to us."

"We'll do just that," Sutton promised.

"One more thing," Jim said. "I really do wish y'all could come with us, especially you, Mr. Holms."

"Why's that?" Holms asked.

"Because, if you were with us out on the prairie, we'd have Holms on the Range," Jim said, laughing.

Smoky threw the rest of his beer at him.

Jim, Smoky, and J.R. decided to stay and have one more drink. After finishing those, they headed back to their hotel. Chuck and Eddie McIlroy walked with them. They stopped the Rangers when they reached the hotel steps.

"Rangers, there's somethin' Eddie and I have been wantin' to ask you," Chuck said.

"Go ahead. We're listenin'," Jim answered.

"We'd like to ride with you, after those Ghost Riders," Chuck said.

"I don't think that's a good idea," Jim said. "First of all, neither of you are lawmen. Second, you're both awful young. Third, we'll be ridin' hard and fast. We'll be settin' a pace I'm not certain you, or your horses, would be able to keep up."

"Besides," Smoky added. "Ain't you two the deputies for this town? Seems to me you're sure actin' like it."

"Nah, we ain't," Eddie said. "We only took on the job because there was no one else to handle it. The county hired a new sheriff out of Uvalde, and he'll be arrivin' day after tomorrow. The town decided, too late, now that the horse is out of the barn, to finally put on a marshal. They hired one of the deputies out of San Saba. He starts next week. So we've got nothin' holdin' us here."

"What about your friends, or any relatives?" J.R. asked. "And do you really want to just get yourselves killed? Seems to me your ma and pa would rather you stayed here, and help rebuild your town."

"The only relatives we have are over to New Mexico Territory," Chuck said. "My pa's brother and his brood. They're pretty much no account.

Pa and ma never did get along with that bunch. Neither did me'n Eddie, for that matter."

"And all the good friends we had got killed in the raid," Eddie continued. "That's why me and my brother want to ride with you. We want to get vengeance for our ma and pa, and our friends."

"I dunno," Jim said. He rubbed his whisker-stubbled jaw. "Ridin' for revenge is never a good idea. Usually just gets a man killed, or turns him into the same kind of hombre he's chasin'."

"Listen, Ranger. If you let us ride with you, we'll obey every order you give us," Chuck said. "That's a promise."

"Besides, you can't stop us from followin' after you," Eddie added.

"Don't be too sure about that," J.R. said. "We can have your butts thrown in jail for obstructin' justice, if you get in our way."

"C'mon. Please let us ride with you," Chuck pleaded. "You can't just expect us to stay here, lettin' what those men did to our ma and pa gnawin' at our guts, while we do nothin' about it. You have to let us come along."

"Me'n Chuck are good shots, too," Eddie added. "You haven't seen what those Ghost Riders can do, but we have. You're gonna need every gun you can come up with to take on that gang. We're two more."

"I still don't know," Jim said.

"I'm beginnin' to think it might not be a bad

idea," Smoky said. "We can use the extra fire-power, seems to me. And just mebbe, if we come across any of the men we're after, one of these boys might spot 'em, whereas we might not. After all, they did get a glimpse of 'em, and their horses."

"I say let 'em come along, too," J.R. said. "Seems to me they're bound and determined to ride with us, anyway. I'd guess if we don't let 'em come along with us they'll just take off after that gang on their own. If they somehow stumbled across 'em before we did, they might spook 'em, if those riders thought the law was finally catchin' up to em. Better to have these two boys with us, where we can keep an eye on 'em. And they seem to have plenty of guts, the way they've been watchin' the town in case any of those raiders returned. If we hadn't spotted 'em ridin' in, they'd have gotten the drop on us. And I have no doubt if we'd made one wrong move they'd have put bullets through our guts. If they can't keep up, or get in the way, we can always send 'em back home."

"There, Ranger Bla . . . Jim. Your pards think it's a good idea. So, what do you say?" Chuck said.

"I say meet us at the livery stable a half hour before sunup, ready to ride," Jim said. "Now go get some sleep. This might just be the last decent night's rest you'll see for quite some time."

140

"Great. Thanks, Ranger," Chuck said. "You won't regret it."

"You sure won't," Eddie added. "We're obliged."

"I hope not," Jim answered. "See you in the morning."

Chuck and Eddie headed for the boarding house where they were staying, while Jim and his partners went up to their room. With only one bed, the sleeping arrangements would be crowded, to say the least. However, several men cramming into one bed in a frontier hotel room was not uncommon. Most lodging in the still mainly untamed West was far from luxurious.

"We gonna flip a coin, as usual, to see who gets stuck in the middle?" Smoky asked.

"Nah," Jim answered. "I'm so dog-tired I'll be fallin' asleep standin' up, any minute now. Don't matter to me where I sleep. I'll take the middle."

"Well, we sure appreciate that, don't we, J.R.?" Smoky said.

"We sure do," J.R. agreed. "Thanks, Jim."

"Don't mention it," Jim answered. "Just try not to snore too loud, either of you. With the thin walls in this place, let's hope none of our neighbors do, either."

The three men pulled off their boots, hats, and gunbelts, then crawled into bed. Within five minutes, Jim had said his evening prayers, and all of them were sleeping soundly.

# 9

Julia Blawcyzk turned from the sink at the sound of an approaching horse and buggy. At the same time, Pal lifted his head and whined. He got up from where he was lying in the corner and trotted to the door. He began scratching at it, and barking furiously.

"Charlie! And Mary Jane!" Julia exclaimed. "Today's the day they're due home." She dropped the dish towel she was holding, hurried to the door, and flung it open. The carriage was just coming into the yard.

"Charlie! Mary Jane!" Julia hollered, and began waving to them. Charlie brought the rig up to the porch rail and reined the horse to a stop. Pal bounded down the steps and jumped into the buggy. He began furiously licking Charlie's face.

"Take it easy, Pal!" Charlie yelped. "Don't drown me. Yeah, I'm home. Lemme down."

Charlie pushed Pal off his lap, jumped out of the buggy, went to the other side, and helped Mary Jane down, then they both climbed the stairs onto the front porch, where Julia was waiting. She wrapped her arms around him for a hug, kissed him on the cheek, then did the same with Mary Jane.

"You're home, at last," she said. "How was Galveston? Did you have a good time? Did you see a lot? How long will you be here? Mary Jane, you look lovely. How was the food, your hotel?"

"Whoa, Ma, just one question at a time," Charlie said, laughing. "First off, I'll probably only be here for tonight, mebbe tomorrow. There was a telegram from Cap'n Storm waitin' for me when we got into town. I have to report back to Headquarters tomorrow mornin'. I'd imagine I'll be riding out right after that."

"So soon?" Julia said. "I'd hoped you'd be able to stay home with Mary Jane for a few days."

"So did I, but we all knew that wasn't likely to happen," Charlie answered. "Look, why don't you and Mary Jane visit for a little while, while I put up the horse and check on Ted and Splash? After that's done, I'll wash up before I come in the house. I won't be long."

"Just like your father. The horses always come first," Julia said, smiling. "You go right ahead. Mary Jane, come inside. Supper's just about ready. You and I can talk while Charlie's busy. I want you to tell me all about your trip."

"I can hardly wait to tell you everything," Mary Jane said. "Wait. Charlie, we nearly forgot. Would you get the package from the buggy, please?"

"I was gonna bring that in with the luggage," Charlie said.

144

"No, I'd like to have it now," Mary Jane answered. "In fact, why don't you just put all the bags on the porch now?"

"That makes sense, I guess," Charlie agreed. "I'll get 'em."

"Thank you, Charlie."

Charlie went back to the buggy. The first item he pulled out was a gaily wrapped, beribboned parcel. He handed that to Julia.

"We got this for you in Galveston, Ma," he said. "Well, I should say Mary Jane did. She picked it out. Now, don't you go openin' it until I come back, y'hear?"

"You know I wouldn't do any such thing, Charlie," Julia said.

"I know that's *exactly* what you'd do, Ma," Charlie retorted. "I can see in your eyes you're dyin' of curiosity. So don't even think about it. You two head inside. I'll be along shortly."

"All right. But don't take too long, or I will open this package," Julia warned. "Let's go, Mary Jane. You can help set the table, if you wouldn't mind."

"I'll be happy to lend you a hand, Mrs. Blawcyzk," Mary Jane said.

"Mary Jane, have you forgotten already? You're part of our family now. Please, call me Julia, as I asked."

"Of course . . . Julia," Mary Jane said. "It's just going to take a bit of getting used to."

"Well, you'll have plenty of time to practice," Julia said, as she took Mary Jane by the arm to lead her inside. "Charlie, don't you dawdle, now."

"Great. Now I've got two beautiful women to give me orders," Charlie said, laughing. "All right, Ma. I'll be quick as I can."

Julia and Mary Jane went in the house, while Charlie took two small carpetbags from the floor of the buggy and set them on the porch. He unhitched the livery stable buggy, then, with Pal bounding along at his heels, he led the rented horse into the first corral.

"I'll brush and feed you in a minute, Taffy," he promised the gray mare. "Just want to check on my boys, first."

Charlie went inside the barn, where his two paint horses, Ted, his first mount, now retired, and Splash, were munching on hay in their stalls, having already been grained and watered by Julia. They nickered a greeting when they spotted him.

"Howdy, Ted, Splash," Charlie called. "I reckon you missed me. I sure missed you fellers. Here, I brought somethin' back for you."

He reached into his shirt pocket, and pulled out two paper-wrapped lumps of sugar from The Beachside Steak House in Galveston. He unwrapped the sugar, gave one piece each to the horses, and scratched their ears.

"I hope you enjoy that sugar," he said. "It cost me an awful lot. Boy howdy, prices are sure high in Galveston, especially on a Ranger's salary. I'll be back to check on you later. Gotta get my own supper. You two behave. And Splash, you be ready to go. We're headed back to work, first thing tomorrow mornin'."

Splash whickered, nuzzled Charlie's cheek, and went back to working on his hay. Charlie cared for Taffy, brushing her down, giving her hay, grain, and a bucket of water, then headed for the pump and washstand behind the house, which he and his father still used for bathing, most of the time, and cleaned up. He picked up the bags from the porch and went inside.

"We were about to start supper without you," Julia said. "You only have two bags?"

"That's all, Ma," Charlie said, as he set the bags on the floor. "Since we're only gonna be here for a night or two, and when I'm on the trail for the Rangers Mary Jane is gonna stay in town with her folks until we get our house built, we left most of our stuff in town with them. We've got everythin' we need. Besides, most of my clothes are still here. The bags are mainly full of Mary Jane's stuff. I never knew how much a woman had to take along on a trip."

"Oh, go on with you, Charlie Blawcyzk," Mary Jane scolded. "I didn't bring all that much."

"I'd hate to see if you had, Mrs. Mary Jane

Blawcyzk," Charlie said. "Boy howdy, I still like the sound of that. Mary Jane Blawcyzk."

"I'm rather fond of it myself," Mary Jane answered.

"That's enough billing and cooing from you two lovebirds," Julia said. "It's time for me to open my present, then we can eat."

"Sure, Ma. Go ahead," Charlie said.

Julia sat down, picked up the package from the table, shook it, and then unwrapped it, to reveal a white silk blouse, with an accompanying scarlet silk scarf.

"Mary Jane, Charlie, it's lovely!" she exclaimed, as she held the blouse against her chest. "I can hardly wait to wear it to the next big social."

"Mary Jane said you'd like it, Ma," Charlie said.

"And you were absolutely right, Mary Jane," Julia exclaimed.

"I know it's not very practical, especially for a ranch wife and horse breeder, but I knew it was perfect for when you get to town," Mary Jane said. "And it's a bit low cut. I wasn't certain it might be too daring for you. I'm so happy you like it."

"Pish tosh," Julia said. "Who cares what some of the old biddies in town might say? I'll bet I can still turn men's heads in an outfit like this."

"I know Pa will appreciate it," Charlie said.

"You might not get outta the house, once he sees you in that. He'll want to keep you all to himself, He sees that blouse and his eyes'll just about pop outta his head."

"Charlie!" Julia exclaimed. "But you're right. And the necklace with the turquoise pendant he gave me for our last anniversary will go perfectly with this blouse. I can't thank the both of you enough. Now, it's time to eat, then after supper we'll talk more about your trip." She set the blouse aside, then got the roast from the top of the stove, where it was keeping warm. The food was placed on the table, then Charlie said Grace.

"Now let's eat!" he exclaimed, once the prayer was concluded. He took several large slices of roast beef and piled them on his plate. Supper was the roast, accompanied by baked potatoes, black-eyed peas, bread and butter, and coffee. Dessert was a freshly baked apple pie.

"Ma, I should have asked you before now, but where's Pa off to?" Charlie asked, between a mouthful of potatoes.

"I honestly don't know," Julia answered. "He, Smoky, and J.R. Huggins are after an outlaw gang called the Ghost Riders. They seem to strike, then disappear, only to turn up again miles from their last attack. Your father could be anywhere from San Jacinto to El Paso."

"I read about that bunch in the Galveston newspaper," Charlie said. "Seems their raisin' all sorts of Cain. Well, I wouldn't worry, Ma. Pa can handle himself all right, especially if he's got Smoky and J.R. sidin' him. They'll handle that bunch."

"I know they will," Julia said, with less conviction than she felt. "Your father will get word to me when he can. Enough Ranger talk. I've only got you here for a day or two, and I don't want to spend the entire time talking about the Texas Rangers."

"All right, Ma," Charlie said. He shoved another forkful of roast beef into his mouth. The rest of the supper was spent in small talk about the news from San Leanna.

"I can't eat another bite," Charlie said, as he shoved back from the table. "Ma, your cookin' is better'n anythin' I ate in those fancy restaurants in Galveston."

"Everything was delicious," Mary Jane added. "Julia, if you wouldn't mind, perhaps you might give me some tips about cooking. My mother's a good cook, and I'm all right, but I'd love to learn to cook and bake like you."

"I'd be delighted to do that," Julia said. "Now, let's not worry about the dishes until later. They can wait. Let's go into the living room. I want to hear all about your trip."

It was close to midnight before the newlyweds and Julia called it a night. Charlie and Mary Jane went to his old room. Charlie knelt alongside the bed to say his nighttime prayers, then undressed and slid under the covers. He turned to Mary Jane, wrapped his arms around her, and began kissing her throat. Mary Jane responded, running her fingers along his ribs, holding him more tightly to her. Without warning, Charlie pulled back.

"Charlie, what's wrong?" Mary Jane asked.

"I . . . I can't," Charlie said, stammering.

"What do you mean, you can't?" Mary Jane asked. "You're not hurt, or sick, are you? Or is it something I did, or said?"

"It's not that at all, Mary Jane. It's just that, well, my ma's just down the hall. What if she hears us? I can't make love to you with her only a few feet away!"

"Charlie, that's just silly," Mary Jane said. "We're newly married. Your mother knows what that means. Besides, do you mean to tell me you don't believe your mother and father made love while you were sleeping right here in this room, just down the hall from them?"

"I don't even want to think about that," Charlie answered. "All I know is making love to you in this house just won't work. I'm sorry, but it won't."

"Well, you're my husband, and I want to make love to you, and I mean right now, Charlie."

"I . . . I just can't do it," Charlie insisted. "But I

151

have an idea. Why don't we go to our own house and make love?"

"Our house?" Mary Jane said. "We don't have a house, not yet. Not even a foundation. All that's out there are the corner stakes and some strings where the walls will go."

"That's right," Charlie said. "Which means we have the soft grass for our bed, the skies, stars, and moon for our ceiling. It can't get more romantic than that. What do you say, Mary Jane?"

"If that's all it will take to get you to make love to me, then why are we still lying here?"

Charlie and Mary Jane hastily threw on their clothes, except for Charlie's boots and Mary Jane's shoes, then tiptoed down the hall, into the kitchen. Pal was sleeping next to the stove. He lifted his head and thumped his tail against the floor.

"Shh, Pal," Charlie softly warned the dog. "We don't want to wake Ma up. Go back to sleep."

He and Mary Jane slipped out the door. Lying in her bedroom, Julia, having heard them trying to walk through the house without waking her, rolled onto her side, with a knowing smile on her face.

"We'd better walk," Charlie said, as he and Mary Jane sat on the porch swing, to pull on their footwear. "The horses would be sure to make a ruckus that Ma would hear, if we tried to get them. Besides, it's not all that far."

"I'd rather walk anyway," Mary Jane said. "It's a lovely evening, Charlie."

Indeed, the night air was warm, with a refreshing breeze taking the edge off the day's heat. Stars were sprinkled across the black curtain of the sky, and a crescent moon was just beginning its climb from the eastern horizon. Eager with anticipation, Charlie and Mary Jane walked hurriedly to where their new house would be built, upstream and across the creek from his boyhood home.

"Charlie, we forgot about crossing the creek," Mary Jane exclaimed, when they reached its bank. "Our clothes will get soaked, and my dress will be ruined."

"That's not a problem," Charlie said. He began to strip out of his clothes, pulling off his shirt, then unbuttoning his denims.

"Charlie! What if someone sees us?"

"Now who's bein' silly? Who's gonna see us? The horses, or mebbe a coyote?" Charlie sat down to pull off his socks and boots. "Of course, we don't have to cross the stream, if you don't want to. We can make love right here."

"No. You put the idea of making love in our new house in my head, and I want to do just that." Mary Jane hastily unbuttoned her dress, and let it slip to her ankles. She stepped out of it, then sat alongside Charlie to remove her shoes. He leaned over and kissed her.

"Not yet, Charlie," she admonished him. "In the

house." She stood up and walked into the creek, which was shallow at this spot. Further upstream it deepened into a good-sized swimming hole.

"Wait for me," Charlie called after her. He splashed into the water. A few minutes later, they were at the site of the new house.

"Where's the bedroom going to be, again?" Mary Jane asked.

"Right over there. That corner," Charlie answered.

"Then that's where we should make love." Mary Jane took his hand and led him to the spot he'd indicated. She turned and kissed him.

"Wait just one minute. I want to look at you first, under the stars," Charlie said. He backed away two steps, and stood there, drinking in Mary Jane's beauty under the dim light of the stars and moon. She seemed to glow under that soft light. All the features of her body were there for him to see. In this light, she appeared even more lovely than Charlie had ever imagined.

"My Lord, you're a beautiful woman, Mary Jane," he exclaimed.

"Why thank you, Charlie," she answered. "And might I say, you are a very handsome man."

For her part, Mary Jane had been studying Charlie's body, his broad shoulders, muscular chest, and flat belly. Sometimes it had been difficult for the both of them, staying true to their vows to remain celibate until after their marriage, especially when Charlie came home after weeks on the trail. However, after their honeymoon, and looking at him now, Mary Jane realized it was worth the wait. She trembled when Charlie hugged her to him.

"Now, we're alone. It's time," he said, as he lowered her gently to the grass, then molded his body to hers.

"Mary Jane," Charlie said, after their lovemaking session was over. They were lying side by side in the grass, looking up at the stars. "Why don't we go for a swim?"

"Now?" Mary Jane said.

"Why not? It will cool us off. And it will be our first swim together. But not our last, if I have anythin' to say about it."

"Well, it seems like a fine idea to me."

"Good. Let's go." Charlie stood up, then pulled Mary Jane to her feet. A few minutes later, they were at the swimming hole. Charlie dove right in. Mary Jane was right behind him. They swam to a boulder which was just underwater, in the middle of the creek, and sat there, letting the gently flowing water wash over them.

"I'm sure glad to see you jump right in," Charlie said. "Most gals won't do that. They'll stand on the side of the creek, dippin' their toes in the water and hollerin' about how cold it is. Them that even swim at all, that is."

"And just how do you know about girls and swimming?" Mary Jane demanded. "How many girls have you gone swimming with, Charlie?"

"None . . . none at all," Charlie stammered. "That's just what I heard tell."

"You're not fooling me one bit," Mary Jane retorted. "Just remember this. I don't care how many girls you've been swimming with in the past. But you're my husband now, and I'd better never catch you swimming with anyone but me, Charlie!"

She pushed him off the rock. Charlie went under, came up spluttering, and pulled her into the water with him. He kissed her, hard.

"Does that tell you how I feel about you?" he asked.

"I'm not certain," Mary Jane answered. "Perhaps you should try again."

"All right." Charlie kissed her again. They clung to each other, letting the current pull them along, until it brought them to the bank.

"Mary Jane, now you look even more beautiful, if that's possible," Charlie said. Her damp flesh glistened in the moon and starlight. Her wet hair hung loosely over her shoulders and down her breasts. "I have to have you again, right here."

"Charlie," Mary Jane said, sometime later. They'd fallen asleep in each other's arms, alongside the creek. "What's that gray light, over near the eastern horizon?"

"That? That's the false dawn," Charlie murmured, sleepily. "C'mere and give me a kiss.

"The false dawn!" Charlie sat bolt upright. "That means it'll be light soon. Mary Jane, we have to go. Now! We've gotta get back before my mother wakes up. It sure wouldn't do for us to walk in on her lookin' like this. And I have to get to Headquarters. Cap'n Storm'll have my hide if I'm late."

"Oh, my goodness!" Mary Jane said. "We'd better hurry."

They jumped up, and raced for where they'd left their clothes.

# 10

Charlie arrived at Ranger Headquarters shortly after eight. He dismounted, looped Splash's reins around the hitch rail, then gave his paint a pat on the shoulder and a piece of leftover biscuit. Splash nickered, then pressed his nose against Charlie's ribs.

"Take it easy there, feller," Charlie said. "I didn't get much sleep last night. I'm so doggone tired a feather could probably knock me over. You just wait here. I don't know how long I'll be." He rubbed some sleep from his eyes, slapped the dust from his hat, shirt and denims, then went inside. A short walk down a wainscoted corridor brought him to Captain Earl Storm's office. Also in the office with the captain was Charlie's long-time best friend, and now fellow Ranger, Ty Tremblay.

"Mornin', Cap'n. Howdy, Ty," Charlie said.

"Howdy, Charlie," Ty answered.

"Mornin', Charlie, it's good to have you back," Storm said, coming from behind his battered walnut desk to shake the young Ranger's hand. "How was your trip? And how's that lovely lady you got hitched to, Mary Jane? How's married life suit you?"

"Our trip was just fine, Cap'n," Charlie said. "Galveston's real pretty. Mary Jane is well, too. Thanks for askin'. And so far married life suits me just fine."

"I can see that," Storm said. He winked, and nudged Charlie in the ribs with his elbow. "From the looks of you, you haven't been gettin' much sleep."

"Not as much as usual, no," Charlie admitted, smiling. To himself he thought, *And it's sure worth it.*

"I'm sorry I had to bring you back to work soon as your leave was up, but with all the trouble in Texas right now, we're short-handed," Storm apologized. "I hated to drag you away from your pretty new bride, but it couldn't be helped."

"That's all right, Cap'n. Mary Jane understands," Charlie said. "And I'm ready to get back on the trail. Guess I'm kinda like my pa that way. I'm fiddle-footed, just like him."

"Fine, fine," Storm said. "Pour yourself a cup of coffee and pull up a chair. I promise you, unless somethin' goes wrong, the assignment I'm handin' you and Ty shouldn't last more'n a couple of weeks, probably less. Then you'll be back here, and should have a few days at home before I need to send you off again."

"All right."

Charlie took a tin mug from the corner shelf, lifted the old and much-dented coffee pot from the stove, and poured himself a cupful of the thick, bitter black brew. He settled into a worn leather chair opposite Storm's desk.

"All comfortable? Good," Storm said. He picked up a single sheet of paper, adjusted the spectacles perched on the tip of his nose, and scanned its contents.

"Boys, it's been a long while since I've had to assign any of my Rangers to prisoner escort duty, but I've got that chore now," he said. "Seems the sheriff up in Brown County has done gone and rounded himself up the Haskell gang."

"The Haskells?" Ty said. "You mean those four brothers, and their two cousins, who are still fightin' the War?"

"That's right," Storm said. "Ezekiel, Joshua, Samuel, and Obadiah Haskell, along with their cousins, Moses and Isaac." He shook his head. "Seems their mamas gave all those boys names straight from the Old Testament, but they sure didn't take. Those hombres are poison mean, ornery as wolves and slipperier than a gator. Is that a word, slipperier? Well, it don't matter, it fits the Haskells. And of course they claim they're still fightin' injustices done to 'em after the war, but that's just an excuse for their robbin', burnin', thievin', and killin'. However, that's all over now, as long as we can get 'em to Huntsville. That's where you two come in. You'll head for Brownwood, take custody of the

161

Haskells, escort 'em to Huntsville, then ride back here. Simple enough."

"If it's all that simple, why can't the Brown County sheriff have a couple of his deputies handle this chore?" Charlie asked.

"Because his jurisdiction ends at the county line. And it would be a real problem tryin' to get the sheriffs of every county from Brown to Walker to provide escorts through each county. Also, of course every exchange at the county lines is more of a chance for those boys to escape."

"Why not just have 'em hauled by rail?" Ty asked. "Or why didn't Huntsville send up a prison wagon and detachment of guards to haul those boys off?"

"It seems none of the railroads want any part of that. The Haskells are plumb dangerous, as you well know, and the railroads don't want them on any trains, seein' as innocent folks might get killed if the Haskells try'n make a break for it. They've still got kinfolk who will probably attempt to help 'em escape. That's also one reason the warden at Huntsville wouldn't send his men to get 'em. That, and like has happened to the Rangers, budget cuts have him short staffed. I should probably also mention the Brown County sheriff lost three deputies and four posse members capturin' that bunch. So the job falls to us."

"That *is* a small detail we appreciate knowin',
Cap'n," Charlie said.

"Seems like this simple little assignment ain't
all that simple after all," Ty said, dryly.

"If I thought you two couldn't handle it I
wouldn't hand it to you," Storm answered. "Just
remember, be careful. At the first sign of any
trouble, you start shootin'. If you have to, bring
in the Haskells' dead bodies, full of lead. Clear
things up after the smoke settles. Now, unless
you have any questions, you should get started.
I won't rest easy until I know the Haskells are
in Huntsville, safe behind bars." He shook his
head. "I can't figure why the judge didn't just
have those good-for-nothin' s.o.b.'s hung, but
he didn't, sentenced 'em to life in Huntsville
instead, so it falls to us to make sure they get
there. I'm countin' on you two. Anythin' else you
need to know?"

"I've got nothin' I can think of," Charlie said.
"Just let Mary Jane know about how long you'll
think I'll be gone."

"I'll do that," Storm promised.

"I've got nothin' to ask either," Ty said.

"Good. Here's your orders." Storm handed the
paper to Charlie. "You'll report to Sheriff Merle
Thornsby up in Brown County. He'll have a
team and wagon ready for you. Make sure you
keep those Haskells in chains at all times, when
they eat, when they sleep, even when they have

to relieve themselves. No matter how much they whine and complain, you keep 'em in those chains, hear? Telegraph me as soon as you reach Brownwood, and every chance you get along the way. It'll be your decision whether you want to put those hombres up in a town jail when you have the chance, or keep 'em out of towns, as much as possible, and away from folks. I'd say the more places you can avoid, the better. The only thing I can add is *Adios*, and good luck."

"Guess we'll be ridin', Cap'n," Charlie said. He got up, and placed his empty mug on the shelf. "Wait a minute. I do have one more question, now that I think of it. My mother tells me my pa is after the outfit callin' themselves the Ghost Riders. Any word from him, or any more news about that bunch? I read about 'em in the Galveston paper. They sound like a rough bunch to tangle with."

"Not recently," Storm said. "Your pa, Smoky McCue, and J.R. Huggins are somewhere west of Brady, tryin' to locate that gang. Far as them bein' ghost riders, folks hung that handle on 'em, although I'm certain it suits 'em. And once your pa and his pardners catch up with those hombres, they'll prove they ain't no ghosts."

"I'm certain of that," Charlie said. "And don't worry about the Haskells. Me'n Ty will get 'em to Huntsville. Bet your hat on that."

"All right, Charlie, Ty. See you in a couple of weeks."

"See you then, Cap'n," Ty said. "C'mon, Charlie, let's head on out."

He and Ty went back to their horses, untied them, mounted, and backed them away from the rail. Ten minutes later, they were loping past the city limits of Austin.

The Blawcyzk and Tremblay families owned adjoining ranches in San Leanna. Charlie and Ty had practically grown up together. They were just about the same age, Ty being a few months older. They had played together, hunted and explored together, swum and fished together. They had fought together, and sometimes against each other, but were always soon fast friends again. They had sampled their first hard liquor together, tried smoking for the first time together, although both quickly decided they wanted no part of tobacco. They'd even been together the first time both of them had kissed girls, behind the schoolhouse after a town social. For years, folks in San Leanna said wherever you found Charlie, you were certain to find Ty, or vice versa. They had even joined the Rangers at the same time, after Charlie's father, Jim, had been shot and badly wounded by a Ranger turned killer. That close friendship was one reason Captain Storm decided to give the pair the assignment of getting the Haskell gang from Brownwood to Huntsville

Prison, despite their relative youth. Each almost always knew what the other was thinking, and could anticipate the other's moves. If they were indeed attacked by any of the Haskells' kin, bent on breaking them free, Charlie and Ty would be certain to act as one man, anticipating what each other would do. If the Haskells somehow did manage to escape, they and their relatives would pay a high price. Several, if not most, of them would die in the attempt, for Charlie and Ty would not stop fighting until bullets finally ripped the lives out of them.

There was no railroad between Austin and Brownwood, so the trip would be made entirely on horseback. Pushing hard, Charlie and Ty hoped to average around forty miles per day, covering the approximately one hundred and forty miles in less than four days. The first night, they made camp shortly after sundown along-side a small waterhole. The spring which fed it would provide just enough water for themselves and their horses, plus it watered a small area of bunch grass, which would give the mounts good grazing for the night. Splash, Charlie's bald faced overo gelding, named for the white splotches which stood out starkly against his black hair, and Bandit, Ty's palomino quarter horse mustang cross, were unsaddled and tended to, before their riders' needs. A Ranger often depended on his horse for his very life, so keeping a mount in top

166

condition was paramount. The two horses were thoroughly groomed, allowed to drink their fills, then picketed to graze before Charlie and Ty turned their attention to their own supper. After washing their faces, firewood was gathered, a fire started, and soon bacon and beans were sizzling in the pan, and coffee boiling. After eating, the dishes and utensils were scrubbed out, and placed alongside the dying fire for use the next morning. With the weather being warm, the fire wasn't needed for warmth while Charlie and Ty slept. They spread out their bedrolls, pulled off their boots, gunbelts, and hats, and stretched out atop the blankets, their heads pillowed on their saddles. Their six-guns were at their sides, loose in their holsters, ready for instant action in the event of any intruders.

"Sure is a pretty night," Ty said, as he looked up at the stars. "Not too hot and sticky, neither. I reckon we'll sleep good tonight, Chip."

"I reckon," Charlie said, unconvincingly. "And don't forget, I'm not called 'Chip' anymore." For a while, the nickname "Chip" had been hung on Charlie, after his being called "a chip off the ol' Blawcyzk" by Texas State Adjutant General W.H. King. Charlie decided he hated the nickname, and wanted no part of it. It took quite some time, and several fistfights with some of the other Rangers, to convince everyone to go back to calling him Charlie.

"I'm sorry. Just a slip of the tongue, that's all," Ty said. "Somethin' wrong, pard? You sound a bit down."

"Just that it's my first night away from Mary Jane since we got married. It's gonna take time to get used to leavin' her behind," Charlie explained. "I'm feelin' kinda lonesome. You'll understand, if you ever decide to finally ask Josie Montrose to tie the knot."

"I'm plannin' on doin' just that," Ty said. "Gonna surprise her with a ring on her birthday. But what do you mean, you're feelin' lonesome? I'm here with you, ain't I? Your old pardner, your buddy and best friend."

"It's about time you asked her," Charlie said. "As far as bein' here with you, I hate to tell you this, Ty, but it ain't the same," he continued. "You're nowhere near as pretty as Mary Jane, and sleepin' next to you ain't hardly the same as lyin' alongside my wife."

"What do you mean?" Ty said, in mock indignation. "I think I've got a pretty good figure. I've been told my face is sorta handsome, too."

"I'm sorry, pard, but your curves ain't in the right places, and your parts ain't the same," Charlie retorted. "And I don't ever plan on kissin' you, nor anyone who has to shave. Not even Moustache Gertie at the Hangman's Saloon."

"I should hope not," Ty said, with a laugh. "Hey, you haven't told me about your honeymoon yet. Was it everythin' you expected it to be?"

"It sure was, and then some," Charlie answered. "Galveston's a real pretty town."

"How about the nights? When you and Mary Jane . . . well, you know." Ty left his question unfinished.

"There's no adequate way to describe it," Charlie said. "And it wasn't just at night, either."

"You mean . . . durin' the day, too?"

"Yup. I think I enjoy makin' love in the afternoon, with the sun shinin', even more than at night."

"You're a lucky man, Charlie."

"You will be too, Ty, if Josie says yes. And I'm certain she will. You two were meant to be together. Now, we'd better get some shut-eye. The sun'll be up before we know it."

"All right. G'night, Charlie."

"G'night, Ty."


Late in the afternoon three days later, Charlie and Ty rode down the main street of Brownwood. Since their badges were in their shirt pockets, and they showed no other signs of being Texas Rangers, but appeared to be merely just two more grubline riding cowboys, most of the passersby paid them no attention. Both were young and lanky, close to the same height and weight, but different in coloring and complexion. Charlie

169

was as fair as his father, with the same blond hair and crystalline blue eyes, while Ty had brown hair and eyes. In addition, unlike Charlie, his usually clean-shaven friend, who now had several days worth of whiskers stubbling his jaw, Ty had grown a full beard. They rode up to the horse trough in the town square, allowed Splash and Bandit short drinks, then rode across the street to the Brown County Sheriff's Office and Jail. They dismounted, tied their horses, then ducked under the hitch rail and entered the office. The young deputy at the front desk put aside the report he was working on and glanced up when they stepped inside. He had a fresh bullet burn across his forehead.

"Can I help you fellers?" he asked.

"Mebbe," Charlie answered. "Is the sheriff in?"

"He is," the deputy confirmed. "But mebbe you don't need to see the sheriff. I can probably handle whatever business you've got with him. I'm Deputy Judd Brandon."

"We appreciate the offer, Deputy; however, we really need to see Sheriff Thornsby," Charlie said. He took his badge from his shirt pocket and showed it to the deputy, then pinned it on his shirt. "I'm Texas Ranger Charlie Blawcyzk. My pardner is Ty Tremblay. We're here to pick up the Haskells and haul 'em down to Huntsville."

"You're here for the Haskells?" the deputy

170

exclaimed. "Boy howdy, will the sheriff ever be glad to see you. Sheriff!"

"What is it now, Judd?" a tired voice called from the back office. "I told you I didn't want to be disturbed."

"There's a couple of Rangers here for the Haskells."

"Why didn't you say so? I'll be right out. Just give me a minute."

"Okay, Sheriff."

"I sure don't envy you boys, havin' to try'n get that Haskell bunch down to Huntsville, no, sir, not at all," Brandon said. "We lost several good men capturin' them. I nearly got killed myself. It was one of them who gave me this scar across my forehead. Another inch and . . . Toughest bunch I've ever come across. And the Rangers only sent two of you?" He shook his head. "Don't see how you're gonna make it all the way. No sir, I purely don't."

Brandon would have continued his rant, but stopped when the sheriff came out from his office.

"Rangers. I'm Sheriff Merle Thornsby," he introduced himself, shaking their hands. "I'm plumb glad to see you." Thornsby was a short, stocky man, in his mid-forties, with dark green eyes and auburn hair, which curled under the flat-brimmed Stetson he wore.

"Charlie Blawcyzk."

"Ty Tremblay."

"Do you have your identification, and orders?" Thornsby asked.

"Got both right here," Charlie assured him. He pulled the paper Captain Storm had given him from his vest pocket, and his commission from his billfold. Ty also took out his badge and commission. Once Thornsby had examined all the documents, he returned them. Ty also pinned his badge to his shirt.

"Well, everything seems to be in order," Thornsby said. "Would you like to see the prisoners now, or wait until a bit later?"

"We'll see 'em now," Charlie said. "We figure this is the last chance we'll have to relax in a town until after we deliver those men to Huntsville, so we'd like to get this part over with. That way, we don't have to deal with 'em again until we pull out in the mornin'."

"That makes sense," Thornsby agreed. "Let's go. Judd, anyone comes in that door until we're back, you don't let him outta your sight. I'm not takin' any chances with the Haskells."

"All right, Sheriff."

"This way, men." Thornsby lifted a large ring of keys from a peg, then gestured to a thick oak door. He unlocked the door, revealing a bank of several cells. Three of those each held a pair of men. They all got up from their bunks and stood glaring at the three lawmen.

"There you are, Rangers," Thornsby said. "Joshua, Samuel, Obadiah, and Ezekiel Haskell. And their cousins, Isaac and Moses. Six of the sorriest excuses for human beings to ever walk the face of the Earth. Obadiah's the ringleader of the bunch, so you'll need to keep a close watch on him, especially."

His statement was met with a round of vicious cursing from the prisoners.

"Settle down, or you might all just get killed tryin' to escape before you ever have the chance to get to Huntsville, if you get my drift," Thornsby ordered. "It wouldn't take much of an excuse for me to plug the lot of you, right here in this jail. No one'd care if I did, in fact, they'd probably give me a medal. Now, in case you're interested, these here are Rangers Blawcyzk and Tremblay. They'll be startin' you on your way to Huntsville, soon as the sun's up tomorrow."

"I wouldn't count on gettin' very far, Rangers," Obadiah said, with a curse. "Our kinfolk ain't gonna let us rot in jail. I'd advise you to make it easy on yourselves, and turn us loose as soon as we're outta town."

Charlie stepped closer to the cells, his blue eyes glittering like chips of ice.

"Mister, let me put this simple enough even someone dumb as an ox like you are can understand it. Anybody who tries to take you from us is gonna end up good and dead. As far as you and your brothers or cousins, as soon as any shootin' starts, you'll catch the first slugs. And I'll make certain you get it first."

Obadiah slammed himself against the bars, reaching for Charlie's throat. Thornsby pulled out his pistol and leveled it at the outlaw's stomach.

"Back off, Obadiah, or I'll gut shoot you right now," he ordered. "Back off, I said."

Muttering curses, Obadiah stepped away from the bars.

"You seen enough, Rangers?" Thornsby asked.

"I reckon so," Charlie said. "Let's go. We'll be back for these men before sunup."

They left the prisoners and went back to the office. Charlie and Ty removed their badges and slipped them back into their shirt pockets.

"What are your plans for the rest of the day?" Thornsby asked.

"We'll want to put up our horses, then get a room," Ty answered. "It'll probably be the last one we see until after we reach Huntsville."

"Fine, fine," Thornsby said. "Tell you what. I'll take you over to the livery stable. Hank Little runs it. He'll take good care of your horses. While we're there, you can look over the team and wagon you'll be transportin' your prisoners with. Then, we'll get you settled in at the Brown-wood Hotel. It ain't much of a place, but it's clean."

"We spend most of our nights sleepin' on the

hard ground, so most any hotel's an improvement," Charlie said.

"I reckon," Thornsby answered, grinning. "Now, as far as your meals, I'd go to the Brown Cow. Best chuck for miles around. And if you want to wet your whistles, head for Whiskey Jack's."

"We'll take your advice on all three, Sheriff," Charlie said. "We've also got to stop by the telegraph office and send a wire to Cap'n Storm, lettin' him know we've arrived."

"Good. Now, let's go meet Hank."

Charlie and Ty retrieved their horses, and Thornsby led them down two blocks, to an old, but well-maintained, stable.

"Hank, you around here somewhere?" he called, when they stepped inside.

"I'm out back, Merle," the hostler called. "Checkin' over this rig that'll be haulin' the prisoners, one last time."

"Good. Keep on doin' just that," Thornsby called back. "The Rangers who'll be escortin' 'em to Huntsville are here. They want to look it over."

He took Charlie and Ty out the back door of the barn. Hank Little was in the wagon bed, checking the restraints which would hold the prisoners one final time. He gave a tug on one chain, then jumped to the ground.

"There she be, boys," he said. "Solid as me and

Pete Houley, the blacksmith, could make her. I guarantee you no one's gonna get loose from those shackles."

Little was in his late fifties, tall and thin, with a toothy smile, teeth stained from years of chewing tobacco, and a whisker-stubbled jaw.

"Rangers Blawcyzk and Tremblay, Hank," Thornsby said. "They'll need stalls for their horses."

"That's not a problem," Little said. "What time are you plannin' on pullin' out tomorrow?"

"Just after sunup," Charlie said.

"I'll be ready and waitin' for you," Little promised. "Let me take your cayuses. I'll get 'em settled while you inspect the rig. You'll want to see the horses that'll be pullin' it, too. They're the big bays in the first two stalls on the right when you come back inside."

"Much obliged," Charlie said. He and Ty handed their horses' reins to Little, who led them into the stable, while they began their inspection of the wagon.

"This sure seems solid enough, Charlie," Ty said.

"It sure does," Charlie agreed. The wagon had been fitted with double oak planks for its sides and floor, to which were secured heavy eyebolts, six each in the floors and sides. Heavy chains connected to those eyebolts would be attached to the shackles fettering the prisoners' wrists and ankles. "I wish it was a covered and barred prison wagon, but it'll do."

"I told Hank and Pete to make is as strong as they possibly could," Thornsby said.

Charlie and Ty went over the wagon with a fine-toothed comb, checking everything from the tongue, to the bed, to the springs, wheels and brakes, and, most importantly, any possible flaw in the restraints.

"Well, is the rig satisfactory?" Thornsby asked, once they were done.

"It's as ready as it's gonna be," Ty answered. "Reckon we might as well head inside to check out the horses."

"Might as well," Charlie agreed. They went back into the barn, where Hank had already unsaddled, rubbed down, and fed and watered their horses.

"Those are the horses you'll be usin', right next to you," Little said. "Mack and Mabel." He indicated two heavy-boned draft animals.

"We'll look 'em over," Charlie said. He checked out Mabel, while Ty inspected Mack. The bays were solid, well-muscled, and appeared suitable for the long journey to Huntsville.

"What d'ya think of them?" Little asked.

"They'll do," Charlie said. "It'll be a slow trip, with them havin' to pull that heavy wagon, but they appear capable of handlin' the chore."

"They will," Little assured him. "There'll be

a sack of oats in the wagon for 'em before you leave."

"That'll sure help. Obliged," Charlie said.

"What'll we do with the rig once we reach Huntsville?" Ty asked.

"The state's already paid for it, so it's Texas's property," Thornsby explained. "You'll leave it at Huntsville."

"Ty, everything's as ready as it can be. Let's get our room and supper," Charlie said. "Haircuts, shaves, and baths, too, if the barbershop's still open. We probably won't get those again until after this job is done."

"Right," Ty agreed. They left their horses, with pats to their noses and chunks of leftover biscuits, in Little's capable hands, and went with Sheriff Thornsby to arrange their own lodging for the night. Knowing they would be getting an early start, Charlie and Ty, after getting shaves, haircuts, and taking baths, then having supper, spent only a short time in the saloon, nursing a couple of beers, declining an invitation to take part in a game of poker. Most of the conversations in town seemed to revolve around the Haskell gang, and the Rangers' odds of actually getting them to Huntsville. Bets were being taken on their chances, with most being placed against the Rangers. For Charlie and Ty, the talk quickly grew tiresome, so they finished their beers, excused themselves, and went back to their room. They were sleeping before the clock struck nine.

Charlie and Ty ate an early breakfast, got their horses, and were at the jail forty minutes before the sun rose. Hank Little brought the wagon over for them. Sheriff Thornsby, along with several heavily armed deputies and volunteers, was waiting.

"We'll bring those boys out whenever you say, Rangers," Thornsby said.

"There's no point in wastin' time. Bring 'em on out," Charlie answered.

"Judd, let's get 'em out here," Thornsby ordered.

"Right away, Sheriff. I'll sure be glad to see those s.o.b.'s taken off our hands." Thornsby, Brandon, and the rest of the deputies went inside to get the prisoners. Charlie and Ty, holding their rifles at the ready, waited near the wagon. A few moments later, the prisoners, heavily shackled at wrists and ankles, surrounded by lawmen, emerged from the jail. They shuffled down the steps and over to the wagon.

"Climb on up there, one at a time. You first, Ezekiel," Charlie ordered.

Muttering under his breath, Ezekiel Haskell clambered into the wagon, then sat down. His shackles were attached to an eyebolt in the sides and floor of the wagon, and locked.

"Your turn, Obadiah," Ty said. Obadiah spit in his face. Ty reversed his rifle and buried its butt in Obadiah's belly. Obadiah doubled over and dropped to his knees, crying in pain. Ty wiped the saliva off his face, then grabbed Obadiah's collar, pulled him to his feet, and shoved him into the wagon, with a kick to the butt for good measure. Obadiah was quickly secured.

"It's a long trip to Huntsville," Ty said. "You men can make it as easy, or as hard, as you like. Your choice."

Isaac and Moses loaded readily enough, their faces stolid. Joshua stopped short when he reached the wagon's tailgate.

"You don't expect me to ride in that thing, trussed up like a hog, all the way from here to Huntsville, do you?" he said. "How'm I gonna eat? What if I have to pee? You think I'm gonna be able to do that with my hands chained?"

Charlie drove the butt of his Winchester into Joshua's groin, jackknifing him, then slammed the barrel of the rifle across Joshua's mouth, smashing his lips and knocking out four teeth. The man dropped like a rock.

"I guess you won't have to worry about either of those for a while now, will you?" he said. "Couple of you deputies, load him up."

The unconscious Joshua, blood dribbling from his mouth, was lifted into the wagon, his shackles secured.

"Anyone else have any objections?" Charlie challenged. He was met with silence.

"Good. Mister, you get up there. And don't say a word," he told Samuel, who shook his head and climbed meekly into the wagon. The prisoners' shackles were given one final check, then Ty tied his horse to the tailgate, and climbed into the driver's seat. He and Charlie had decided one of them would drive, while the other rode horseback, scouting ahead and behind, looking for any signs of an ambush. They would switch places every four hours, and travel, weather and roads permitting, for approximately twelve hours each day, more if the horses held up. At that pace, they should reach Brownsville in seven or eight days.

Charlie mounted up.

"Good luck, Rangers," Thornsby said. "I still feel bad I can't spare any men to go with you as far as the county line, but with the ones that got themselves killed or shot up bringin' in this bunch, I really don't have any I can spare."

"Don't fret about it, Sheriff," Charlie answered. "Ty and I can handle this bunch. Sometimes fewer is better than more."

"You're right about that," Thornsby agreed. "Well, vaya con Dios."

"Adios, Sheriff," Charlie said.

"Yep. Adios," Ty added. He clucked to the team and slapped the reins on their rumps, putting them into a slow walk. Charlie, his rifle across the pommel of his saddle, heeled Splash to just ahead of the wagon. He made the Sign of the Cross, and uttered a silent prayer that he and Ty would, indeed, deliver their prisoners to Huntsville Prison without incident.

For the first few miles, they would head due east, into a blood-red sunrise, before cutting slightly more southeast. The next town of any size they would hit would be Waco, four days hence.

The first three nights on the trail were, much to Charlie and Ty's surprise, uneventful. Their prisoners gave them little trouble, not much more than the usual grumbling almost all prisoners made. The Haskells rode mostly in silence, and protested but little when, one at a time, they were unchained to eat, drink, and relieve themselves. After supper, the four brothers were chained to the wagon wheels for the night, while their two cousins remained secured in its bed. Despite the apparent acquiescence of the Haskells to their fate, Charlie and Ty remained constantly vigilant, whichever was on horseback riding ahead and behind, making a wide loop, taking advantage of any ridgetops to survey the surrounding countryside, always on the alert for any possible spots suited for an ambush. Whichever was driving had his eyes in constant motion, scanning the horizon for any signs of approaching riders. And at night, one or the other was always on watch.

They were camped for the night alongside an unnamed stream, a tributary of the Brazos River. Charlie had just returned to the fire after making certain the prisoners were secure, for one last time. He would be taking the first watch this night. He poured himself a cup of coffee, then hunkered on his heels. Ty was already stretched out on his blankets, lying on his back, his Colt at his right side, his Winchester at his left.

"Somethin' botherin' you, Charlie?" he asked. "You seem a mite uneasy."

"Yeah, there sure is," Charlie answered. "This whole trip, up 'til now, has gone far too smoothly. Soon as we left Brownwood, these hombres settled right down. They've been real quiet ever since. Too quiet."

"I know what you mean," Ty replied. "It's almost as if they want to lull us into a false sense of security. Tryin' to get us to relax, and let down our guard."

"That's what I'm sayin'. I figure their kinfolks are gonna hit us, hard, sometime before we reach Huntsville. Sure wish I knew where. When I checked on 'em just now, they were whisperin' to each other. Clammed up right quick as soon as they saw me comin'. Just gave me some sly grins. They're expectin' help, all right."

"We'll just have to be ready for 'em, whenever they come," Ty said. "Anyway, I doubt it'll be tomorrow. We'll be in Waco tomorrow night. I don't expect they'll try anythin' this close to a city of Waco's size. I figure it'll be somewhere between Waco and Huntsville. And at least we'll be halfway there, once we cross the Brazos."

"That's another thing that's stickin' in my craw," Charlie said. "Havin' to run this bunch right through town. You know people'll be followin' us, squeezing in close, tryin' to get a good look at the Haskell gang. And there's bound to be some reporter pesterin' us for a story for his paper, and photographers wantin' pictures. I sure wish we could go around Waco altogether."

"I feel the same way, Charlie, but you know that's not possible. We have to take the bridge over the Brazos at Waco. We sure can't chance puttin' the wagon on a ferry. That'd leave us sittin' ducks, if the ambush we're expectin' took place along the river. And we can't float the rig across, not with all that iron attached to it. It'd sink for certain. We also need to send a wire to Cap'n Storm, lettin' him know how we're doin'. We've got no choice but to go through Waco."

"I know, I know. But Ty, I sure wish I could think of another way."

"We could just unhitch the horses, let the wagon roll into the Brazos, and drown the whole sorry lot of 'em," Ty suggested, half-seriously.

"Say we were gonna spend the night on this side of the Brazos, and when we unhitched the team the brakes let loose."

"It's a temptin' thought," Charlie admitted. "But neither one of us is built that way. Sometimes, I have to admit, I sure wish we weren't."

"That makes the two of us," Ty said. "But we ain't. And there's no use stewin' over what might or might not happen, and losin' sleep over it. I'm gonna get some shut-eye right now. Wake me in four hours. G'night, Charlie."

Ty pulled his Stetson over his eyes, and let out a yawn.

"G'night, Ty." Charlie picked up his rifle and tool up his post, sitting down and leaning against the trunk of a cottonwood.


Close to sunset the next day, they had reached the city limits of Waco. A branch of the Chisholm Trail crossed the Brazos here, over the Waco Suspension Bridge. When it opened, the bridge, designed by the Roebling Company, the same firm which would go on to build the Brooklyn Bridge in New York City, was considered an engineering marvel. It was the longest of its kind in the world, with a span of four hundred and seventy five feet. Its support towers were built of over three million, locally produced bricks. With the nearest railroad to Waco over a hundred miles distant, most of the rest of the materials used in the bridge's construction had to be brought to Galveston by ship, then unloaded onto river steamers, which would haul them as far as Bryan. From Bryan, the materials would then be hauled by oxen-pulled wagons nearly one hundred miles to Waco, over one of the worst roads in Texas.

Cattle herds being driven north to the Kansas railheads became more numerous as the Rangers and their prisoners neared the city. Charlie and Ty gave most of them a wide berth. They were a half mile from the river crossing when Charlie reined Splash to a halt. Ty, who had taken over driving three hours previously, stopped the wagon alongside him.

"Ty, let's palaver a little, where these hombres can't hear us," Charlie said.

"All right, Charlie." Ty climbed down from his seat. Carrying his rifle, he followed Charlie about fifty feet from the wagon, where they could speak softly and not be overheard, yet still be close enough to put a bullet in any of the men who might try and break loose.

"What do you want to talk about, Charlie?" Ty asked.

"I'm not certain," Charlie replied. "I've just got a gut feelin'. Mebbe it's nothin', but it seems to me our prisoners have been gettin' more and more uneasy, the closer we get to Waco."

"I noticed that, too," Ty said. "They're on edge, kinda like they expect somethin' to happen, at any time now. I can't quite put my finger on it, but I've got the same hunch you do. What do you think we should do?"

Charlie thumbed back his Stetson, and rubbed his whisker-stubbled jaw.

"I dunno," he admitted. "You think mebbe I should ride on ahead, and scout out the crossin'?"

"That wouldn't be a bad idea," Ty answered. "That way, if anyone is layin' in wait for us, you might spot 'em."

"You think you'll be okay, handlin' this bunch alone until I get back?" Charlie asked.

"I'll be just fine," Ty said. "And if anyone does make the mistake of tryin' to bushwhack me, they'll have six dead Haskells on their hands. They might get me, but not before I take care of their kin, permanently."

"Good. Then that's what we'll do," Charlie agreed. "Give me forty-five minutes. If I'm not back by then, start headin' for the Brazos. And if you hear any gunshots, come on the double."

"Same goes for you, if you hear any shots back this way," Ty said.

"Of course. You'd best get back to the wagon. I'll return quick as I can."

Charlie heeled Splash into a lope. As he walked back to the wagon, Ty carefully observed their prisoners. The Haskells were exchanging startled looks. Obadiah was muttering under his breath.

*There sure is trouble ahead,* Ty thought. *I just*

*hope Charlie can figure out what it is, before we find ourselves filled so fulla lead we'd crash through that bridge and sink clean to the bottom of the Brazos.*

Charlie was less than a quarter mile from the bridge when he came across a herd of longhorns, being circled and bedded down for the night. He called out a greeting to one of the cowboys bunching the cows.

"Howdy," he said. "What outfit is this?"

"It's the Circle M," the cowboy answered.

"Who's ramroddin' the outfit?"

"George Cummings, the hombre wearin' the black hat, ridin' that roan over yonder," the cowboy answered. "But I wouldn't bother him if I were you, Mister. We don't need any more hands, and the boss is in a real foul mood."

"I'm not lookin' for a job," Charlie answered. "Just want to talk with him for a minute. Much obliged for pointin' him out."

He put Splash into a jog, and rode up to the Circle M foreman.

"Mister Cummings?" he said.

"I'm George Cummings, yeah. What do you want, cowboy? We're not takin' on any more hands, if that's what you're askin'."

"Nothin' like that. Just wanted to know how many other cattle outfits are between yours and the Brazos. I've got a wagon I'd like to get across the bridge before it's closed for the night."

"Then you're plumb out of luck," Cummings answered. "The bridge is already shut down for the night." He added a curse for good measure. "That's why we're stuck here, on this side of the Brazos, until mornin'. We'd planned on makin' the crossin' tonight, and beddin' the herd down in the stock yard corrals on the other side the river, so I could let the boys have some fun in town, but the blasted bridge keeper has the gates down, and says they won't open again until eight tomorrow mornin'. I offered to pay him a dime a head, double the usual toll, but he still said no."

"That makes no sense," Charlie said. "The sun won't set for another eighty minutes or so, and the bridge never closes before full dusk. A herd your size would be across well before dark."

"I sure know that, but that blasted bridge keeper wasn't havin' none of it," Cummings answered. "Said he was too sick to open the gate, and count our beeves. We're not gettin' across, and neither are you. Now, if you're done jabberin', I'm real busy here tryin' to settle these cows."

"Understood. Much obliged," Charlie said. He touched the brim of his hat, then turned Splash back to the road.

"Somethin' funny's goin' on, Splash," he said to his horse. "Somethin's real wrong. And we're gonna find out what it is." He headed the paint for the bridge, riding at a slow walk. Two hundred yards before reaching the span, he stopped, dismounted, and tied Splash to a live oak.

"You wait here, and keep quiet," he told the horse, as he pulled his rifle from its boot. "I'll be right back." He removed his spurs from his boots and hung them from his saddlehorn, so their jingling wouldn't give him away, then started toward the bridge.

Charlie had crossed the Waco Suspension Bridge several times in the past, so he knew its approaches, and how to get close to it without being seen, despite its location close to the center of a bustling cow town. He wouldn't approach the bridge directly, but would circle around to a location on the Brazos' bank, just downstream. He took advantage of the cover of barns, sheds, and outbuildings to make his approach. The lengthening shadows of the setting sun also helped conceal him. Once he drew near the river, where the vegetation grew more thickly, he took to the brush, blending in as best he could, dropping to his hands and knees to crawl most of the remaining distance, then falling to his belly and dragging himself by his elbows the rest of the way. He hit the riverbank two hundred feet below the bridge. Still concealed by the tall grass and thick brush which grew alongside the river, he studied the bridge. Sure enough, as Cummings had said, the gates were down, and the bridge keeper was nowhere in sight.

"What the devil's goin' on?" he muttered. As Charlie continued to watch the bridge, he caught a slight movement, at the top of the nearest tower, on its right side. As he looked more closely, he could barely make out the top of a hat, and the sun glinted off a gun barrel, for just a split second.

"Someone's up there, with a rifle," he whispered. "Bet that wasn't the bridge keeper Cummings talked to at all."

He studied the bridge further. At the top of the left hand side of the farther tower, where the suspension cables entered, he could now make out the face of someone who had made his way up the tower, or crawled along the cables, and concealed himself inside, lying hidden just inside the opening.

"Two of 'em, at least," he muttered. "I'd bet my hat there's one inside the keeper's cottage, too. That'll make three of 'em."

He studied the bridge a bit longer, spotting the form of one more man, lying flat atop one of the cables where it curved upward from the bridge deck, about three-quarters of the way up.

"One more. That's all I can see. There's three on the bridge. Figurin' there's at least one, mebbe more, in the cottage, that makes at least four men waitin' to plug me and Ty, and help the Haskells escape. They're dug in real good. Gettin' past 'em'll be well nigh impossible, and shootin' 'em off that bridge even tougher. I've gotta think of somethin', and fast." He glanced at the westering sun. "It's gonna be dark soon, and we can't wait until mornin' to cross this bridge. I'd better get back to Ty, before he starts thinkin' somethin's happened to me. Mebbe between the two of us we can come up with an idea."

Charlie slithered out of the brush, hurried back to Splash, jerked loose the reins and threw himself into the saddle. He put the big paint into a hard gallop. A few minutes later, he had to slow his horse to a walk to avoid startling the resting Circle M cattle, possibly starting a stampede.

"Splash, I've got an idea," he said. "Mebbe we can get some help from this outfit." He looked for the trail boss, Cummings, and spotted him behind the chuck wagon, where he was just dismounting. Cummings glared at Charlie when he rode up.

"I thought I told you to quit botherin' me, Mister," he said. "And you just couldn't take my word for it, could you? Had to go and see for yourself the bridge is shut down."

"Mr. Cummings, what would you say if I told you there was a way you could get your herd across the Brazos tonight? Would you be interested?"

"Darn certain I'd be interested," Cummings replied. "But just how do you think you can pull that off?"

Charlie reached into his vest pocket, pulled out his badge, and pinned it to the vest.

"I'm a Texas Ranger, name of Charlie Blawcyzk. Me'n my pardner, Ty Tremblay, are haulin' six prisoners to Huntsville. Ty's holdin' 'em in a wagon about a half mile back. That ain't the bridge keeper who told you the bridge was closed. There's at least four men on that bridge, waitin' to ambush me'n Ty and take our prisoners from us, if we try'n get across. They'll plug us, easy, once we set foot on the bridge."

"Why, those . . ." Cummings issued a curse. "But how can we help you, if they're up on the towers, which I'd guess they are. They'd gun me and my men down, too. And much as I'd like to help you, this ain't really my problem."

"Two of 'em are on the towers. One's on the cables," Charlie confirmed. "There's at least one in the bridge keeper's house, mebbe more. My guess is they either killed the keeper and his family, or have them tied up and are holdin' 'em hostage. As far as it not bein' your problem, no, it's not, except you can't get across the bridge. Did I forget to mention it's the Haskell gang we've got?"

"The Haskells? You sure didn't say who it was, Ranger. That makes a difference. Just about everyone in Texas has heard of 'em. They should've been hung, long ago. Yeah, now I'd be plumb happy to give you a hand. Seems like it'll be nigh impossible to outfox their pardners. But you think you have a way to get past 'em?" Cummings answered.

"I do," Charlie answered. "I'd like to borrow about fifty head of your cows, and a couple of your men. You see, if me'n Ty attempt to cross the bridge by ourselves, the first thing those hombres'll do is shoot our horses, leavin' us easy targets. We'll be sittin' ducks. What I want to do is put the wagon carryin' our prisoners in the middle of those cows. Surround it on all sides by beef. Then, once we're set, we'll stampede the cows across the bridge. With us in the middle, those bushwhackers won't be able to get a clean shot at us. So, what d'ya say? You'll be helpin' yourselves, and us, at the same time."

Cummings took off his hat and ran a hand through his hair.

"I dunno," he said. "I sure would like to help you, but this herd's my responsibility. I can't chance losin' any of my boss's, Mr. Montrose's, beef. I wouldn't want to see any of my men get shot, either."

"That won't be a problem," Charlie answered. "If you lose any of your cows, the state of Texas will reimburse you for 'em. Far as you and your men, you don't need to get in the line of fire. All you need to do is start those cows runnin'. After that, me'n Ty'll just take our chances."

"As long as you guarantee I'll get paid for any cows we lose . . ."

"You have my word as a Texas Ranger on that," Charlie said, before Cummings could even finish.

"Then we have a deal. And since we'll be workin' together, you might as well call me George," Cummings said. He called over two of his men, one of them the cowboy who had directed Charlie to him.

"Purdy. Mavis."

The cowboys got up from their places next to the fire, and sauntered over.

"Yeah, boss?" one said.

"Boys, this here is Charlie Blawcyzk. He's a Texas Ranger, with almost the same problem we have. He has to cross the Brazos, pronto. The only catch is there's some men holed up on the bridge, waitin' to ambush him and his pardner. They're the ones who've shut it down. We're gonna give him some help. Charlie, this is Shep Purdy and Floyd Mavis. They're the two best shots in the outfit."

"Ranger." The two men nodded, then shook Charlie's hand.

"Shep, Floyd. I'm right pleased to meet you, and I'm obliged."

"You want to tell us what this is all about, Ranger?" Purdy asked.

"I'll ask your boss to do that," Charlie said. "George, if we're gonna get this done before it's too dark, I'd better get started back to where I left my pard. I'll let you explain what's goin' on. I'll be back in twenty minutes."

"Fine," Cummings answered. "Here's hopin' your horses don't get spooked by bein' in the midst of a stampedin' herd. Shep, Floyd, saddle your horses. We've gotta cut out fifty or so cows from the bunch. I'll tell you what our plans are while we do that. Charlie, we'll see you in a bit."

"All right, and gracias."

"Por nada."

Charlie turned Splash and put him into a lope. A few minutes later, he was back at the wagon. Ty was standing alongside it, holding his rifle.

"Thought I'd take advantage of the wait, and stretch my legs a bit," he said.

"Can't blame you for that," Charlie answered. "These boys behavin' themselves?"

"Hasn't been a peep out of 'em," Ty said. "They've been real quiet. Too quiet. I was just gettin' ready to start after you. You see any sign of trouble?"

"I sure did. Plenty of it. There's at least four men waitin' on the bridge to bushwhack us. Gotta be some of the Haskells' kin. I figure they've either killed the bridge keeper, or are holdin' him prisoner. Soon as we try'n cross the bridge, we'll be gunned down."

"That ain't exactly the news I wanted to hear," Ty said. "What're we gonna do? Any ideas?"

"Matter of fact, yeah. We got a stroke of good luck. There's a herd belongin' to the Circle M up ahead. They need to get across the Brazos tonight, just like we do. We're gonna use some of their cows to break through that trap."

"How we gonna do that?"

"By stampedin' those beeves," Charlie said. "We're gonna put ourselves right smack in the middle of those cows, and use 'em for cover to get across the bridge."

Ty scratched his chin.

"That just might work, except whoever isn't drivin' can't be in the middle of the herd. He'll have to stay clear, so he can try'n pick off a couple of those hombres. Best thing would be for him to stay right on those cows' tails."

"I reckon you're right. I didn't think about that," Charlie admitted. "Only question now is, which one of us drives, and which one rides. Whoever drives will have his hands full, tryin' to keep the team under control. He'll be gettin' shot at, but won't be able to shoot back. I reckon it's only fair we leave that up to chance. We'll flip a coin."

"Don't bother," Ty said. "My shift drivin' doesn't end until we're settlin' down for the night. I'll stick with it."

"Are you certain?" Charlie asked.

"I'm positive. You'll be more of a target up there on your horse than I'll be on the wagon seat . . . especially since none of the Haskells are gonna want to plug any of their kin by mistake. Besides, you're a better shot with a rifle than I am."

"Okay, as long as you don't mind, that's what we'll do," Charlie said. "We'd best get movin'."

"All right." Ty clambered back onto the wagon, then turned to the Haskells. He gave them a grin, which was almost a sneer.

"I reckon you hombres imagined we wouldn't figure out your little trap, didn't you? Well, sorry to tell you this, boys, but we did, and we're gonna spring it."

"You ain't got across that bridge yet, Ranger," Obadiah retorted. "And I wouldn't plan on it. I reckon before it's dark, you and your pard'll have your guts filled fulla lead, and we'll be on our way to Louisiana."

"Only if you're in a pine box," Ty shot back. "A bullet might find me, but before I'm done, I'll put one of my own right between your eyes."

He picked up the reins and slapped them on the horses' rumps, putting the team into a trot.

"We're all ready, Charlie," Cummings said, when Charlie and Ty reached the Circle M camp. "Got fifty of the most ornery, rankest, spookiest, high-tailed longhorns out of the herd for you. They'll run like the Devil hisself was on their heels."

"Good. George, this is my pard, Ty Tremblay.

Ty, George Cummings, the Circle M's trail boss, Shep Purdy and Floyd Mavis."

Ty and the Circle M hands traded nods.

"Sun's sinkin' fast, so we'd best get this fandango on the road," Purvis said.

"You're right," Charlie agreed. "You boys ready?"

"We are," Cummings answered.

"Gimme just one minute," Ty said. "I've gotta untie my horse. Wouldn't do to have Bandit bein' dragged along behind the wagon, in the middle of a stampede. He'd fall and get trampled for certain. I'll leave him here, and pick him up later."

"Okay," Charlie said. Bandit was untied, and left in the care of a Circle M hand.

"We're all set. Just remember, George, this is me'n Ty's play. Once you boys get the cows runnin', fall back."

Cummings shook his head.

"There ain't a chance of that, Charlie. We're in this, all the way. You think we're gonna let you Rangers have all the fun? Not hardly. We'll be crossin' the Brazos with you."

"You certain?"

"Absolutely."

"Then let's move out."

Cummings, Mavis, and Purdy pushed the longhorns toward the bridge, keeping them at a walk. Charlie and Ty were just behind. They would push the wagon into the herd just before reaching the bridge, then gunshots over their heads from the Circle M men would send the cattle into maddened, headlong flight.

"What . . . what are you intendin' to do, Ranger?" Joshua stammered, as the Circle M hands began to press the longhorns into a quicker pace.

"Even someone dumb as spit like you should be able to figure that out, Haskell," Ty answered. "We're gonna use these cows to get across the bridge."

"You mean you're gonna try and follow 'em?"

"Nope. We're about to put this wagon right in the middle of the herd."

Joshua blanched. Sweat broke out on his brow. He began to pull wildly at the chains shackling him.

"You can't mean that!" Isaac screamed. "We'll all be killed."

"Do I look like I'm joshin'?" Ty asked. He slapped the reins on the team's rumps and clucked to them, matching their pace to the now trotting cattle.

"Ranger, you . . . you ain't gonna do . . . you're . . . you're plumb loco," Isaac shouted. He grabbed the shackles holding his ankles and yanked on it, as hard as he could.

"Never been accused of bein' sane," Ty

retorted. "Besides, it's us crazies who have all the fun."

The towers of the bridge had just come into view. Mavis and Purdy rode into the center of the herd, clearing a space for the wagon. Ty slapped the reins again, sending the horses leaping ahead. Once they were amongst the cattle, the herd closed back around them. The Circle M hands pulled out their pistols and began firing them into the air, giving Rebel yells. The startled cattle, already on edge from being pushed so hard, broke into a dead run. The horses pulling the wagon were forced to keep up, or get trampled.

As the herd swept ahead, Charlie fell back and unshipped his rifle. The first of the cows thundered onto the bridge. Its wooden deck reverberated and shook under their hooves, terrorizing them even further.

The bushwhacker on top of the nearest tower gave a startled yell, and a curse, when he realized what was happening. He came to one knee, and leveled his rifle at the driver of the hard-charging wagon. He fired just a split second after Ty bent low, making himself less of a target. Instead, the bullet he'd meant for Ty's chest burned across his shoulder, then punched through Samuel Haskell's forehead. It exited from the back of his skull in a spray of blood, bits of bone, and brain. Before he could fire again, Charlie pulled Splash to a crow-hopping stop, took careful aim, and fired. His bullet tore into the would-be killer's stomach. The man half-rose, dropped his rifle, doubled over, and toppled off the tower, onto the backs of two of the stampeding cows. They tossed him off, only to be caught on another cow's horns. He hung there for a moment, then fell, his body disappearing, to be trampled under two hundred hooves.

"Keep movin', Ty!" Charlie shouted, needlessly. Ty couldn't hear him over the clattering hooves, the gunfire, the bawling of the cattle, and the shouts of the men in any event. The team was now out of control, as they raced along with the frenzied cattle. Two men holding rifles appeared in the windows of the bridge keeper's house. They aimed at Charlie's side. Cummings, Purdy, and Mavis fired as one man. Their bullets ripped into the men, driving them back. Charlie waved his appreciation to the Circle M cowboys. A bullet whined just past his left ear, reminding him there were still two bushwhackers to be dealt with. The one on the cable presented a fairly easy shot, when he rose up to take aim at Cummings. Charlie slammed a bullet into his chest, knocking him from his perch. With a scream of terror, the man fell. His scream was cut short when he landed, with a huge splash, in the Brazos, nearly one hundred feet below.

The bushwhacker in the cable opening was a much more difficult target. One of his shots knocked Floyd Mavis out of the saddle. Knowing if the man ducked back inside the tower, it would be impossible to get him, Charlie took a hasty shot. Luck was with him. His bullet clipped the bricks at the base of the opening, then ricocheted up into the man's throat, through the roof of his mouth and burying itself in his brain. He slumped over the ledge, dead.

The panicked cattle, and the prisoner wagon, swept across the bridge and onto the opposite riverbank.

"I think we've done for 'em all," Charlie shouted. "Let's stop those runaways." He put Splash into a dead run, with Cummings and Purdy at their heels.

The north bank of the Brazos, where the bridge crossed, was still mostly undeveloped, a tangle of brush and trees alongside the road. By the time Charlie and the Circle M hands caught up to them, the cattle, tiring after their run, had slowed, scattered into the brush, and dropped their heads to graze. Ty had stopped the team, and was checking over the exhausted, lathered horses for injuries. In the wagon, the Haskells, except for Samuel, slumped dejectedly, stunned at the failure of their escape attempt. Samuel's lifeless body was sprawled at his brothers' feet.

"You all right, Ty?" Charlie asked, as he rode up.

"Yeah. Yeah, I'm fine," Ty answered. "The

horses came through in pretty good shape, too. Only got a couple of scrapes from a cow's horns. How about you?"

"I'm okay," Charlie answered. "A few of those bullets came too close for comfort, though."

"Boy howdy, don't I know that," Ty said. He pointed to a bullet tear across the left shoulder of his shirt. "That one burned a little."

Charlie whistled.

"Can you handle these boys while I go back and check the ones on the bridge?" he asked.

"I'll manage. One of 'em tries anythin', and I'll put a bullet through him. Not that I think any of 'em are in the mood to pull any shenanigans." Ty gave a grim laugh. "I know Samuel sure ain't."

"All right, then I'm gonna head back to the bridge."

Cummings and Purdy were alongside Charlie.

"We need to start roundin' up these cows," Cummings said. "Long as you're goin' back, will you check on Floyd? I dunno how bad he got hit. And can you get word to the outfit they can start movin' out? There's not a lot of daylight left. Tell Fred Pride, he's my segundo, we'll wait here."

"Be happy to," Charlie said. "And much obliged for all your help. I'll get word to your outfit quick as I can. First thing I've gotta do, after seeing to Floyd, is find out what happened to the bridge keeper and his family. I'd imagine the ruckus we just raised will attract the local law, bet your hat on it. You might have to answer a few questions before you can leave. I'll try'n convince whoever shows up to find you at the stock yards, if they need to talk with you. I reckon I'll be able to answer most of their questions, without havin' to get you too involved."

He turned Splash back to the bridge, and put him into a lope. A moment later, he was again riding onto the bridge. Floyd Mavis, holding his left arm, was riding toward him.

"Floyd!" Charlie called. "Glad to see you're not hurt all that bad, seems like."

"I'm not," Mavis confirmed. "Took a slug through my arm. Should be fine, once I get it patched up. How about everyone else?"

"They're all right," Charlie said. "You feel up to ridin' back to your outfit, and tell 'em they can head out? George and Shep are roundin' up the cows we borrowed. They'll meet you on the other side of the bridge. Bring my pard's bronc along, too."

"Sure am, Charlie. This arm can wait a bit," Floyd said. "I guess we gave these hombres what for, didn't we?"

"We sure did," Charlie answered. "See you in a bit."

As Charlie had expected, a crowd was starting to gather. He removed the badge from his vest and held it up.

"Texas Ranger!" he called. "All of you, just

stay back. And someone send for the town marshal."

"I'll go for him, Ranger," one of the men answered.

With the drygulchers who had been on the bridge clearly dead, Charlie pulled out his pistol, rode up to the bridge keeper's house, and dismounted. The door was locked, but a quick kick shattered its dry-rotted frame. The door swung inward. Charlie stepped inside, to see the two bushwhackers who had hidden in the house lying face up and bullet riddled. From the kitchen came a muffled cry. Charlie hurried into the room. The keeper, his wife, and their two daughters were there, tied to chairs, gags stuffed in their mouths. Their eyes were wide with fear.

"It's all over," Charlie said, putting up his gun. "I'm a Ranger. You're safe."

He pulled the gag from the keeper's mouth, then untied him.

"Gimme a hand lettin' your wife and kids loose," he said.

"With pleasure, Ranger," the keeper said. "And boy, you don't know how glad I am to see you. What was this all about, anyway?"

"I'll explain once everyone's untied," Charlie said, bending to loosen the rope binding one of the girl's ankles. Swiftly, the keeper's family was freed. Now that the danger was over, the girls broke into tears.

"There, there, Sally, Delia. We're all right now," their mother comforted them. "Everything is just fine."

"Ranger, I'm plumb grateful to you," the keeper said. "Guess I should introduce myself. The name's Les Hollings. My wife, Beulah, and my girls, Sally and Delia."

"Charlie Blawcyzk. I'm plumb glad y'all weren't harmed. The hombres who did this were after me and my pard. We're takin' the Haskell gang to Huntsville. We'd been expectin' an ambush, just not certain when or where it would happen. We were real lucky to spot this one before we rode into it."

"I'd say," Hollings agreed. "Sounded like Shiloh all over again, with all the gunfire. And I heard a bunch of cattle runnin' over the bridge."

"We used those as cover," Charlie said. "The rest of the herd'll be along shortly, now that the way is clear. It belongs to the Circle M outfit. I'd recommend you let 'em cross for free. If it hadn't been for their help, we never could have sprung that trap. And most likely, once they'd done for us, the bushwhackers would have finished you and your family, too. They wouldn't want to leave any witnesses."

"I'll do that," Hollings agreed. He and Charlie turned, as a man wearing a city marshal's shield, and carrying a shotgun, walked into the house.

"Evenin', Marshal," Hollings said.

"Les," the marshal answered, then settled his gaze on Charlie.

"Ranger, what in the blue blazes happened here? There's a body, or what's left of a body, lyin' in the middle of the bridge, I see two more in here, and folks tell me there was quite a gun battle goin' on."

"Howdy, Marshal. Glad you got here so fast. My name's Charlie Blawcyzk. There's also another body up in one of the towers, and still one more floatin' down the Brazos. Me'n my pard, Ty Tremblay, are takin' the Haskell gang to Huntsville. Some of their kin set up an ambush for us, right here on the bridge. We were able to bust through it, with some help from a cattle outfit."

"Seems like you had a time doin' that," the marshal answered. "I'm Alf Neill. I'll need a few more details than that."

"I'll be happy to give you those, Marshal, but I have to get back to where I left Ty. He's by himself with our prisoners. I can't leave him there for long. Can you get a few men to take care of the bodies? That way, you can come along with me. We'll want to put the prisoners up for tonight in the city."

"I can arrange all of that, sure," Neill said. "Meet you outside."

He went to press some of the bystanders into service, removing the dead outlaws.

"All right. Mr. Hollings, Mrs. Hollings, I'll need to talk with you a bit later," Charlie said. "If you need anything, just let me know, when I get back."

"We'll be just fine, now, thanks to you, Ranger," Hollings said.

"Yes. We're very grateful," Mrs. Hollings added.

"It's all part of the job," Charlie answered, with a shrug. "I'm just sorry you folks got caught in the middle."

Charlie had to wait a few minutes for Neill to get two men willing to climb the tower to retrieve the body of the man inside, then he and the marshal headed back to where Ty was waiting. Cummings and Purdy had rounded up most of the cows, which were now peacefully munching grass alongside the trail.

"Everythin' all right back there, Charlie?" Ty asked.

"Sure is," Charlie answered. "The keeper and his family were tied up. I turned 'em loose. They weren't hurt, just frightened out of their wits. George, Floyd will be all right. He only took a slug through his arm. He'll be along shortly, with the rest of your outfit. Everythin' quiet here?"

"Quiet as a church on Monday mornin'," Ty answered. "I think losin' their chance to break loose has taken the starch out of our boys. That, and seein' their brother's brain blasted out."

"Good," Charlie said. "This here's Waco Marshal Alf Neill. He's got some men pickin' up the bodies we left behind. He's also gonna hold the Haskells in the town jail for us tonight. Dunno about you, Ty, but I could stand a night in a hotel room, and a good meal."

"Boy howdy, you've got that right," Ty said. "Obliged, Marshal."

"Always happy to help the Rangers," Neill answered. "I see you've got one more body for the coroner. One of you plug him?"

"Nope. One of the men tryin' to get me got him by mistake," Ty explained. "It was close, though. Reckon I've got to buy me a new shirt, if any of the stores are still open."

"Quite a few of 'em stay open late, to accommodate the drovers comin' up the Chisholm," Neill explained.

"That's good to know," Cummings said. "We were plannin' on pickin' up supplies tonight, until we found out we couldn't get across the river. Guess we'll still be able to do that after all."

"You will be," Neill said. "But I will need to talk with you and your men, to get the information I need for my report. I assume you'll be runnin' your herd into the stock yard corrals for the night?"

"That's right, Marshal."

"Fine. Tell you what. Why don't you do that,

while me'n the Rangers get these hombres locked up for the night? After your cows are settled, meet us at the Frontier Saloon. They serve a mean steak, the drinks are good, and the gals ain't hard on the eyes, either. We can palaver while you eat, and wash the dust from your throats."

"That sounds like a good plan to me, Marshal," Cummings said. "We'll get there soon as we can."

"You get all your cows back, George?" Charlie asked.

"All but two, that broke their legs," Cummings answered. "Don't worry about reimbursin' the Circle M for two cows. We'll butcher 'em for the boys to eat along the trail. And it was worth losin' two cows to bust that Haskell outfit."

"Couldn't have done that without you," Charlie said. "See you in town. Ty, Marshal, let's get movin'."

The surviving Haskells, still uttering little pro-test, were ensconced in the Waco jail. Once they were locked up, Neill took Charlie and Ty to the Brazos Bend Mercantile, where Ty purchased a new shirt, and both replenished their cartridges. After giving Alf Neill their reports, then having supper and a few beers, they left their horses at the Waco Livery. Now, they were in their room at the Hueco Hotel. Ty was sitting in a straight backed chair. He had slipped off his ruined shirt, washed out the bullet burn along the top of his shoulder, and was now coating it with salve. Charlie was at the wash stand, cleaning up.

"Boy howdy, it's been a day, hasn't it, pard?" Ty said.

"It sure has been," Charlie agreed. "I hope we don't have another one like this, for a long, long time. I'm bushed. How's that shoulder?"

"It'll be fine," Ty answered. "I skinned my knees worse'n this when I was a kid, lots of times."

He replaced the top on the tin of salve, pulled off his boots, then stretched out on his bed.

"This is the softest mattress I've been on in a coon's age," he said. "I'm gonna sleep real good tonight."

"I sure hope I can," Charlie said, as he ran a washcloth over his chest. "There's somethin' stickin' in my craw, though."

"What's that?"

"How'd those hombres know when we'd be crossin' the Brazos?"

"That's been gnawin' at my guts, too. You reckon someone tipped 'em off? Mebbe some-one back in Brownwood?"

"I wouldn't bet my hat against it, Ty. Mebbe even one of the deputies. And we're sure gonna find out."

"You figure one of the Haskells can tell us, Charlie?"

"Yup. And we'll get it out of 'em, any way we have to."

"Not here in Waco, though."

"No. Not here in Waco. We'll wait until tomorrow night, after we set up camp."

"After what they put us through today, I'm lookin' forward to that."

"So am I, Ty. So am I."

Charlie finished washing, then toweled himself off. He sat on the edge of his bed, removed his boots, and settled in the bed, lying on his back and gazing at the ceiling, while reciting his evening prayers. Exhaustion soon claimed both he and Ty. Despite their still-jangled nerves, both were soon fast asleep.

The next day passed uneventfully enough. The surviving Haskells rode sullenly for the most part, although by late afternoon they had regained some of their bravado, and were once again claiming they would break loose before ever reaching Huntsville.

Camp that night was a dry one, in a shallow wash cut through the mostly level prairie. There was no sign of rain, and this far away from the hills no threat of a distant thunderstorm suddenly filling the wash with a flash flood. The wind had been blowing hard, and hot, all day, so the low walls of the wash would provide at least some relief.

"About time to find out how those drygulchers knew when we'd be crossin' the Brazos, ain't it, Charlie?" Ty said, once supper was finished. He gazed balefully at their prisoners.

"I reckon it is at that," Charlie agreed. "How about it?" he called to the Haskells. "Any of you care to explain how your friends knew *exactly* when we'd be hittin' the Waco bridge?"

He was met with stony silence.

"It's up to you boys," he said. "There's still three more days from here to Huntsville. We can make 'em as easy on you, or as hard, as you'd like."

"And I, personally, hope you sidewinders choose the hard way," Ty added.

Again, they were met with silence.

"Okay, if that's the way it's gonna be," Charlie said. "Pick out one of 'em, Ty."

"With pleasure." Ty looked over the prisoners, then walked up to Isaac.

"I think you'll do just fine," he said. He unlocked the chains holding Isaac in the wagon, but left his wrists and ankles shackled.

"Out," he ordered.

"What if I say no?" Isaac retorted.

"That's not an option." Ty cracked the barrel of his pistol across Isaac's jaw, then dragged him out of the wagon and dumped him to the dirt. The gun's sight tore a long gash across Isaac's chin.

214

"Now, get up," he snarled.

Isaac rolled onto his belly, then pushed himself up to his hands and knees. He shook his head, sending blood splattering from his ripped-open chin.

"I ain't goin' . . . nowhere, Ranger," he muttered. Ty kicked him in the gut, driving the air from his lungs. Isaac rolled onto his back, moaning. Ty aimed his six-gun right between his eyes.

"I said get up, or I'll kill you right here and now. No one'll be sorry about that, and no one'll doubt my story that I shot you while you were tryin' to escape. What's it gonna be?"

His eyes filled with hate, Isaac managed to pull himself upright. He stood hunched over, struggling for breath.

"This one yours, or mine, Charlie?" Ty asked.

"You chose him, so he's all yours, pard," Charlie answered.

"Thanks," Ty said. "Let's go, you." He grabbed Isaac by the shoulder, spun him around, and marched him around a bend in the wash.

"What . . . what's your pardner gonna do to my brother, Ranger?" Moses stammered.

"Depends." Charlie shrugged. "If he answers Ty's questions, nothin'. If he doesn't, then . . ."

As if in answer, a screech of pain came from down the wash.

"You get the idea?" Charlie concluded.

• • •

"What the devil was that all about, Ranger?" Isaac asked, after Ty let loose with that blood-curdling yell.

"Far as your kinfolk know, that was you doin' the screechin'," Ty said. "That's to give 'em somethin' to think about. You, too. Now, how can I convince you to tell me what I want to know . . . how those drygulchers knew when to wait for us back in Waco."

"You . . . you can't, Ranger. Besides, I don't know."

"Why don't I believe you?" Ty said. He slapped Isaac across the mouth.

"It don't matter whether you believe me or not," Isaac insisted. "I just don't know."

"I guess I'll just have to make you talk." Ty took his Bowie knife out of its sheath, and poked its sharp tip into Isaac's belly, just above his belt buckle. A splotch of blood appeared on his shirt.

"You want me to gut you, like a hog bein' butchered?"

"No . . . no, Ranger."

"Then are you gonna talk?"

"I told you I don't know nothin'!" Isaac cried. "Don't do this, Ranger. Please, don't shove that knife in my guts."

"Why shouldn't I, after what you and your outfit have done to so many innocent folks, and after you tried to have us drygulched?"

216

" 'Cause . . . 'cause you're a Ranger. You ain't built that way."

"Boy howdy, have you got *that* wrong," Ty said, with a wicked grin. "I'd as soon gut you as look at you. But mebbe you're right." He pulled the knife away from Isaac's belly.

"Thanks . . . thanks, Ranger," Isaac gasped. Sweat was beading on his forehead, and made dark circles under his armpits. A dark stain appeared on his pants, where he had wet himself.

"Mebbe I'll just slit your throat from ear to ear, instead."

Ty put the point of his knife against the soft tissue at the base of Isaac's throat. Again, he pricked the skin, just enough to draw blood.

"Go ahead and kill me, Ranger," Isaac whimpered. "You're gonna do it anyway, so get it over with. But you're not gettin' another word out of me."

"Have it your way, then, Mister," Ty snapped. He drove his knee into Isaac's groin, jackknifing him, then kneed him in the chin as he doubled over. Isaac fell to his face, out cold.

"Reckon I underestimated you," Ty muttered. "I figured you as the weak one of the bunch, the one who'd most likely break. Guess I was wrong."

He grabbed the unconscious man by the collar and dragged him back to the campsite. Once there, he let go of his grip. Isaac dropped limply to the ground.

"He tell you anythin'?" Charlie asked.

"Nope. Claimed he didn't know anythin'," Ty answered. "So I cut out his lyin' tongue. Reckon it's your turn to give 'er a whirl."

"I was kinda hopin' he wouldn't talk, so I'd have a chance to work on one of these skunks," Charlie said. "Only question is, which one?"

He looked over the other four prisoners. They all looked at him stoically, but he noticed Ezekiel swallowing hard. Fear shone in the man's dark eyes. Charlie pointed at him.

"You."

"Me. I don't know nothin'. Nothin' at all," Ezekiel answered.

"Let's find out exactly how much you 'don't know'," Charlie retorted. He unchained Ezekiel from the wagon wheel, then pushed him toward a mesquite, fifty feet away. Once they reached it, he spun Ezekiel around, shoved him up against its trunk, and jabbed his Colt into the man's gut.

"I ain't gonna waste as much time with you as my pardner did with your worthless cousin," Charlie growled. "I know every one of you was waitin' for that ambush to happen, which means you also knew how your friends would know when to find us at the bridge. Either spill your guts, right now, or I'll let my gun spill'em for you."

"I can't . . . I mean, I didn't know there was gonna be an ambush," Ezekiel stuttered. "You gotta believe me, Ranger."

"Wrong answer." Charlie stepped back, thumbed back the hammer of his gun, pulled the trigger, and sent a bullet into the mesquite's trunk, just alongside Ezekiel's head. The slug took a chunk out of his left ear, and deafened it.

"You want to try and give me the right answer this time?"

"Can't . . . can't." Ezekiel shook his head.

Charlie aimed lower, this time putting his bullet between Ezekiel's legs, just below his groin. It burned a path through the crotch of the prisoner's pants before burying itself in the mesquite's trunk.

"I've got four bullets left in my gun, and a cartridge belt chock full of 'em," Charlie said, coldly. His eyes, so much like his father's, glittered like chips of blue ice. "My next shot's gonna be an inch or so higher than that one. The one after that'll be another inch higher. You're gonna die real slow, hard, and painful, if you don't talk . . . and I mean right now."

"All right, all right," Ezekiel said, sobbing. "Just don't shoot any more, Ranger. Please. We set up that ambush."

"How?"

"Our cousin, Jude, was watchin' the jail ever since we got caught. The others were camped in

219

the brush outside of Brownwood, waitin' for him to tell 'em we were bein' moved. We knew the odds were whoever took us to Huntsville would cross the Brazos at Waco, and that the bridge would be the perfect spot for a drygulchin'. We figured we had a foolproof scheme."

"The others were your kin, too?"

"Yeah, yeah. All cousins."

"They trailed us from Brownwood?"

"That's right. Jude can trail without bein' spotted as good as any Comanche. He stayed about an hour behind. The rest hung back of him, about two hours. Once Jude saw where we stopped for the night, he rode back to the others. That way, they were far enough behind you wouldn't discover 'em, but were close enough they wouldn't lose us. Once we were a day out of Waco, they rode on ahead, so they'd be waitin' for you."

"Which one was Jude?"

"The one you shot into the Brazos."

"Any more of your kinfolk waitin' to bushwhack us between here and Huntsville?"

"I . . . I can't tell you, Ranger."

"You'd better."

Charlie stuck the barrel of his pistol up Ezekiel's left nostril.

"All right, all right. Don't kill me, Ranger," Ezekiel pleaded, then broke down, blubbering. "There's no more left. They all got killed, back in Waco."

"That's what I wanted to know," Charlie said. He pulled Ezekiel away from the mesquite, shoved the barrel of his gun against his spine, and walked him back to the wagon.

"Well?" Ty said.

"He spilled his guts. We were bein' trailed, all the way from Brownwood," Charlie answered. "He claims they've got no kin left, after we got those bushwhackers. Says there won't be any more ambushes. But we're gonna be real careful. Somehow, I don't believe that, one bit. Soon as I get him secured, I'll give you the whole story."

Ezekiel was chained back to a wagon wheel, then Charlie told Ty everything the Haskell brother had divulged to him.

"You're right, Charlie," Ty said. "I reckon they've got some more friends, or kin, who are gonna make one more attempt to help 'em escape. Well, at least we've only got three more days to Huntsville. Once this bunch is safely behind bars, we'll finally get to relax. Speakin' of which, since you've got first watch tonight, I'd better try'n get some shut-eye. I'll see you in four hours."

"See you then," Charlie said. He poured himself a cup of coffee, picked up his rifle, and settled with his back against a fallen cottonwood. Ty went over to his bedroll, spread out his blankets, and crawled under them.

• • •

Despite the Rangers' trepidations, the next two days passed uneventfully. They made their final camp of the journey about twenty miles outside Huntsville. Their prisoners had been fed, and now Charlie and Ty were having their own suppers.

"Last night," Ty said. "I'll sure be glad to see the walls of that prison tomorrow."

"So will I, bet a hat on it," Charlie said. He took a swallow of his coffee. "One night in Huntsville, then we'll be on our way home, me back to Mary Jane, and you back to Josie."

"Hey, Ranger," Obadiah Haskell called.

"What d'ya want, Haskell?" Charlie called back.

"I've gotta pee, real bad. Can't hardly do that chained to this here wagon wheel. You mind turnin' me loose, so I can go?"

"Reckon I'd best let him up," Charlie said. He put down his coffee cup and got up, with a sigh.

"I'm comin' Haskell."

"Hurry it up, Ranger, before I pee my pants."

"Be careful, Charlie," Ty urged. "He might be tryin' to pull somethin'."

"Don't worry. I'll be ready if he tries anythin'," Charlie reassured him. "You just keep a sharp lookout."

"You can count on that," Ty said.

"C'mon, Ranger!" Haskell pleaded.

"I told you, I'm comin'. Just keep your pants on," Charlie answered.

Ty looked at him and chuckled.

"I can't believe you just said that, pardner."

"What can I say? Some of my pa rubbed off on me."

"More than you know, Charlie. More than you know."

Charlie walked over to the wagon and unlocked Obadiah's shackles from the wheel. Obadiah got slowly to his feet.

"I thought you were in a hurry," Charlie said. He kept his six-gun trained on the man's chest.

"I am. Just got to get my circulation goin'. My feet are plumb numb."

"Just get movin'." Charlie shoved Obadiah toward the clump of brush they were using as a privy. They had just walked behind it when Charlie stepped on a loose rock. His foot shot out from under him. He tried to recover, twisted, and fell on his stomach. Instantly, Obadiah was on him. He drove a knee into the small of Charlie's back. Charlie arched in pain. Obadiah looped the chain shackling his wrists around Charlie's neck. He pulled back hard, choking him. Silver spots swam before Charlie's eyes as his air was cut off.

Ty, concentrating on the other prisoners, didn't hear the commotion. Charlie still had his six-gun in his hand, and squeezed off one shot.

"Charlie!" Ty headed for the brush on the run. He circled behind it, to see Obadiah on Charlie's back, his shackles digging into his neck. Charlie's head lolled, limply. Evidently, he was already unconscious, or close to it. Perhaps even dead. "Turn him loose, Haskell!" Ty ordered.

Obadiah's only response was to pull back harder on Charlie's throat.

"I said turn him loose!" Obadiah gave another jerk. Ty aimed his rifle at the middle of his back and fired. The bullet took Obadiah square in the middle of his shoulder blades, severing his spine. He slumped on top of Charlie. Ty rushed over to them.

"Charlie!"

"Get him . . . get him offa . . . me!" Charlie gasped, his voice raspy. Ty lifted Obadiah's arms over Charlie's head, pulling the chains away from his throat, then shoved his body aside.

"You all right?"

Charlie rolled onto his back, rubbing his throat. The chains had dug deeply into his flesh. Livid welts were rising where they had been wrapped around his neck.

"I am . . . now. Obadiah?"

"Dead. I had no choice but to plug him. He wouldn't let loose, and you looked like you were already a goner. What happened? How'd he get the drop on you?"

"Doggone loose stone. I stepped on one,

twisted my ankle, and lost my balance. He was on top of me before I even knew it. Thanks, Ty. Reckon you saved my life."

"Don't even mention it. That's why we're pards. Lemme help you up. We'd better get back to the others."

"I reckon we'd better."

Ty grasped Charlie's hand and pulled him upright. Charlie stood, shakily.

"You gonna be able to walk?" Ty asked.

"Yeah. I'll be fine," Charlie said. He tested his weight on the ankle. A twinge of pain shot through it, but he was able to walk, albeit with a bad limp.

Ty looked at Obadiah, lying dead, his face locked in a grimace of pain.

"Well, I reckon he don't need to pee after all," he said, with a laugh. "Let's go."

When they returned to the wagon, they found the remaining prisoners just as they had left them.

"Where's our brother, Ranger?" Joshua asked.

"He's dead. Tried to choke my pardner," Ty answered. "All he got for his trouble was a bullet in the back. Any of you make even the smallest wrong move, and you'll get the same. Now just settle down."

Ty's answer was met with a string of oaths. He sent a bullet into the wagon's side, just over Joshua's head.

"I said settle down, or the next one'll be through your stomach."

"Ty, I'm gonna get some salve, and take care of these scrapes on my throat," Charlie said.

"You'd better," Ty agreed. "They're lookin' kinda raw. I'll bet it'll be a few days before you get your voice back, too. Boy howdy, that was a close call for you. Soon as you're done, I'll get Obadiah's body. Figure we should wrap it up and haul it the rest of the way to Huntsville, bein' as we're less'n a day aware. He won't start stinkin' too bad before we get there."

"All right."

Charlie cared for his hurts, then Ty dragged Obadiah's body back into camp, wrapped it in a tarp, and loaded it into the wagon.

"You want me to take first watch, Charlie?" he asked.

"No." Charlie shook his head. "My neck's hurtin' so bad I won't be able to sleep anyway. You get some rest. Mebbe by the time my watch is up, the pain won't be quite so bad."

"Okay, pard."

Ty rolled up in his blankets, while Charlie settled against a juniper. He shuddered, thinking on just how close he had come to dying this night.

"Oh, well, it's all part of bein' a Ranger," he whispered. "Never know when your time'll come. But that goes for just about anyone." He sighed, and let his rifle drop into his lap.

• • •

The last twenty miles passed with no sign of anyone attempting to free the Haskells, nor any sign on their part they were even expecting any help. They rode sullenly, eyes downcast. By four o'clock in the afternoon, they were safely behind the forbidding high brick walls of Huntsville prison. Obadiah's body was consigned to the prison graveyard. Now, Charlie and Ty were headed for town.

"There's still some daylight left. You want to start back tonight, soon as we wire Cap'n Storm and have our supper, Ty?" Charlie asked.

"Nah," Ty answered. "We wouldn't get all that far before dark. I'm as eager to get home as you are, but I'd sure like to have a nice, hot bath, get a shave and haircut, then a good meal and a few beers. A night in a stall, with a good feedin', will do our horses some good, too."

"That's exactly what I was thinkin'," Charlie said. "We'll get a good night's sleep, and start out fresh in the mornin'. C'mon, Splash, step lively there."

He and Ty heeled their horses into a lope.

# 11

"Well, we certainly had a busy day, even with the rain and fog," Mike Jarratt said to his wife and daughter, as he turned the key and locked the store's front door. "A lot of goods left the place. We'll have to decide whether to work late tonight, restocking the shelves, or get up early and do the stocking before we open in the morning."

"Father, why can't we just refill the shelves after we open tomorrow morning?" Mary Jane asked. "If a customer comes in looking for an item that's not out, we can always get it from the stock room for him, or her."

"Mary Jane's right, Mike," Bethea agreed. "It's been an exhausting day. We never stopped waiting on customers, all afternoon. I think we should just have our supper, and get to bed early. That way, we'll be refreshed and rested come morning."

"You know very well we can't do that," Mike answered. "Jarratt's store has always prided itself on having a complete selection of merchandise, out where the customers can examine it. That's the way my grandfather ran the store, the way my father ran the store, and the way I run the store. Our customers expect it, and we will not disappoint them. It won't take all that long to get this done, working together."

"All right," Mary Jane said, with a sigh. "I don't have anything else to do tonight anyway. Charlie isn't due home for a few more days. I might as well work, rather than sit around moping, while I wait for him to return."

Mike winked at Bethea before answering Mary Jane.

"Young lady, did it ever occur to you the reason we've been so busy these past few weeks *is* you? Why do you think all those young cowboys come in here all the time? It's not because they need so much tobacco, or shirts, or boots. It's because they enjoy looking at a pretty young lady."

"Father!" Mary Jane exclaimed.

"It's true," Mike insisted. "Isn't it, Bethea?"

"Just like a young woman enjoys watching good-looking young cowboys. An older woman, too, for that matter," Bethea said.

"Mother! You and father are both so . . . so exasperating," Mary Jane said. "Well, it doesn't matter how many cowboys come into this store. I married Charlie, I'm deeply in love with him, and there will never be another man for me. So there!"

"We were just teasing you, daughter," Mike said. "You and Charlie are a perfect match. Everyone in town knows that. I must say, however, that I will regret seeing him ride up. That means I'll lose my best helper. You'll disappear for days."

"Or weeks, if I'm fortunate," Mary Jane retorted. "I hope Charlie has enough time on leave so we can at least start building our new home."

"I'm certain he will, darling," Bethea assured her.

"And if we don't get to work, these shelves will still be empty when he gets here," Mike said.

"All right, husband. We get the hint," Bethea said. "Mary Jane, why don't you work on the women's dresses, while I restock the yard goods?"

"Fine, Mother."

"I'll get started on the lanterns," Mike said. "We had a run on those today, for some reason."

An hour later, they were nearly finished with their work.

"Bethea, will you and Mary Jane please . . ." Mike stopped short, at the sound of hard ridden horses galloping up the street. He looked out the window, to see a group of white-robed horsemen race by.

"Mary Jane, Bethea! Get in the back room. Now!" he ordered.

"What is it, Mike?" Bethea asked.

"Don't question me! Just get out of sight, quick!" He reached for a Winchester on the display rack. Just as he grabbed it, four of the raiders peeled off from the rest. One tossed a burning torch through the front window. It wedged itself between two kegs of black powder, its flames licking hungrily at the wooden barrels. Another man shot Mike in the back. Mike yelled, arched in pain, then slumped to the floor.

"Michael!" Bethea screamed. She and Mary Jane ran to him, and knelt alongside her dying husband.

"Go . . . go . . . get outta here," Mike gasped. "Go."

"No!" Bethea said, sobbing. "I'll not leave you."

"Go . . . go! Mary Jane, take your mother out of here."

"Yes . . . yes, Father," Mary Jane answered. She took her mother's arm and began to drag her under a table.

The four men attacking the store dismounted and walked inside. Mary Jane's eyes widened with fright. She screamed.

"Screamin' won't do you any good, girlie," one of the men said. He pulled off his robe, and tugged at his belt.

Fear for her daughter's safety overcame Bethea's shock at the murder of her husband. She pulled out of Mary Jane's grasp and lunged at the two raiders.

"Don't you dare touch my baby," she shouted,

gouging at the man's face. She ripped off his mask.

"You hadn't ought'a done that, lady," he snarled. He brought the barrel of his six-gun down on Bethea's head. She grabbed at his neck as she crumpled to the floor, pulling off a turquoise medallion he wore on a leather string. He put two bullets into her back.

"Now, girlie, me'n you are gonna have a real good time," the man said to Mary Jane. He fumbled with the buttons of his denims. A bandanna still masked his face.

"We don't have time for that, Cannon," one of the other men said. "You'll make the boss awful mad, wastin' time with that gal. And if he finds out you took off that robe, so these women got a look at you . . ."

"Neither of 'em'll be able to do any talkin'. And this won't take long, Stonefield," Cannon answered. "You start lootin' the place while I have some fun with this pretty young filly."

He grabbed Mary Jane and pulled her body against his. She twisted in a futile effort to break his grip. She yanked off his bandanna, revealing his features.

"A spunky one. I like that in a woman," he growled. He ripped open Mary Jane's blouse, then dropped his pants to his ankles.

"You're gonna enjoy this, girlie," he said, tugging at her skirt.

"No . . . no," Mary Jane pleaded. "Please, no."

"Don't bother beggin'," the raider said. He squeezed her arm, digging his fingernails into the flesh. Mary Jane whimpered.

"No. Please, don't." Then her eyes blazed with fury, she bit his arm, and slapped him across the face.

"Why, you little . . . I'll teach you." The raider shoved her to the floor, then leveled his gun at her forehead.

"Cannon, we've gotta get outta here," one of the others yelled. "This place is liable to blow any minute."

"I'm takin' this here gal with me," Cannon shouted back. He pulled his pants up. "C'mon, Stonefield, gimme a hand with her."

He dragged the struggling Mary Jane to her feet. Stonefield grabbed one of her arms, Cannon the other. They pulled Mary Jane outside, the other two men close behind.

The flames had eaten their way through one of the powder kegs. It exploded with a tremendous roar, setting off the others on the shelf.

"Drop that gal, you fools! We're pullin' out, right now," someone ordered. Mary Jane was released, and fell to the street. That voice, those blasts, the crackle of flames, and the sounds of exploding ammunition were the last things Mary Jane heard, before she sank into a sea of black.

As in all the other towns they had attacked, the Ghost Riders did their work in San Leanna with deadly efficiency. Two of them headed straight for the marshal's office. When Tom Colburn ran out, having heard the commotion when the raiders galloped into town, they cut him down in a hail of lead. Others went to O'Malley's restaurant. Two sticks of dynamite were thrown through its windows, the subsequent explosion obliterating the building. Others methodically hit every business in town, gunning down anyone they came across. When they raided the Shenandoah Saloon, Beau Stanton held them off from behind the bar, for a few moments. When he ran out of ammunition, he grabbed the Confederate cavalryman's sword which hung over the bar, whirled, and ran it through a raider's belly, just before several bullets ripped the life out of him.

"Grab the liquor and cash, then set the place afire," the apparent leader of the group ordered.

"What about Walt?" one of the others asked.

"Just leave him lyin' there. The fire'll take care of him. No one'll be able to identify him. When they find his bones, they'll figure he was just one of the customers."

"If you say so."

The shelves were cleaned of liquor, the cash drawer emptied. Two coal oil lamps were smashed on the floor, their fuel soaking into the sawdust. A match was tossed into the oil-soaked wood, quickly taking hold.

"Let's head for the hotel," the leader ordered. "The others should be waitin' by now."

As with almost all the other businesses, the Duncan Hotel was burning furiously. The flames luridly illuminated the white-robed horsemen gathered in front of it.

"Where's Drake and Brennan?" the leader asked.

"Dunno, boss," one man answered. "Last I saw of 'em, they went into the store, along with Cannon and Stonefield. I saw those two come runnin' out, draggin' a gal along, but didn't see a sign of Drake or Brennan. I yelled at Cannon and Stonefield to drop the gal. Then the place blew up. I reckon they got caught in the blast."

"Where's those two fools now?" the leader asked.

"We're right here, boss," Stonefield called, as they rode up. "Our horses run off when that store exploded. We had to catch 'em. Didn't want to leave 'em behind, with our gear."

"What about Drake and Brennan? And where's your mask and robe, Cannon?"

"They were still inside," Cannon answered. "I'd reckon they're in as many pieces as the store, right about now. Far as my disguise, the gal's mother ripped 'em off me. Don't worry about her seein' my face. She's dead. I made sure of that."

The leader cursed, then said, "We'll have to leave 'em. There won't be anythin' left of 'em to recognize, so we should be all right. And if either of you two idiots try takin' a gal alive, ever again, I'll cut you into bits even smaller'n what remains of your two pardners. Let's go!"

"Hey, I had nothin' to do with that woman," Stonefield protested. "That was all Cannon's idea."

"It don't matter whose it was, it was stupid. You'd better hope that gal can't identify you," the leader snapped.

"Don't worry," Cannon answered. "She's dead, too, under what's left of the store."

"You're lucky you ain't," the leader answered. "Now let's ride."

Twenty minutes after the raid started, it ended just as suddenly. Most of San Leanna was ablaze. Bodies were scattered in the streets. All the horses had been driven out of Munson's Livery by the attackers, no animal left for any possible pursuers. Smoke, along with the hoof beats of the retreating Ghost Riders' horses, drifted into the night sky.

Jim, Smoky, J.R., and their new riding companions, Chuck and Eddie McIlroy, had spent several frustrating days trying to find any sign of the Ghost Riders. It seemed as if the renegades had disappeared from the face of the Earth without a trace. However, they had just run across four white-robed men, who were hunkered down in the brush overlooking a small ranch, apparently preparing to attack once night fell. The four had no idea the Rangers had spotted them, until Jim's voice cut through the air like the crack of a whip.

"Don't move a muscle, any of you, unless you want bullets in your backs," he ordered. Two of the startled men leapt to their feet.

"That's far enough! There's five guns pointed at you," Jim growled. "Just get your hands up over your heads. You two on the ground, get up, slow and easy. Raise your hands, too. Texas Rangers. You're under arrest."

"All right, all right," one of the men said. "Don't shoot us, Ranger, please. We weren't meanin' any harm. We're not even wearin' any guns."

"Chuck, Eddie, you want to take those masks off of 'em?" Jim asked. "Mebbe you'll recognize 'em."

"Gladly, Ranger," Chuck said. He and his brother stripped the masks off the captives, to reveal the faces of four teenagers, none more than sixteen years old. Their eyes were glassy with fear. Two of them stood trembling.

"Those ain't any of the Ghost Riders," Smoky said, with a curse. "They're just a bunch of snot-nosed kids."

"You'd better explain yourselves. Start talkin'," Jim ordered. "Names first."

"Sure. Sure, Ranger," the oldest one answered. "I'm Dave Houston. This is my brother Paul, and our buddies, Oscar Prentiss and Roberto Quinones. Our friends Bobby and Bret Coombs live at that ranch over yonder. We was just gonna scare 'em, pretendin' to be the Ghost Riders. We wanted to get even with 'em for stealin' our clothes when we were swimmin' in the creek a while back. We had to try'n sneak back home and get other duds without anyone seein' us, plumb naked as we was. Only thing, Bobby and Bret had told the Lennox sisters, there's three of them, what they'd done. Those gals waited for us, and laughed their fool heads off when they saw us. It was downright embarrassin'. So, we were just tryin' to get back at Bobby and Bret."

"Did it ever occur to you that you might have gotten your fool heads shot off?" J.R. asked.

"No, Ranger, it sure didn't," Dave shook his head. "I reckon we was plumb foolish."

"I'd reckon you were," J.R. agreed.

"Take those robes off, so we can make certain you're not armed," Jim ordered.

"Yessir, Ranger," Dave answered. "Right away."

The four boys pulled off their robes. As Dave had said, none of them wore a gun.

"I guess you're tellin' us the truth," Jim said.

"Go on, get outta here. And you might think twice before you try'n pull a stunt like that again. Not only might those folks down below have shot you, if anyone had come along and seen you in those getups they could very well have plugged you, and asked questions later. You'd better get rid of those outfits, too. Folks are on edge, and if they had any thoughts you four were involved with the Ghost Riders . . ."

"Okay, Ranger. You made your point," Dave answered. He and his friends gathered up their robes, retrieved their horses, mounted, and rode away.

"Another dead end, Jim," Smoky said. "Where do we go now?"

"We're not all that far from Junction," Jim answered. "We'll head there, and wire Headquarters. Maybe Cap'n Storm's got some new information for us. Mount up."

The Western Union office in Junction was in a room of the Texas Central Railroad station. After sending their message to Captain Storm, Jim and his partners went across the street, to have a quick dinner at the Railroad Café. They were halfway through the meal when the telegrapher hurried in. He looked around the room, spotted the Rangers, and rushed over to them.

"Rangers. I'm certainly glad I found you," he said. "I've got a reply to your wire. It seemed too important to wait, so I brought it over to you. Here."

He handed Jim a yellow flimsy. Jim read the contents, his blue eyes darkening with anger, glittering like chips of ice.

"Jim. What's that say?" Smoky asked.

"See for yourself." Jim handed Smoky the paper.

*Ghost Riders hit San Leanna four days ago STOP Wives safe STOP Cp E Storm* it read.

"Oh, my Gawd!" Smoky exclaimed.

"What is it, Smoke?" J.R. asked.

"The Ghost Riders attacked San Leanna," Smoky said.

"Your home town?"

"That's right, J.R.," Jim said. "Let's go."

They left their meal unfinished, paid their bill, and headed for the train station. A single ticket agent was working the counter.

"May I help you gentlemen?" he asked, when Jim and his partners walked up to his window.

"You sure can," Jim said. "What time does the next train leave for Austin?"

"There's one leaving in two hours. The Number 47. It does make one stop between here and Austin, in Fredericksburg. It will arrive in Austin about seven tonight."

"We'll need five seats," Jim said. He pulled out his railroad pass and shoved it under the grate.

"Certainly, Ranger." He glanced at the pass,

241

then the badges pinned to Jim's, Smoky's, and J.R.'s vests. "Now, of course, you Rangers ride on your state passes, but what about the two young'ns with you? They'll need to purchase tickets."

"They're deputies from McCulloch County, and they're with us on assignment," Jim answered. "They'll ride on our passes. I'll sign the voucher."

"That's fine, Ranger." The agent stamped five tickets for the train to Austin. "Is there anything else I can help you with?"

"Yeah," Jim answered. "We've got five horses that have to ride with us. We'll need a cattle or box car added to the train."

"That's rather irregular, but I'll see what I can do," the agent said.

"Just make certain it gets done," Jim ordered. "We're on the trail of the Ghost Riders."

"The Ghost Riders?" the agent echoed. He paled slightly. "The worst outlaw scum to darken the face of Texas in years? You'll have that box car, Ranger. I guarantee it."

"Much obliged," Jim answered. He took the tickets and shoved them in his vest pocket. After that, he and his partners returned to the telegraph office, where Jim composed a message to Captain Storm telling him they had arranged passage on the first train to Austin, and the time it was due to arrive.

"Nothin' to do now for a couple of hours, until our train pulls in," he told the others. "There's a saloon across the street. We might as well get ourselves some liquid refreshment."

The two hours seemed like an eternity to the anxious lawmen. What exactly had happened in San Leanna? How many people had been killed, people who were friends of Jim and Smoky? How many businesses and homes had been destroyed? And what exactly did Captain Storm mean by "wives safe"? Had Julia and Cindy been in town when the raiders hit? Were they safe, but injured? Or worse? Mary Jane, too, crossed Jim's mind. And where was Charlie? Did he know about the attack? Perhaps most important, had the raiders left any clues behind? Did anyone have an idea where they might be headed next, and was there a posse, or hopefully a company of Rangers, on their trail? The answers would have to wait until they reached Austin.

Jim's sarsaparilla, and the others' beers, were without taste to them. They merely sipped at the drinks, each lost in his own thoughts. Finally, fifteen minutes ahead of schedule, they heard the whistle of the approaching Number 47.

"Time to go, boys," Jim said. They took last swallows of their drinks, then went to the station. Twenty-five minutes later, their horses were settled in a box car, the men seated in the rearmost passenger coach. With a hissing of steam, clanking of couplers, clanging of the locomotive's bell, and a blast on its whistle, Number 47 chuffed out of San Leanna, eastward bound for Fredericksburg and Austin.

# 12

Despite their anxiety about what had happened to their home town, Jim and Smoky, as well as the others, did manage to snatch some sleep on the ride to Austin. They awoke at the conductor's call of "Next Stop – Austin." When the train rolled into the station, they saw Captain Storm on the platform, waiting for them. They were already standing on the car's steps while the train was still rolling, and jumped off even before it came to a complete stop.

"Over here, men," Captain Storm called to them. They hurried up to him.

"Howdy, Cap'n," Jim said.

"Same goes for me," Smoky added.

"And me," J.R. said.

"Who's the youngsters you've got there?" Storm asked.

"These boys here are Chuck and Eddie McIlroy," Jim answered. "Their pa was sheriff of McCulloch County. Both he and their ma were killed by the Ghost Riders. They asked if they could ride with us, and I said it'd be okay. How bad are things in San Leanna?"

"Glad to meet you boys," Storm said, as he shook Chuck's, then Eddie's hands, "I'm not

gonna sugarcoat things, Jim," he continued.
"They hit your town real hard. Let's get your
horses, and I'll tell you more as we ride."

"Okay, Cap'n."

The horses were unloaded, cinches tightened,
bridles slipped into place, then the men mounted.
Captain Storm's blue roan, Major, was tied out
front of the station. Once Storm was in the
saddle, they put the horses into a fast lope.

"All right, men," Storm said. "Here's what we
know, so far. First, Jim and Smoke, neither of
your wives was in town when the raid happened.
They're both safe. And I let them know you'd be
comin' home tonight. That said, Jim, I've got bad
news about Charlie's wife and family. Her mother
and father are dead. Mary Jane's still alive, but in
real bad shape. It's real questionable whether or
not she pulls through."

Jim stiffened in his saddle, but didn't say a
word in reply. He stared straight ahead at the
horizon.

"How many others, Cap'n?" Smoky asked.

"A dozen, so far, that we're certain of," Storm
answered. "The Jarratts, the marshal, Tom
Colburn, and the dressmaker, Emma Pullium.
The other bodies we've recovered were burned
beyond recognition, or in so many pieces they
didn't even look human. But we're positive two
of them were the O'Malleys, who owned a restaurant, and another is Beau Stanton, the saloon

owner. At least we're as positive as we can be. They're all missin', and the last anyone saw of them they were in their businesses. There were a few bones left in the saloon, so we're assuming some of them were what's left of Stanton. The other remains were most likely customers. The restaurant and Jarratt's store were dynamited. The saloon was burned to the ground, as was most of the town. I'm sorry to be so blunt, but there's no other way to describe what happened."

"Has Charlie gotten the news yet, Cap'n?" Jim asked, his voice thick with anger.

"Not yet." Storm shook his head. "He and Ty Tremblay delivered some prisoners to Huntsville. They weren't gonna communicate with me until they got back. They left there three days ago, which means they'll be arrivin' home sometime late tomorrow. Jim, I'm glad you got here first. What happened's gonna be real hard on your boy. You bein' here for him will help cushion the blow, at least a little. Not that I'm sayin' it ain't also rough on you and Smoky. I know you've lost a lot of friends."

"Not as rough as it's gonna be on those s.o.b.s, when we catch up to 'em," Smoky said. He took a long drag on the quirly dangling from his lips.

"Cap'n, you have any idea which way those men went after the raid?" J.R. asked. "Is anybody on their trail?"

"Yes, and no," Storm answered. "With the

marshal dead, along with so many other folks, no one was able to go after that outfit until some of us Rangers got there. Josiah Stubbs, the banker, told us they headed north. We did find some tracks which led out of town, toward Austin. Once they hit the main road, those hoof prints got mixed in with all the others. What little sign was left got obliterated by all the traffic, of course. You know how many freight wagons roll over that road. I'm certain once those raiders rode out of town, but before they got to the road, they pulled off their robes and stuffed 'em in their saddlebags, then rode along as if nothin' had happened, as if they didn't have a care in the world."

"But they'd have to be haulin' a heap of stolen goods, not to mention horses," Smoky said.

"We thought of that," Storm answered. "All they'd need was a couple of pack horses to carry whatever they took. As far as the stolen horses, you know horse herds are always bein' moved around, as they're bought and sold. Unless those hombres made a slip, there'd be no reason for anyone to suspect they were drivin' a bunch of rustled horses. Also, I'd wager after they attack they only ride at night, and hole up somewhere before the sun rises. I'd also imagine they switch out some of their horses for darker ones they stole. That way, if anybody did happen across 'em, they wouldn't still be mounted on all light horses, which would raise some suspicions. And I don't need to remind you they don't leave many witnesses. And pickin' on small towns, easy targets, they're long gone by the time any effective pursuit can be organized. I'm afraid we're up against a tough one, Jim. And of course we've got men out there, plus every lawman in Texas is on the lookout for that outfit. But so far, no luck. I figure that's about to change, though."

"How's that, Cap'n Storm, if you don't mind my askin'?" Eddie questioned.

"Because with Jim Blawcyzk, Smoky McCue, and J.R. Huggins on their trail, it's only a matter of time before those so-called 'Ghost Riders' are run to ground," Storm answered. "As Jim would say, I'd bet my hat on that."

"Let's get movin' faster," Jim said. He kicked Sizzle into a gallop.

A little more than an hour after leaving Austin, the five men rode into San Leanna. This time of year, mid-summer, the sun set well after eight o'clock, so there was still enough light for them to see the destruction the Ghost Riders had wrought. Nearly every building in the small town had been destroyed or severely damaged. Some of the rubble had been removed, but most of it still remained, piles of burnt timbers and ashes. Mercifully, it seemed many of the homes had somehow survived, but of the businesses, only

Hal Munson's livery stable seemed unscathed. There was nothing at all left of O'Malley's Restaurant or the Shenandoah Saloon. The Duncan Hotel had collapsed, only its rear wall still standing, blackened and charred. The few establishments which had not been burned had their windows shattered, their contents looted. The First State Bank of San Leanna still stood, but it had been gutted by fire, its windows were gaping holes, its stone walls blackened by smoke. Even the town's three churches had not escaped the attack completely. The cross had been shot off St. Cecelia's steeple, the First Methodist Church's front windows were blown out, and the Union Baptist Church, which was located closer to the center of town than the others, had one side scorched from the flames which had destroyed the harness shop. The town was eerily quiet. Not one person was in sight, although some of the homes had lamps glowing behind drawn curtains.

As they rode down the main street, a young man stepped from the shadows. He was holding a rifle, and wore a Ranger's badge.

"Howdy, Cap'n," he called. "Jim, Smoky, J.R. I figured you'd be comin' along any time now. Who's that with you?"

"Chuck and Eddie McIlroy," Jim answered. "They lost their folks to this same bunch, up in Brady. They've been ridin' with us."

"I'm glad to see you're keepin' a sharp eye out, Bert," Storm said, to Ranger Bert Kline. "The last thing we'd need here is looters . . . not that there's much left to loot. But there's always some low-lifes ready to take advantage of others' misfortunes."

"Smoky, Jim, I'm sure sorry about what happened here," Kline said.

"Thanks, Bert," Smoky answered.

"Same here, Bert," Jim added.

"Where is everybody?" Chuck asked.

"The few folks that are left have already called it a night," Kline answered.

"There's no reason for 'em to stick around, with most of the town gone," Captain Storm said. "Everyone's undoubtedly worn out, after what happened, plus havin' to start to clean up this mess. And, they just held the last of the funerals yesterday. I'm certain everyone needs to rest. We'll come back in the morning. Folks'll be out and about, gettin' ready to rebuild. We could stop in at the doctor's to check on Charlie's wife, and a couple of others who are there, but they're probably sleepin', and I'd hate to disturb them."

"Are you certain Julia's not with Mary Jane?" Jim asked.

"No, she's not. I was here in San Leanna when I got your message. Doctor Watson insisted she go home and get some rest. Cindy, too. They've both been here, helping out, since the attack took place."

"Make that we'll be back at sunup, Cap'n," Jim said. "I don't want to bother folks tonight either, and the sun'll be settin' soon, which means no light to look around. But I want to begin diggin', soon as it's light enough to get started. Meantime, I want to get home to Julia. The rest of you can spend the night at my place. Except you, Smoke. I've got a feelin' you'd rather sleep in your own bed."

"I think Cindy would rather that, too," Smoky answered, with a tired smile. "Let's go home."

He put Midnight into a slow jog.

After leaving Smoky at his ranch, the others continued on to Jim's small horse ranch, the J-B Bar. It was full dark when they arrived. The only light in the house shone through the kitchen window. Hearing the approaching riders, Julia came onto the porch, holding a rifle. Charlie's collie Pal was alongside her, barking a warning. As soon as he spotted them, Jim called out.

"Julia! It's me, Jim. Pal, be quiet. I've got Captain Storm and some friends with me."

"Jim!" Julia dropped the rifle and flew off the porch. Jim was out of the saddle before Sizzle came to a stop. He grabbed Julia and held her tightly. Pal bounded in circles around them, barking joyfully,

"Jim. Jim, thank God you're here," she said. Tears streaked her cheeks. "I thought you'd never get back home."

"It's going to be all right, Julia," Jim said. He kissed her gently, then stroked her long brown hair. "Those hombres made one big mistake when they attacked San Leanna. We'll be on their tails like ticks on a hound until we catch 'em."

"Oh, Jim. What happened was so awful. The Jarratts. And Mary Jane. How will we ever tell Charlie?"

"Shh. Just take it easy as you can," Jim said. "We've already come through town, and we saw what was done to it. I told everyone they could spend the night here. Let us care for the horses, then we'll have all the time you need to talk. All right?"

"All right, Jim. I made a pot of stew, and kept it warmed for you." She glanced at the other men. "I hope it's enough."

"It'll be plenty," Jim assured her. "These boys ridin' with us are Chuck and Eddie McIlroy. They lost their folks to the same outfit. You know J.R. and Captain Storm, of course."

"It's good to see you again, J.R.," Julia said. "You also, Captain. And I'm pleased to meet you boys. You're welcome here, naturally. I am very sorry about the loss of your parents."

"Thank you, ma'am," Eddie answered.

"Pish tosh. My name's Julia."

"Thank you, Julia," Chuck added. "We're both obliged to your husband for lettin' us ride with him and his pardners. Me'n my brother won't rest easy until those men pay for what they did to our ma and pa, and so many other decent folks. And we don't want to put you to any trouble. We can rustle up some grub for ourselves, and sleep outside, or in the barn."

"Nonsense. It's no trouble at all," Julia answered. "Where would you find anything to eat? Or stay? Certainly not back in town. And it's far too late to do any hunting. There's enough room in the house for all of you. Jim, go care for the horses. I'll put a fresh pot of coffee on. By the time you're done, I'll have supper on the table."

"All right," Jim said. "C'mon, boys, I'll show you where to put your horses."

Sam, Jim's aged paint, now retired, had been standing at the main corral's fence, nickering to his rider. Now, as Jim approached, he whinnied a loud greeting.

"Howdy, Sam," Jim called. "I missed you too. Soon as I get the gear off Sizzle, I'll be with you."

He opened the corral gate, so the horses could be led inside. Sam trotted over to him and buried his nose in Jim's belly, then nuzzled his hip pocket.

"Of course I saved you a peppermint, pal," Jim said, with a laugh. "Here ya go." He pulled two candies from his pocket, gave one to Sam, the other to Sizzle, then loosened Sizzle's cinches and pulled off his saddle.

"Just hang your gear on the fence," he told the other men. "It's gonna be a dry night, so they won't get wet. There's grain in a bin in the tack room, and I'll fork down some hay soon as I finish with Sizzle and Sam here."

Once the horses were cared for, the men quickly cleaned up at the washbench behind the house, then headed inside to eat. Julia already had the table set.

"Anythin' we can help you with, Julia?" Jim asked.

"Just sitting down and keeping from underfoot is the best help you can give me," Julia answered. "You boys can hang your hats and gunbelts from those pegs. I'll start dishing out the stew. And Jim, why didn't you invite our guests to take a nice, hot bath? We do have the tub, you know."

"It slipped my mind, with everythin' that's happened, and bein' in such a hurry," Jim answered. "Besides, we're all starved, and wanted to wash up fast as we could."

"That's all well and good," Julia said. "So that leaves it up to me. Captain Storm, J.R., Chuck, Eddie. Jim's probably trying to keep it all to himself, but some months back I had a bathtub installed. It has hot and cold running water. Now, I'm certain you'd all like to take a nice, hot soak, to get off some of the trail grime and ease your aches. There are enough washcloths, towels, and soap for all of you, so I hope you'll take advantage. All I ask is you wipe down the tub after you're finished, so it will be clean for the next man."

"A tub? With hot water, right in the house?" Chuck said. "I've never heard of such. I've gotta try it."

"Me, too," Eddie added. "Thanks, Julia."

"That's an offer I can't pass up," J.R. said.

"I reckon I could stand to clean up a little more, too," Captain Storm said.

Jim sniffed. "I think you could stand to clean up a *lot* more'n just a little, Cap'n," he said, laughing.

"And I reckon you're lookin' to be knocked down to Private, Lieutenant," Storm retorted.

"Then it's settled," Julia said. "After supper, you can take baths. But now, will you please sit down so I can dish out the stew?"

"All right, Julia," Jim said. "Boys, those first two chairs are ours. Take any of the others you want.

"We always say Grace before meals," Jim explained, once everyone was seated, and the stew dished out. "So, if you all will join me."

Everyone folded their hands and bowed their heads.

"Bless us, O Lord, and these Thy gifts, which

we are about to receive from Thy bounty, through Christ Our Lord. Amen," Jim prayed.

"Amen," everyone answered.

"And Lord," Jim continued, "I'm gonna add a bit to my prayer tonight. First, I'd like to ask You to grant healing to everyone hurt by the Ghost Riders, eternal rest to those they have killed, and comfort to all the victims and their families. And Your help in bringing those Ghost Riders to justice. Amen."

"Amen."

"Now, dig in," Jim said.

Despite Julia's worry there wouldn't be enough of the leftover beef stew to go around, there was plenty, accompanied by bread and butter, and of course lots of hot, black coffee. Everyone had seconds.

"Julia," J.R. said, "that's the best meal I've had since I left home. Of course, after eatin' mostly your husband's bacon and beans for the past weeks, just about anythin' would taste good. But your stew was delicious."

"Thanks, J.R.," Julia said.

"Hey, I didn't hear you complainin' about my cookin'," Jim protested. "As a matter of fact, you seemed to down quite a bit of it."

"That's because it was eat your cookin' or go hungry," J.R. answered. "You might not've heard me complainin', but you sure had to have heard my belly grumblin' . . . and why do you think I spent so much time behind the bushes?"

"I've got to agree with Lieutenant Huggins," Eddie said. "My apologies, Jim, but your food ain't the best."

"Then next time, one of you can cook," Jim said. "I didn't notice anyone else volunteerin' for the job."

"Enough," Julia broke in. "J.R., I neglected to ask about your family. How's Cora doing?"

"She's just fine, Julia," J.R. answered. "Thank you for asking. She's still teaching."

"How about your children?"

"They're both doing well. Laura's very happy, being married to Tanner and running their horse ranch. Dan's off with the Rangers, down around Del Rio."

"I'm happy to hear that. Now, is anyone ready for apple pie?"

"I think that question should be is anyone *not* ready for apple pie, Julia," Jim said, with a laugh. "I reckon we'll all have some."

"I reckon Jim's right," Captain Storm agreed.

After supper, everyone went to the living room, where the attack on San Leanna was discussed in great detail. As the night wore on, each man took the opportunity to avail himself of the tub in the back room. Finally, close to midnight, everyone was ready to turn in. Chuck was the last man to bathe.

"Boy howdy, that tub purely beats all," he said, when he returned to the living room.

"It sure does," Eddie agreed. "I've never seen the likes of it. Hot water and everythin', piped right inside the house. We're much obliged, Julia."

"You're more than welcome," Julia answered.

"Mebbe now I can finally get to take *my* bath," Jim said.

"Jim, you can take a bath anytime you like, whenever you're home," Julia said. "Our guests can't. As soon as I have them settled for the night, you can take yours."

"Which is exactly what I plan on doin'," Jim said.

"Chuck and Eddie, you two boys can sleep in our son Charlie's room," Julia said. "His bed's already made up. Captain Storm, you can have the sofa. I'll get some blankets for you and J.R. J.R., I'm sorry, but you'll either have to sleep in Jim's chair, or on the floor."

"The floor will be fine," J.R. assured her.

"I'll get an extra blanket, and a pillow, so you'll be a bit more comfortable," Julia answered.

Soon, everyone was settled for the night. Jim took his bath, then he and Julia retired to their room.

"See, it wasn't so bad after all, having to wait for your bath," Julia said. "This way, you didn't have to get dressed again, then undress all over."

"I guess," Jim said. "But it was a mighty lonesome one."

"Jim! You know I couldn't take a bath with you . . . not with people in the house."

"I don't see why not," Jim answered.

"Go on with you, Jim Blawcyzk," Julia said. "You know perfectly well why not. Now, come to bed."

"I thought you'd never ask." Jim knelt down, said his evening prayers, then slipped into bed, alongside his wife. He drew her close and kissed her.

"I've missed you so much," he said. "Then, when I got the wire from Captain Storm . . . He said you and Cindy were safe, but that didn't help much. I had to see for myself. And he never mentioned Mary Jane, until we got to Austin. I still don't know for certain how badly she's hurt. The cap'n wouldn't tell me."

"I can't tell you a whole lot either," Julia said. "She was very lucky, actually. Some men found her in the street, under a counter that had fallen on her, and was covered with rubble. The counter is what saved her. It protected her from the falling debris. However, both her legs are broken, so is her right arm, she's got several fractured ribs, internal injuries, and a bad concussion. But worst of all, she's blind."

"Blind?"

"Yes, blind. Doctor Watson isn't certain

whether or not she'll regain her sight. It depends on what the damage is that's causing her blindness, whether it's pressure from swelling of the brain, or the eyes themselves, that may go down, just bruising, or permanent damage to the optic nerve. Doctor Watson says there's nothing more to be done. All we can do is wait . . . and pray."

"And hope Charlie doesn't go completely loco when he finds out what happened," Jim said. "I don't know if it'll be worse him not findin' out until he gets home, or if Cap'n Storm had been able to reach him, so he already knew. At least that way, he'd have had some warnin'. And what about Josie Montrose, Ty's gal? What happened to her?"

"Josie's fine. So's her family," Julia said. "They were visiting kin over to Buda, so they weren't at home when those raiders struck."

"And the Tremblays?"

"They're all right too. Mark, Michelle, and Brianna are fine. The raiders came in the opposite direction from their place, so they were never threatened. And of course Ty's off with Charlie. Charlie! Jim, exactly how hard do you think Charlie will take the news, once he's found out what happened to Mary Jane?"

"I'd imagine just exactly as hard as I did when you and him were nearly killed, by those raiders who were tryin' to put me in the ground," Jim answered. "That's another reason I want to be in town as early as possible tomorrow mornin'. I'm sure Charlie's not gonna head for Austin first, or here, but straight into San Leanna to be with Mary Jane. I want to make certain I'm in town when he gets back. It'll just about kill him when he discovers what happened, and I don't want to see him do anythin' foolish."

"You mean like you did, riding off after those men left me and Charlie for dead, even though you were half dead yourself, Jim?" Julia said.

"That's precisely what I mean. Charlie's gonna want to go after those men, there's no question about that, but I want him ridin' with me when he does. I don't want him runnin' off half-cocked and gettin' himself killed."

"I'll be going into town with you," Julia said.

"Of course. I expected that," Jim answered. He yawned and stretched. "Reckon I'm more bushed than I realized. Guess I'd better try'n get some shut-eye. It'll be sunup before we know it. Good night, Julia."

He kissed her cheek, then settled back on his pillow, his arm around her shoulder.

"Good night, Jim."

Soon, Julia was asleep, but Jim lay there, staring at the ceiling, wondering what the morrow would bring. Would he finally come up with some clue that would lead him in the direction of the Ghost Riders, or would they just seem to disappear into thin air, as had happened so many times before?

Would he be able to keep Charlie in line, hoping the boy would realize he would need to keep a cool head, and his wits about him, to have any hope of bringing the murderous gang to justice? Or perhaps Charlie would want to stay with Mary Jane while she recovered. If he did, that would be one less thing Jim would have to worry about. And while he hoped Charlie would, deep in his gut Jim knew better. Charlie was like him in so many ways. And, just as Jim had gone after the outlaws who had attacked his ranch, leaving Julia and Charlie for dead, Charlie would be certain to go after the men who had so badly injured his wife, and murdered her parents. And, just like his father, Charlie would not rest until those men were behind bars . . . or dead.

Jim looked at Julia and sighed deeply. After weeks on the trail, his body ached for hers. Whenever he returned home, those long absences made their lovemaking that much sweeter, their passion more intense. Not this time, however. Not after the tragedy which had struck San Leanna. There would be no chance to make love to his wife, nor any rest, until the Ghost Riders were brought to justice. He rolled onto his side, and slipped into a troubled sleep.

Before the gray light of the false dawn even touched the eastern horizon the next morning, the men had gulped down the huge breakfast which

Julia cooked, the ranch's stock was fed, and the horses were saddled. Julia had hitched Ben and Jerry, the draft team, to a buckboard, which she'd loaded with food and supplies people in the burned out town would need, and would drive into San Leanna. The dew was still dimpling the grass, the morning mist still rising, and the coming sunrise just beginning to paint the eastern sky pink and rose when they rode away from the J-B Bar.

"Jim," Captain Storm said, as they headed for town, "I know I'm the ranking officer here, as well as your commanding officer; however, I gave you the job of tracking down the Ghost Riders. That hasn't changed just because I'm here. This is still your investigation, so you're still in charge. And, since it's your town that was attacked, I figure it's only right you and Smoky should talk to your neighbors, and get what information you can. They'll probably open up more to you two than me, or anyone else."

"I appreciate that, Cap'n," Jim answered. "Of course, my first stop's gonna be at Doc Watson's, to see how Mary Jane is doin'."

"I wouldn't have thought anythin' else," Storm said.

After stopping at Smoky's, to get him and pick up his wife, who would be helping Julia with her mission, they rode in silence the rest of the way to San Leanna, the only sounds the clopping of the horses' hooves, the jingling of bits, harness, and spurs, and the rattling of the wagon. When they reached town, a half hour after sunrise, it was already bustling with activity, as the survivors of the Ghost Riders' raid continued to remove debris and rebuild. Joe Jones, who owned the hardware store, had set up a tent to temporarily replace the burned-out shell that had been his business. Planks set on empty packing barrels and crates served as counters. Several freight wagons were pulled up, waiting to unload lumber, hardware, bolts, nails, and tools, everything which would be needed to start reconstructing the town. Josiah Stubbs, the town banker, had set up temporary quarters for the bank in his home.

"Howdy, Jim, Smoky," Jones yelled, as they rode past. "Heard you were in town. Now those Ghost Riders'll have somethin' to worry about. And they ain't gonna kill our town. No sir, they sure ain't."

Jim and Smoky returned his greeting, but kept their horses at a steady pace, as they headed for Doctor Watson's office. When they reached it, Bert Kline was sitting on the porch, in a tilted back chair. The young Ranger cradled a rifle in his arms.

"Mornin', Bert," Captain Stone said. "Everythin' quiet?"

"Mornin', Cap'n, and everybody," Bert answered. "Quiet as a church on Tuesday mornin'. I'm keepin' my eye out for trouble, just in case, but I don't expect none. Those raiders didn't leave enough to make it worthwhile for any other renegades to come here."

"All right, Bert," Storm said. "You go get yourself some breakfast, and some sleep. I'll see you later."

"All right, Cap'n." Bert wandered off in the direction of Mrs. Hastings' boarding house, where he and Storm were staying. Jim and his partners dismounted and tied their horses, then Jim helped Julia from the buckboard.

"Jim, that looks like Father Clermont's buggy in Doctor Watson's carriage shed," she said. "I hope nothing has happened to Mary Jane."

"I doubt it," Jim said, trying to reassure her, despite the sinking feeling in his own gut. "Bert would've told us if anythin' had."

"Julia, I'm positive Jim's right," Cindy added. "But there's only one way to know for certain. You hurry inside. I'll wait here for you."

"We'll stay here until you come back, too, Jim," Captain Storm added.

"All right. Be quick as I can," Jim said. He and Julia hurried into Doctor Watson's house, where he maintained his office. Father Clermont was in the parlor with the physician.

"Good morning, Jim," he said. "I'm certainly pleased to see you're home. How long will you be staying? And good morning to you, Julia."

"Mornin', Father," Jim answered. "I'm afraid I'll only be here long enough to try'n pick up a lead as to where to find the hombres who did this."

"I see. Well, please stop by the rectory before you leave. I'll bless you and your men. I'll pray the Lord keeps you safe, and grants you success in your endeavor."

"I'm obliged, Father."

"Father, how's Mary Jane?" Julia asked.

"She's pretty much the same, but she is awake. She's aware both her parents are gone. Learning that was very hard on her, of course. As far as her condition, Doctor Watson can tell you more," Father Clermont answered.

"Mary Jane is doing quite well, considering the extent of her injuries," Watson said. "Her recovery is still very much in question, as well as whether or not she regains her sight, but I'm pleased with the progress she has made, so far. And she has been asking for Charlie. Do you have any idea when he'll be home?"

"He should reach town sometime later today," Jim answered. "Doc, it's important I speak with Mary Jane, if it's at all possible. I'm hopin' mebbe she saw or heard somethin', anythin', which might help us track down the outfit which is behind all these raids."

"Of course," Watson said. "I can only allow you a brief visit with her, however. She needs lots of rest to regain her strength."

"I won't need long," Jim said. "Just enough time to ask her a few questions."

"Jim, Julia, I have to get back to the church to say morning Mass," Father Clermont said. "Jim, don't forget. Stop and see me before you leave town."

"Count on it, Father."

"Good. Doctor, I'll return this evening to visit with Mary Jane again."

"You're welcome anytime, Father. Quite often, what I as a physician can't heal for the body, the Lord seems to heal for the soul. Good day."

"Good day, Doctor. I'll see myself out."

"Jim, right this way," Watson said, once the priest had left. "Julia, you know the room." He led them to a back room, brightly lit by the rays of the rising sun streaming through the east-facing windows. Mary Jane lay covered with blankets. Her face was a mass of bruises, and a cloth, held in place by a bandage wrapped around her head, covered her eyes.

"Mary Jane, it's Doctor Watson again. Jim and Julia are here."

"Jim's here? Oh, Jim, I've been praying for you and Charlie to get home. Is he with you?" Mary Jane asked. Her voice was hoarse from the smoke she'd breathed in, while trapped in the burning store.

"He's not, but he'll be here sometime today," Jim said. "I'm certain his first stop will be to see you. Mary Jane, I'm so sorry for the loss of your mother and father. They were my good friends, and I'm certain I'll miss them almost as much as you will. Doc Watson tells me you're starting to recover. You just listen to him, and you'll be better before you know it."

"Mary Jane, you already look a bit better than you did yesterday," Julia added.

"I wish I felt better," Mary Jane said. "And I wish I could see you."

"You will, in time," Julia assured her. "And once Charlie's here, I'm certain that will help speed your recovery."

"Jim, I need to remind you this visit has to be brief," Watson said. "We can't overtax my favorite patient. Mary Jane, Jim wants to ask you some questions about the night of the raid. I told him that would be all right, as long as he didn't take too long. You still need plenty of rest."

"All right, Doctor."

"Mary Jane," Jim said. "I've really only got one question, but you may have more than one answer for it. Do you recall anythin' about that night, or anythin' about the men involved? Anythin' at all?" Mary Jane hesitated before replying.

"I'm . . . I'm not certain," she said. "It's all so hazy. We were just closing the store when the town was attacked. The raiders threw a torch into the store, and shot my father through the window. Then, four men came inside. One of them tried to . . . tried to . . ." She broke down, sobbing.

"It's all right, Mary Jane," Jim said. "Take your time."

"He tried to molest me!" she burst out. "My mother tried to stop him. She pulled off his mask before they killed her. I ripped off his bandanna when I tried to break free of him. I saw he had a scar on his left cheek, from just under his eye, almost to his chin."

"Mary Jane, that's the first real clue we've had about any of those hombres," Jim said. "Thank you. Did you happen to notice anythin' else about him?"

"Yes. He was tall, but not thin. He had a good-sized belly. I remember that from him pressing up against me. He had reddish hair, and light brown eyes. They looked almost yellowish. He also had another scar, just above his . . . his . . ."

"Where, Mary Jane? Where?"

"I, I can't say it," Mary Jane stammered. "I just can't."

"Mary Jane, this is important. Anythin' you can tell me might lead me to the man who did this to you. Now, where was that other scar?" Jim insisted.

"It . . . it was . . . on his belly . . . just above . . . his . . ." Mary Jane struggled to find the proper word she could use. "His . . . manhood. In fact, the scar ran a little way down the side of that. I noticed it when he tried to . . ."

"You don't need to say any more, Mary Jane," Jim said. "Thank you. I know that wasn't easy for you to tell me. You're doin' just fine. Can you recall anythin' else?"

"I . . . think so. One of the other men tried to stop his partner from attacking me. He said they didn't have enough time, and their boss would get angry if he found out what he was tryin' to do to me. He called him Cannon. And Cannon, the one who tried to molest me, called his partner Stonefield."

"Did they survive the explosion?"

"I believe they did. No, I'm positive they did. They pulled me into the street. Another man told them to let me go. They did, and ran for their horses."

"That's two names, and a description," Jim said. "Mary Jane, I'm really impressed you recollected all that, especially after what was done to you. What you've given me just might be the information I need to run those renegades to ground, once and for all. If the Rangers ever take gals into the outfit, you'd make a fine one. One to ride the river with. I'd bet my hat on it."

"A fine gal?" Mary Jane said, with a weak laugh.

"There, that's better. You're smiling," Jim said. "That's a good sign. And no, I meant a fine Ranger. As far as you bein' a fine gal, there's no question."

"Jim, Julia, I hate to cut your visit short, especially since you really haven't had any time with Mary Jane, Julia, but I can't allow her to become overtired," Watson said. "You can come back this afternoon, if you'd like."

"We will be back, and Charlie will be with us," Jim said. "Mary Jane, you rest until then."

"Yes," Julia added. "We'll see you again, later today."

"Thank you," Mary Jane said. Her eyes closed.

"Doctor?" Julia said, alarmed.

"She's just drifted back to sleep. That's not unexpected," Watson explained. "Most patients who have had traumatic injuries such as Mary Jane has suffered will fade in and out of consciousness, quite a bit. It's nothing to particularly worry about. Jim, before you leave, I have something for you. It's right here."

Watson opened a cabinet drawer and removed a circular object, which he handed to Jim.

"There wasn't much left of any of the bodies in Jarratt's store, mostly just a few bones. Four were found, the skeletons of three males and one female. The males were most likely Mike Jarratt and two of the raiders. Marcy Pratt was hidin' across the street. She saw four men go into the store, but only two came out. They had Mary Jane, but dropped her just before the explosion. Marcy said they tried for their horses, but the animals ran off, and they chased after them. The female skeleton, I can only assume it was Bethea, had that clutched in its hand. I don't know if it means anything or not."

"That confirms what Mary Jane said, that two of the men who hit the store survived," Jim said. "Lemme take a closer look at this thing."

Jim examined the object, a round, smoke smudged, turquoise stone. He turned it over in his hand. Marks on the back seemed to indicate it had been mounted on something, most likely silver, which had melted away from the intense heat of the fire that had consumed Jarratt's store. "I don't know if it means anythin' either, Doc," he said. "But I've never seen anythin' like this in Jarratt's store. Did you, Julia?"

He showed Julia the stone. She shook her head.

"No, I've never seen a stone like that in the store."

"That means it was most likely bein' worn by one of the raiders," Jim said. "Probably the one who tried to rape Mary Jane, the one she said was called Cannon. I'd wager Bethea yanked this off him when she pulled the mask off his face. Doc, I'm gonna take this along. Mebbe someone, somewhere, will recognize it. Now, I really need to get goin'. I've got a lot more people to question. I'll see you this afternoon."

"Of course, Jim."

Jim and Julia both kissed Mary Jane lightly on the cheek, then took their leave.

"Julia, how's Mary Jane?" Cindy asked, as soon as they came outside.

"She seems a bit better," Julia answered.

"More importantly, she was able to give me the first real leads on those Ghost Riders," Jim said. "Julia, where are you two headed now?"

"We're going to the Methodist Church," she said. "Cindy promised Reverend Patterson we'd help him set up a shelter for those who have lost their homes. That's what all the food I've brought is for, to help stock its shelves."

"Okay. I'm going to see Banker Stubbs next. I understand he's doin' business out of his house, until the bank is rebuilt. Then I've got a few more people to talk to. I'll come get you at the church as soon as I'm done. Or once I see Charlie and Ty ride in."

"All right. I'll see you later." Julia gave him a quick kiss, then climbed to the buckboard's seat and picked up the reins. She slapped them on the horses' rumps, putting the team into motion.

"What do you want us to do, Jim?" Captain Storm asked.

"I figure it'd be a good idea to comb through what's left of the buildings," Jim answered. "Mebbe one of you'll come up with somethin'. Chuck, Eddie, you stick with the captain. Smoke, you take J.R. with you. We'll meet at the livery stable, say in about two hours."

"That seems like as good a plan as any,"

Storm said, with a shrug. "C'mon, boys, let's go."

Jim interviewed every person in town who had survived the attack of the Ghost Riders. However, not one of them was able to provide more information. It was a very frustrated Ranger who met his partners at Hal Munson's Livery Stable.

"Howdy, Jim, pull up a barrel and have a seat," Hal invited, when Jim arrived. The rest of the men were already there. "I'd offer you a pull on the jug, like these boys just had, but I know you don't drink anythin' harder'n sarsaparilla." He spat out a long stream of tobacco juice. "Got coffee keepin' warm on the stove if you'd like."

"You mean that coal tar you try'n pass off as coffee?" Jim said, with a laugh. "Sure, I'll get myself a cup." He went inside, got his coffee, then returned and sat down.

"I hope some of you had better luck'n I did," he muttered. "Except for what Mary Jane gave me, and the stone from Doc Watson, no one else was able to give me any information at all."

"We didn't do any better," Smoky admitted. "I talked to a few folks, too, just in case they might've recollected somethin' after they spoke with you, and we went through every buildin' we could. Didn't find a thing that'd help."

"How about you, Hal?" Jim asked. "You see

anythin' of those men? And how'd they miss your stable?"

"Plain, dumb luck, Jim. Tad Purdy, that boy who's a bit touched in the head, came by for a visit the night everythin' happened. He left the barn door open and all the horses got loose, except for my Becky. They took off outta town like the devil hisself was after 'em. The entire bunch was two miles away from here before I was able to catch up with those ornery cayuses. By the time I was able to round 'em up and drive 'em back to town, those Ghost Riders had been and gone. It was sure lucky for me I guess they figured, without any horses to steal, it wasn't worth burnin' down my barn. Even luckier they came from the opposite direction from which the horses went."

"I'd say," Jim said. "Hal, supposedly some of those hombres didn't make it, but got killed. What happened to their horses? You have any of 'em?"

"Nope." Munson shook his head. "There were two in front of the store that got killed by the explosion. Any others must've been taken along by the raiders, because there weren't no more. Reckon they didn't want to chance anybody findin' out who they were by somethin' in the dead men's saddlebags."

"Before you ask, Jim, Hal did take the gear off those dead mounts," Captain Storm said. "Me'n

276

Bert have already gone through it. There was nothin' we could use."

"So we ain't a whole lot better off than we already were," J.R. said.

"No, we sure ain't," Jim agreed. "You know, one thing's really been stickin' in my craw. Why'd those raiders hit San Leanna, of all places? Every last one of their other attacks has been much farther west. Why'd they ride so many miles to strike here?"

"That's been gnawin' at my guts, too," Smoky said. "There's a lot of towns between here and Brady they could've hit. And San Leanna's darn close to Austin. They took an awful long chance, hittin' a place so close to a big city, let alone the state capital. Seems it would've been a lot safer for 'em to stay out in the tall and uncut, where the law's stretched real thin, and it'd be easier for 'em to just disappear into the brush. Makes no sense, them hittin' here." He took a last drag on his quirly, then tossed the butt into the street.

"I dunno." Jim thumbed back his Stetson and wiped sweat from his brow. "All I do know is this is the most aggravatin', frustratin' assignment I've ever been handed. After all the time we've spent lookin' for 'em, with no luck, those so-called Ghost Riders, now havin' killed a bunch of my friends, includin' my boy's in-laws, are still ridin' high, wide, and handsome out there somewhere, probably laughin' at us, and gettin' ready to hit another settlement. And we have no idea where."

"Jim, I know it's got to be drivin' you half out of your mind, not bein' able to come up with that bunch," Storm said. "Heck, I've been rackin' my brain, tryin' to figure out their next move. I still don't have any more idea about that than you."

"Wait a minute. I just thought of somethin'," Smoky said. Excitement gleamed in his dark eyes. "Jim, remember that night we came to town, to have supper at O'Malley's, then some drinks at Beau's place?"

"Yeah, I sure do, Smoke," Jim said. "Our nice, relaxin' evenin' in town that was ruined by the hombres who tried to rob the O'Malley's restaurant."

"Yeah. And remember what that one man said, just before he was hauled down to Doc Watson's? The one Don stuck in his gut with that meat fork?"

"Sorta. He said the town would pay for what we'd done," Jim answered. "That don't mean anythin'. Lots of men make threats like that all the time."

"Yeah, but what if those three were part of the Ghost Riders, mebbe just passin' through, mebbe scoutin' out places to raid," Smoky replied. "That'd explain why San Leanna was their target. Once word got back to the rest of the outfit their pardners had been killed right here in this town, they'd be bound and determined to get revenge, just like that hombre said would happen."

"You could be onto somethin', Smoke," Jim said. "Hal, you took in those three men's horses, to sell 'em for the town to cover the buryin' costs for those hombres. You happen to recollect what color those broncs were?"

"I sure do, Jim," Hal answered. "Two were gray, and one was a real light blue roan."

"The same color mounts as the Ghost Riders use," Jim exclaimed. "That's gotta be it. Good work, Smoke."

"I'm just glad I recalled what the dyin' renegade said that night," Smoky answered.

"So we've got two last names, one man's description, and a turquoise stone," J.R. said. "And now the reason they attacked San Leanna. That's not much to go on. But it's still more'n what we had yesterday."

"It's a start," Jim said. "All we have to do is keep pluggin' away, and we'll come up with the Ghost Riders. Bet your hats on it, all of you."

Jim and his partners left their horses at the livery stable for feed and rest, then spent the next several hours poking around the ruins of San Leanna, hoping against hope to come up with a few more clues. At noon, he and the other men met Julia and Cindy at the United Methodist

Church, where Cindy and Smoky were members of the congregation, for dinner. Cindy introduced the Rangers, as well as the McIlroy boys, to the church's pastor, Reverend Donald Patterson, his wife, Elizabeth, and their daughters, Elisha and Ruth, as well as several other parishioners who were helping prepare the shelter.

"I'm glad to see you home again, Smoky. We miss you at services when you're gone," the Reverend said, once the introductions were completed. "The same goes for you, Jim. And it's a pleasure to meet the rest of you. I'm glad you stopped by. Y'all look like you could use some rest. We have plenty of sandwiches, lemonade, and lots of hot coffee. Help yourselves."

"Much obliged, Reverend," Captain Storm answered. "You heard him, men. Chow down."

Not having eaten since before sunrise, the men made quick work of the ham or roast beef sandwiches, which were accompanied by deviled eggs and pickles.

"Reverend, are you certain you should be serving these deviled eggs?" Jim asked, laughing.

"Jim, we don't call those deviled eggs," Reverend Patterson replied, also laughing. "Those are angel eggs."

"Well, whatever you call 'em, they're mighty tasty," Eddie said.

"I can tell you like 'em, Eddie," J.R. answered. "You've eaten half a dozen already."

"We've also got peach cobbler for dessert," Elizabeth said.

"Peach cobbler? Now you're talkin'!" Chuck exclaimed. "Let me at it."

"Reverend, if you'd like, once we're finished eating, we can help you out here," Captain Storm said. "We won't be doing much until Charlie and Ty reach town."

"That isn't necessary, although we do appreciate the offer, Captain," the Reverend answered. "We have more than enough help. And I'm certain you have plenty of your own work to do, despite what you claim."

"We can keep ourselves occupied, that's for certain," Storm said. "But right now, I'd like to occupy myself with some of that cobbler. And I know Jim will have some."

"I sure will," Jim said. He picked up a plate from the table, then quickly put it down, when the hoof beats of two horses sounded. Hoof beats that suddenly, and rapidly, increased in tempo.

"The cobbler can wait. That's gotta be Charlie and Ty."

He started down Main Street on the run. Sure enough, Charlie and Ty were sliding their horses to a stop in front of the lot where Jarratt's store had stood. Shock was apparent on their faces.

"Charlie! Charlie! Ty! Over here," Jim called.

"Pa!" Charlie shouted back. He turned Splash

and loped him over to Jim. "What happened here? Looks like almost the entire town burned down. Where's Mary Jane? Where's her folks?"

"Mary Jane's at Doc Watson's," Jim answered. "She's been waitin' for you to get back. Charlie, wait!" he yelled, to no avail, as Charlie ripped his horse around and galloped for Watson's office.

"Ty, give me a ride, quick," Jim ordered. He jumped up onto Bandit's rump and settled in place. Ty needed no urging to take off after Charlie. Bandit's quarter horse and mustang blood meant he was extremely quick in a short sprint. They overtook Charlie just as he reached the doctor's office. Jim slid off Bandit's rump, and when Charlie dismounted grabbed him by the shoulder and spun him around.

"Charlie, hold on a minute. You have to listen to me before you go in there. It was the Ghost Riders who did this. I won't go into details now, but they just about destroyed San Leanna, as you can see. Mike and Bethea are dead. Mary Jane was badly hurt. Doc Watson says she should recover from most of her injuries, but it will take time."

"What do you mean, most of her injuries, Pa? And why are you here? Why aren't you after that bunch?"

"To answer your first question, Charlie, right now, she's blind. The doc doesn't know if she'll regain her sight or not."

"Blind?" Charlie echoed.

"Blind," Jim confirmed "But it might not be permanent. Just pray it isn't. As far as your second question me, Smoky, and J.R. just got into town yesterday. We were over in Junction when we got the news the Ghost Riders had struck San Leanna. We got here as fast as we could, after findin' out what happened. I've been talkin' to folks, tryin' to get more information. So have Smoky and J.R. Mary Jane was able to give me the names of two of those men, and a pretty good description of one. However, we have no idea which way they headed, except toward Austin. They could be almost anywhere. But we'll find 'em, you have my promise on that. Right now, you need to be with your wife, and let me worry about the Ghost Riders."

"Jim's right," Ty said. "I'd wager Mary Jane will be just fine. You'd better go on in, Charlie."

"Yeah. Yeah." Charlie took the stairs two at a time and burst into Watson's office. Jim and Ty followed, more slowly. Jim stopped Ty on the front porch.

"Ty, I didn't get the chance to tell you, but your family is fine. So are Josie and her family," Jim told him. "I just left them, down at the Methodist Church. They're working on a temporary shelter for the folks who have lost their places. Julia and Cindy are also there."

"Thanks, Jim. I appreciate you're lettin' me

know," Ty answered. "I'll head over there right now. Tell Charlie I'll see him later."

"I will," Jim said. "Like I told Charlie, we have found out a little about this Ghost Rider outfit. I think we'll talk everythin' over tonight, back at my place. If you have enough time after visitin' with your folks and Josie, ride on over. When we go after this bunch, I want you ridin' with us."

"You know you won't be able to keep Charlie out of this fight either, Jim," Ty said. "Not after what they did to Mary Jane and her parents, and our friends."

"I know that," Jim said. "I'm kinda hopin' he won't want to go with us, but would rather stay here with Mary Jane."

"There's not a chance of that," Ty said. "And I'll be at your place tonight. Count on it."

"Thanks, Ty. I'll see you then."

"See you tonight, Jim."


"Charlie," Doctor Watson said, as soon as the young Ranger came through the door. "Hello, and am I certainly happy to see you."

"Howdy, Doc," Charlie said. "Where's Mary Jane? Is she awake? How is she? Can I see her?"

"She's right out back," Watson answered. "Yes, she's awake, and has been asking for you. That's why I'm so glad you're here. Seeing you home safe is probably the best medicine for her right now. She's doing quite well, considering how badly she was injured, and the shock from the loss of her parents. And of course you can see her. I do need to caution you, however. Her injuries are quite extensive. Her face is considerably bruised and scraped. There are also some slight burns, as well as several broken bones. She also has fairly extensive internal injuries. And she's blind, at least temporarily, so her eyes are bandaged to protect them."

"My pa told me all that," Charlie answered. "None of it matters. I just want to see my wife."

"Certainly," Watson said. "I'll take you to her, right now."

He led Charlie into Mary Jane's room. Charlie had to keep his emotions in check at the sight of her. Her face was swollen and bruised, her eyes covered. Her right arm was splinted, and in a sling. Under the blankets covering her, both of her legs were splinted, and her fractured ribs were swathed in more bandages.

"Mary Jane, you have a visitor," he said.

"Who is it, Doctor?"

"I'm not certain you know him. He says his name's Charlie. He's a Texas Ranger, and he claims he's married to you."

"Charlie! Charlie's here?"

"I sure am, Mary Jane," Charlie answered. He rushed over to the bed, slid an arm under her shoulders, and hugged her carefully, not wanting to hurt her further. "Everythin'll be all right now. You'll see. I promise you that."

"Oh, Charlie. How I've missed you. I never thought I'd see you again." She ran her hands over his face, then down his neck, pausing over the still-healing scab Obadiah Haskell's chains had left.

"You need a shave," she said. "And what happened to your neck? You didn't get shot, did you?"

"I was plannin' on takin' a bath and shavin' tonight," Charlie answered. "Seems now like that'll have to wait. As far as my neck, I didn't duck fast enough when Splash ran under a low-hangin' live oak branch," he fibbed. "It ain't nothin' to worry about. And you ain't gonna believe this, but Ty's grown himself a full beard. I don't know how Josie's gonna like that."

"She probably won't," Mary Jane said, then broke down, weeping.

"It's all right. Cry as much as you want," Charlie said. He held her, silently, until she was once more able to speak.

"Charlie, what happened . . . it was so awful. Those horrible men killed my father, then my mother. She was trying to protect me, and they killed her for it. I really don't remember anything after that, until I woke up here. I must look awful."

"You look perfectly beautiful to me, just as you

always have, Mary Jane. Black and blue always did look good on you," Charlie tried to reassure her, with a soft laugh. "And don't worry about me leaving. I'll stay here with you as long as you need me."

"Do you mean that, Charlie?"

"I sure do."

"I'm so happy to hear that," Mary Jane said. "But I have something to say to you. Don't say a word until I'm finished."

"All right."

"You just said two words," she chided. "Charlie, I can't tell you how happy and relieved I am to have you home. However, when we decided to marry, I promised you I would never interfere with your job as a Ranger. I know how important it is to you. And right now, it's also important to me. I understand, more than I ever did before, how essential the Rangers are to this state. I want you to help find the men who did this. They've killed my parents, and many of our friends. They have to be stopped, Charlie. You have to help find them. You must."

"Are you certain, Mary Jane?"

"As certain as I ever have been about anything. I don't want to see anyone else hurt by those men. I especially don't want to see another woman confronted by the man who . . . who . . . tried to force himself on me. No woman should have to go through what I did."

She started sobbing again.

"Wait a minute, Mary Jane. One of those hombres tried to have his way with you?" Charlie exclaimed.

"Yes. Yes, one of them did. I gave Jim a description of him and his partner. That's why he shot my mother, because she tried to stop him."

"Mary Jane, I'll track down that man if it's the last thing I do on this Earth," Charlie promised. "And when I find him, I'll make certain he can never harm another woman, ever again."

"That's what I needed to hear you say. Just promise me you'll be careful."

"I'll be as careful as I can," Charlie said. "And I'm not going to leave right away. I'll stay here with you tonight. I need some rest. So does Splash. I want to talk with pa and the other Rangers, to find out exactly what they know. I need every bit of information I can get to find that man."

"Charlie, Mary Jane, I hate to interrupt, but you do need to rest now, Mary Jane," Watson said. "Charlie, you can spend as much time as you want with your wife. Stay the night if you wish. But right now, I need to give her some medication, so she'll rest more comfortably."

"That's all right, Doc," Charlie said. "Mary Jane, if it's okay with you, I'll go talk to pa now. I'm gonna try'n clean up some, too, and mebbe get a bite to eat. I haven't had anythin' since breakfast, and that wasn't much. I'll come back quick as I can."

"That's fine, Charlie. I am feeling tired again, and will probably still be sleeping when you return. Go on ahead, take as much time as you need, and don't fret about me. Just knowing you're here will help me to rest."

"I'll always worry about you, Mary Jane. I love you too much not to. You just get some rest, and listen to Doctor Watson, so you'll get well as quickly as possible."

"I will, Charlie."

"Thanks for everything, Doc," Charlie said. "I'll leave you with your patient now. Take good care of her."

"I'll do exactly that," Watson said. "I'll see you later."

Charlie kissed Mary Jane, his eyes moist. He turned and left. When he reached the living room, he found Jim still waiting for him. Julia was also there. She stood up, gave Charlie a kiss, and hugged him.

"Charlie, I'm so happy you're home," she said. "I hope you'll stay. Mary Jane needs you by her side. Was she awake? Were you able to speak with her?"

"I'm happy to see you too, Ma," Charlie said. "Yes, she was. We had a nice talk. As far as me stayin', we'll talk about that in a minute."

He turned to Jim, his fists clenched and eyes blazing.

"Pa, why didn't you tell me one of those men tried to rape Mary Jane?" he asked, his voice low with anger.

"First, because it was more important for you to see her first," Jim answered. "Second, you didn't give me the chance. It wasn't somethin' you needed to know right off. I was gonna tell you after you saw her, as soon as we had the chance to sit down. There's a lot you need to know."

"There sure is," Charlie said. "But you only need to know one thing, Pa. I'm goin' after the men who did this. Whether it's with you, or on my own, I'm goin' after 'em. And when I find 'em, they'll wish the Devil himself had caught up with 'em first."

"Charlie, I wouldn't try'n stop you, even if I could," Jim said. "All I ask is that you wait for me to try and get some more information as to who those men might be, and where they might turn up next. Then you can ride with us. Ty too, if he's willin', and he says he is. I'll clear it with Captain Storm."

"Charlie, are you certain?" Julia asked. "What about Mary Jane?"

"That's what she and I talked about, Ma. I told her I'd stay here with her, if she wanted. She made it plain she'd rather I go after those men. She wants to make certain they don't do to anyone else what they did to her, and this town."

"However, even if she didn't, you wouldn't have stayed," Julia said, with a sigh. "You're just like your father that way. And I guess that's part of what makes me love you both so much . . . and hate you just as much, sometimes."

"That's right, Ma, I wouldn't have stayed. And thank you for understanding."

"Charlie," Jim said. "I'm sure you're plannin' on spendin' the night with Mary Jane. However, if you want, come out to the ranch tonight. Me, Cap'n Storm, and the rest of the men are gonna go over everythin' we've learned about these Ghost Riders. Much of which, I might add, Mary Jane gave us. Ty'll be there. When we ride out, he's comin' with us."

"Sure, Pa. I'll be there. What time?"

"We're gonna have supper, which I'm certain you'd like to have," Jim said.

"I sure would. I haven't tasted Ma's cookin' since me'n Mary Jane returned from Galveston."

"Good. Figure around seven o'clock."

"I'll see you around seven. Until then, I'm just gonna stay with Mary Jane. I'll stop by Mike and Bethea's graves and pay my respects, on the way home."

Julia absolutely refused to allow any discussion of the Ghost Riders, or any of the crimes they had committed, at supper that night. She insisted the men needed the time just to relax, enjoy themselves, and clear their heads. It was only after the buttermilk pie was served, the table cleared, and the men in the living room, while she cleaned up the kitchen, that any mention of the Ghost Riders was allowed. Once everyone had cups of coffee, those who smoked had lit their cigarettes, and everyone was comfortably seated before the topic was brought up.

"All right men, now that we've all got bellyfuls of Mrs. Blawcyzk's fine cookin', it's time we got back to the business at hand," Captain Storm said. "This bunch folks have taken to callin' the Ghost Riders."

"That name sure seems to fit the outfit," J.R. said. "They always strike on a cloudy or stormy night, they dress to look like ghosts, even their horses are all light colored, to look like ghost mounts. That preys on superstitious folks, and if enough of those get scared soon more'n more people start thinkin' they're up against a bunch of real spooks . . . except they ain't."

"That's right," Storm said. "Now, since Jim's in charge of trackin' down that bunch, I'm gonna let him take over. Jim . . ."

"Thanks, Cap'n," Jim said. "Unfortunately, we still don't have a lot to go on, although we did pick up a bit more information, mostly from Mary Jane, Charlie's wife. First, until they attacked here in San Leanna, the outfit had committed most of their depredations over in west Texas. Thanks to Smoky, we have a pretty good idea why they hit here. We think three of their members were here in town, some weeks back. They happened to try'n rob the same restaurant where me'n Smoke were havin' supper. The three of 'em died in the attempt. Once the rest of the outfit found out what happened to their pardners, they came for revenge. Once that was done, they hightailed it on outta this territory. We figure they're probably already back in west Texas somewhere, and will hit some small settlement over that way. The only problem is, we have no idea where."

"And that's a whole lot of territory to cover," Ty said.

"You're right about that," Jim agreed. "Now, we know these hombres have no consciences whatsoever. They kill without compunction, take everything what they can and destroy most of what they can't. Even worse, so far they've been operating with impunity. When we do finally catch up with 'em, keep that in mind. These aren't the kind of men who'll surrender. They'll fight until they're dead . . . or we are."

"I don't plan on takin' any prisoners anyway," Charlie said.

"Neither do me'n Chuck," Eddie added.

"I don't think any of us do," Smoky said.

"All right, that's clear," Jim said. "Now, Mary Jane was able to give us two names, and a good description of one of the men. One is called Stonefield, accordin' to what she heard. The other one is Cannon. Now, Cannon's a pretty common name, so that's not much help. Stonefield's not nearly heard of as much, and that name's kinda familiar to me. I just can't place it. Any of you familiar with a Cannon or Stonefield you think might be connected with this outfit?"

Jim's question was met with a shaking of heads and murmuring of "nos".

"That's what I suspected. Well, mebbe this description of Cannon which Mary Jane gave me might jog someone's memory. He's tall and heavy. Has a good sized gut, accordin' to what she said. He's got sorta reddish hair, and light brown eyes that look kinda' yellowish. But what's most noticeable is he's got two scars, probably knife scars, from Mary Jane's description. The first one runs down his left cheek, from under his eye almost to his chin. The second one's down low on his belly. It slices across his groin, and a little way down the side of his penis. Mary Jane saw that when he attempted to force himself on her. My guess is both those scars came from an angry husband, or boyfriend. I'd bet my hat this Cannon snake has molested women before. We know both of them survived. Mary Jane said they did, and so did Marcy Pratt. When I talked to her, she confirmed Mary Jane's story."

"That's all well and good, Jim, but I don't

think, if we run across this Cannon hombre, we'll be able to convince him to drop his pants so we can take a look," Smoky said. "I think he might object to that."

"That don't matter," Charlie answered. "When we do find that lousy son of a bitch, I'll tear his pants clean off. Then I'll cut off his nuts and feed 'em to him. He'll never touch another woman again. Sorry, Dad, for the language. I know you don't like cussin'."

"Charlie, I think this is one time I can make an exception. I know exactly how you feel," Jim said, then continued. "Unfortunately, that's about all we have to go on. I know it's eatin' at each and every one of us, feelin' so helpless, but unless those Ghost Riders make a slip, or someone stumbles across 'em and lives to tell about it, we'll just have to wait until they hit again before we can pick up their trail."

"However, we're not just goin' to sit around on our butts, waitin' for that to happen," Captain Storm said. "I've already wired Headquarters, and telegrams are being sent to every law enforcement agency in the state, with the descriptions of the men Jim just gave you. Also, tomorrow morning, I'm heading back to Austin. I've already got several clerks working on pulling the files of anyone who may be in our records with the name of Cannon or Stonefield, or anyone who might match Cannon's description.

I want you men to remain here in San Leanna, for one more day, to see if there might be something we've overlooked. Then, I'll expect you in Austin first thing the next mornin'. I want you ready to move the minute we receive any possible information about the whereabouts of the Ghost Riders. Charlie, that doesn't apply to you, if you'd rather remain here with your wife. We'd all understand."

"Me'n Mary Jane have already had this discussion, Cap'n," Charlie answered. "I'll be ridin' with the rest of you."

"Bueno," Storm said. "Now, unless there are any questions, I'd highly recommend y'all get some rest. I have a feelin' you're gonna need it."

Charlie went back to town to be with Mary Jane. Smoky and Ty returned to their own homes, while the men staying at the J-B Bar settled into their beds for the night. Knowing there would only be one more night with his wife before he left, for who knew how long, Jim made passionate love to her, not worrying about their house guests.

The next morning they returned to San Leanna. Jim's first stop was at Doctor Watson's, for a brief visit with Mary Jane and Charlie. Watson reported that Mary Jane was improving every day. Jim, Smoky and Ty took the time to visit the graves of their friends who had been killed in the raid. After that, they rejoined their partners, to once again question the survivors of the raid, and comb yet again through the ruins, hoping to find the least little clue which might bring them closer to finding the Ghost Riders. They turned up nothing.

With their search for the murderous gang stymied, the anxious lawmen spent a restless night. Ordinarily, the Rangers went about their jobs stoically, not losing sleep when a hunt became frustrating, where every lead seemed to turn into a dead end. However, the Ghost Riders were by far the worst outlaws Jim and his partners had ever come across. They wanted to stop them before they could strike again. And, of course, for Jim, Smoky, and especially Charlie, the attack on San Leanna, the killings of so many of their friends, and the near rape and near murder of Charlie's wife, made this assignment personal. None of them would rest until the Ghost Riders were run to ground.

Knowing the rest of the men would arrive in San Leanna shortly after sunrise, Charlie awakened early. He lay next to his still sleeping wife, gently stroking Mary Jane's hair while he watched her. Finally, sensing Charlie's gaze, she awakened. He gave her a quick kiss.

"Good mornin', darlin'. How are you feelin'?" he asked. "Better, I hope. You look a bit better. Some of those bruises are startin' to fade."

"Good morning to you, husband of mine," Mary Jane answered. "Mrs. Charles Blawcyzk. I still can't get used to my new name. And I still have trouble pronouncing it, even after all this time."

"You'll have plenty of time to practice," Charlie said. "Years and years. And you still haven't answered my question."

"I certainly hope so, Charlie," Mary Jane said. "And yes, I am feeling a bit better." She glanced out the window, at Doctor Watson's still dark back yard. "What time is it? And why are you up so early?"

"It's just before dawn," Charlie answered. "And I have to leave for Austin today, with my pa and the rest of the men. Remember?"

"I do now," Mary Jane said. She sighed.

"Mary Jane, it's not too late to change your mind. I can still stay here with you, if you'd like," Charlie assured her.

"No, Charlie, I meant what I said when I told you that you had to go after the men who put me here," she answered. "It's just that, well . . ."

"Just what, Mary Jane? Tell me."

"Charlie, if you don't want to come back to me, you don't have to. I'll understand."

"What do you mean, don't come back to you, Mary Jane? Have you gone loco? Of course I'll come back to you, once my work is done, and the Ghost Riders are dead, or behind bars, waitin' to be hung."

"Charlie, I'm blind," Mary Jane said, her voice breaking. "I may always be blind. Doctor Watson says he can't be certain I won't be crippled, and I'll almost certainly have scars. If you want me to set you free, I will. You don't have to stay married to me out of some misplaced sense of duty, or loyalty . . . or worse, pity."

"Mary Jane, I married you. Not your eyes, or your legs, or any one part of you. I married the whole woman. Besides, by the time I get back, you'll be able to see again. I just know it. And just to set things straight, I still love that whole woman, and always will. Although I have to admit, you do have mighty pretty eyes. And a real cute nose, too."

He kissed her on the tip of that pert, slightly turned-up nose.

"Do you really mean that, Charlie?" she asked.

"Let me put it to you this way. Suppose I come home some day, with a bullet or knife scar on my face, or mebbe crippled up by some Kiowa's arrow or renegade's slug. Would you leave me because of that?"

"Of course not, Charlie," Mary Jane answered, her voice indignant.

"And I won't leave you because of what those outlaws did to you," Charlie replied. "So, that's enough of this kind of talk. Let me just hold you, until it's time for me to go. We can talk about our future, if you'd like. And we do have one, you know, despite how bleak things look at the moment. All right?"

"All right. I love you, Charles Edward Blawcyzk."

"And I love you, Mary Jane Jarratt Blawcyzk."

All too soon, it seemed, Jim was knocking at Doctor Watson's front door. When Watson admitted him into the house, he went straight to Mary Jane's room.

"Pa? You're here already?" Charlie said.

"I'm afraid I am," Jim answered. "We've gotta get ridin'. Mary Jane, how's my favorite daughter-in law this mornin'?"

"I'm feeling a lot better, Jim," Mary Jane answered. "And I'm your only daughter-in-law."

"You're still my favorite," Jim answered, smiling. "Charlie, all the others are outside, waitin'. We'll give you a few more minutes, but then we have to get ridin'."

"All right, Pa."

"Charlie, don't make them wait," Mary Jane said. "I'll be fine, really. The sooner you go, the sooner you'll come back to me. Just make certain you do."

Charlie glanced at Jim.

"As my pa'd say, and I would too, you can bet your pretty feathered and flowered bonnet on that, Mary Jane. Yeah, you sure can."

He leaned over and kissed her.

"Reckon it's time to go. C'mon, Pa."

# 13

Captain Storm was already waiting when they arrived at Ranger Headquarters, a little over ninety minutes later.

"Mornin', Cap'n," Jim said, as he walked into Storm's office, followed by the others. "Beggin' your pardon, but you look terrible. Appears like you haven't slept all night."

Storm was unshaven, his eyes red and swollen. He still wore the same rumpled clothes he'd had on for the previous two days.

"Mornin', Jim. Mornin', boys," Storm replied. "And I did manage to snatch a few minutes sleep. But you're right, Jim. I've been up most of the night, along with two of my clerks, diggin' through records, then burnin' up the telegraph wires. It appears all that hard work just might have paid up. Pour yourselves some coffee, pull up a chair, and I'll tell you what I've learned."

The men got mugs from the shelves, poured them full of the thick, black coffee always kept warm in a pot on the stove, then settled onto chairs, or the worn leather sofa Storm kept in one corner. Smoky, as always, lit a quirly, while Storm filled and lit his pipe. Once everyone was set, Storm put on his spectacles, then opened one of the files on his desk.

"Charlie, before I begin, how is Mary Jane this mornin'?"

"She's doin' a bit better, Cap'n. Thanks for askin'."

"Good, good. I'm glad to hear that, especially after what I've uncovered. If we do manage to bring in the Ghost Riders, it'll be because of the information your wife gave us."

"You mean you know who those men are, Cap'n?" Charlie said, excitement rising in his voice.

"Just rein in, son, and listen to what I have to say. That'll answer all your questions," Storm answered. "Yes, I've got a pretty good idea who those men are. The first one, Stonefield, is most likely Ike Stonefield. He's a half-breed, Kiowa and white. His family owns a good-sized spread, the Cross SF, up in the Panhandle, about twenty miles north of Quitaque. The place sits between the Caprock canyonlands and the Prairie Dog Town Fork of the Red River. I don't need to tell you that's mighty rough country. Ike's father, Morris, is a prominent citizen of Briscoe County. Even though his wife is a full-blooded Kiowa, they're both well respected up that way. Morris and his wife are as fine as they come. So are their two youngest sons, and their daughter. However, Ike sure didn't turn out like the rest of his family.

302

Five years back, he got caught wide-loopin' cattle. He spent four years in jail for it. He swore he'd get revenge for that. My guess is he has, by joinin' the Ghost Riders."

"Now I know where I'd heard that name," Jim said. "It was Ranger Hank Field who brought Ike in. But, accordin' to what Mary Jane told me, Stonefield ain't the leader of the outfit. He's just one of the gang."

"Mebbeso, but he probably helped organize the bunch," Storm answered. "I'm waitin' for responses to messages I've sent, to see who Stonefield might've associated with, either while he was in or after he got out of prison. With luck, that'll give us a few more names."

"What about the other hombre? Cannon?" Charlie asked. "He's the one I want to line up in my sights. I'm gonna put a bullet right between his legs, blow his balls clean off, let him suffer awhile, then put another bullet right in the middle of his forehead and blast his brains out." He shook his head. "Sorry, Pa, I'm cussin' again."

"I can't blame you for feelin' that way, Charlie," Storm answered. "But we've got to try'n bring this bunch in alive . . . not that I think there's much chance of that. I do have a first name for him. Took a while, but I tracked it down. His full name is Emerson Cannon, out of Natchitoches, Louisiana. He raped and almost killed a woman there, just like he tried with your wife. Her husband came home just in time to stop him. He's the man who gave Cannon those scars. He half killed him. While Cannon was awaitin' trial, he broke jail. Last anyone had seen of him was over in Throckmorton. A deputy recognized him from a wanted poster, and attempted to arrest him. Throckmorton killed that deputy, and made good his escape on a stolen horse, headed west. He just might've met up with Ike Stonefield. They'd be the kind to throw in with each other."

"That's all well and good, Cap'n, but that still doesn't give us any idea as to who's leadin' the outfit, and where they hole up," J.R. said. "Seems to me someone's protectin' 'em, too, the way they can just up and disappear. You reckon it's Ike's father? He might be providin' a way for Ike and his pardners to sell off the livestock they've rustled, too."

"Anything's possible, but I doubt it," Storm answered. "Morris Stonefield paid for his son's lawyer, but once it was proved Ike was behind a whole passel of cattle rustlin', he cut ties with the boy. No, I don't think it's him. And the only reason I think Ike didn't go after his father when he got out of jail is it would've been too obvious."

"Although now, that some time has passed, he just might be thinkin' of doin' exactly that," Smoky said. "It'd be easy enough for Ike to do, especially ridin' with the Ghost Riders, then the whole outfit could make their way into the Indian Territories, or over to New Mexico, out of our reach. They've got to know we're gonna close in on 'em, sooner or later. I'd wager they're startin' to think they've grabbed enough money, and it's time to hightail it out of Texas."

"That's likely, Smoke," Storm agreed.

"Cap'n, did you get a description of this Stonefield hombre?" Ty asked.

"Yep, it's right here. Lemme read it to you." Storm picked up another sheet of paper. "He's twenty-eight years old, stands about five foot nine, weight about one hundred and seventy pounds. Has brown hair and eyes. Wears a moustache."

"Then why're we just sittin' here?" Charlie demanded. "We should be on the trail of those hombres, right now."

"Because, right now, we don't have any idea of where to look for 'em," Storm answered. "Sure, I could have you boys ride up into the Panhandle, but what good would that do? The Ghost Riders might well turn up somewhere else. When I get the answers I'm waitin' on, then I might be able to put you back on the trail. For now, hard as it is, we'll just have to wait, and be patient."

Charlie jumped up from his chair.

"I ain't waitin' around any longer. I'm goin' after those hombres, right now."

He started for the door. Jim grabbed him by the shoulder and spun him around to face him.

"Charlie, you ain't goin' anywhere, not until . . ."

Jim's words were cut off when Charlie drove a punch to the point of his chin, sending him staggering backwards. When Charlie swung again, Jim ducked the punch, and sank his own fist into Charlie's belly. Charlie doubled over and fell to the floor, arms wrapped around his middle and struggling to pull air into his lungs.

"Charlie, I might be gettin' a bit long in the tooth, while you're still a young'n, but I sure ain't too old to whup you," Jim said, standing over his son, his fists clenched. "You hear me?"

"Yeah . . . yeah," Charlie gasped.

"All right." Jim pulled Charlie to his feet. "That's enough of this foolishness about takin' off on your own. We'll wait until we have some idea which way to head. Once we have that, we'll stick to the trail like white on rice." He paused. "Charlie, I know exactly how you feel. When our ranch was attacked, while you were still a young'n, you and I were shot, your mother was beaten and raped, and all of us left for dead, I couldn't wait to take off after the men responsible."

"And you did just that," Charlie retorted. "You caught those men, too. So why're you tryin' to stop me from doin' the exact same thing?"

"Because what I did was wrong, Charlie," Jim explained. "It was wrong then, and it's still wrong now. It took me a long time to admit that to myself. Also, don't forget, I might've found those men, but I still needed help to round 'em up. I couldn't have done it alone. All I would've accomplished is gettin' myself killed, leavin' your ma a widow and you without a father. If you insist on goin' after Cannon and the rest of his bunch single-handed, that's what will happen to you. None of us want to see that happen. Think about Mary Jane. Do you want to leave *her* a widow, before you're even married three months? You need to listen to me, Charlie, and ride with us, not alone. Can I count on that?"

"I'll go along, for now," Charlie muttered. "But when we do finally catch up with that bunch, Cannon is mine. Don't any of you get in my way."

"I promise you that, Charlie," Jim said.

"Those two are sure exactly alike," J.R. half-whispered to Smoky.

"They sure are," Smoky answered, softly. "Charlie takes after his pa, in both looks and temperament."

"I'm sure glad you're takin' your pa's advice, Charlie. I understand your being so anxious to find those men," Storm said. "However, if you'll wait a while longer, you'll have a much better idea where to start lookin' for 'em. Do you

307

understand that? Am I gettin' through to you?"

"I reckon," Charlie mumbled. "I'm still not happy about it, though. Not with Mary Jane lyin' in that bed, all busted up, and not bein' able to see. And her ma and pa dead. Those men have hurt an awful lot of folks. Don't forget, Chuck and Eddie here lost their ma and pa, too."

"None of us are, Charlie," Storm agreed. "Now, we have some other business to attend to. Chuck, Eddie, you've been ridin' with Jim and his pardners for quite a few miles now, and I reckon you both intend to see this hunt through to the end."

"That's right, Cap'n. We sure do," Chuck answered.

"That's for certain," Eddie answered.

"Well, then, I reckon we'd better make this legal," Storm said. "It's time I swore you in as Rangers. I couldn't do that before, until I checked into your backgrounds, and made certain you weren't part of the Ghost Riders, and mebbe spyin' for the gang."

"You thought we might be part of the Ghost Riders?" Chuck said. "Those men killed our ma and pa, and tried to kill me'n Eddie. What made you think we'd ever be hooked up with a bunch like that?"

"I didn't, but I had to be certain," Storm answered. "You could've been in cahoots with the outfit, and wanted your folks killed. I've seen odder things than that happen, many times. And you're both forkin' gray broncs. That did look a bit suspicious."

"Well, now that you know we ain't, we appreciate your takin' us on as Rangers," Eddie said. "We're obliged, Cap'n."

"I'm happy to make you part of the outfit," Storm said. "Now, you both look like you might be a bit young, so don't tell me your birth dates."

"You don't have to worry about that, Cap'n," Chuck said. "I turned nineteen last month."

"And I'm eighteen. Well, near to it, anyway," Eddie added.

"We'll leave it go at that," Storm said. "Once you're sworn in, I have some more files we can go over, until I get the answers I'm waitin' on."

It was shortly after noon when Captain Storm pushed back from his desk, and pulled off the spectacles perched on the edge of his nose.

"Boy howdy, I don't know about the rest of you boys, but I can't look at another file," he said. "Tell you what. Why don't we head over to the Silver Star for some grub, and a couple of drinks? Mebbe that'll help clear our heads. We've gotta celebrate the McIlroy brothers here bein' made Rangers, so we'll do that too. I'll leave word if any messages come in to bring 'em over to the saloon."

"Sounds good to me, Cap'n," J.R. said.

"Same here," Smoky added.

"Good," Storm said. "They've got a new singer over at the Silver Star, name of Lacey Burns. She does some entertainin' for the dinner customers, besides her regular show at night. We'll catch her act. She's got a fine voice, and she's real easy on the eyes, too."

"Not to mention the Silver Star Saloon serves a mean steak," Jim said. "And a real fine dried peach pie. It's about time we got some chuck, Cap'n. My belly button's pushin' up against my backbone, it's been so long since I ate."

"Yeah, it's been all of five hours since you put away a stack of hotcakes, half a pound of bacon, another of ham, and half a dozen eggs, Jim," Smoky said, laughing. "That's not even countin' Lord knows how many biscuits you ate, and four or five cups of coffee. I'm surprised you ain't done starved to death."

"I will, if I don't get some food in my belly, right now. Bet a hat on it," Jim answered. "Let's go."

The Silver Star Saloon was the unofficial Rangers' bar in Austin. Most of the men stationed at Headquarters, except those who were married and had their own homes, took the majority of their meals there, as well as spending evenings relaxing over drinks, perhaps enjoying the company of one of the percentage girls, for a dance

310

or other pleasures. Teddy Mahoney, the chief bartender, knew the preferences of each and every one of his regular clients. By the time Captain Storm and his men made their way to a back corner table, Stacy Marie, one of the girls, had already brought over glasses of beer for the captain, Smoky, J.R., Charlie, and Ty, and a bottle of sarsaparilla for Jim. She was a red-head, with laughing green eyes, a smattering of freckles across her nose, and full-figured. She wore a red satin gown which emphasized every curve of that figure.

"Howdy, boys," she said. "Smoky, Jim, J.R., Ty, it's been too long. Charlie, I'm certainly sorry to hear about your wife, and your in-laws. Please tell me she's doing better."

"She is," Charlie assured her. "Thanks for askin' about her."

"That's good news," Stacy Marie said. "Earl, who's these two handsome new fellers you've got with you?"

"This is Chuck McIlroy, and his younger brother, Eddie," Storm answered. "They just signed on with the Rangers. They lost their folks to the Ghost Riders, up in Brady. Their pa was the county sheriff."

"I'm sure sorry to hear that, boys. And I am pleased to meet you. Since you've joined the Rangers, I hope I'll see quite a bit of you in here."

"Thank you, ma'am," Chuck said.

"Ma'am?" Stacy Marie laughed. "I'm not that old. No one 'ma'ams' me, not ever. The name's Stacy, or Stacy Marie. That goes for you too, little brother."

She kissed Eddie, full on the lips.

"Did that feel like a kiss from a 'ma'am'? Or perhaps your sister?"

"No. No ma'am, I mean Stacy Marie," Eddie stammered. "It sure didn't."

"I should hope not," she answered, laughing. "Now, what's your pleasure? For drinks, that is."

"I'll have a beer," Eddie answered.

"Same here," Chuck added.

"Comin' right up."

"Stacy Marie, put in an order of steak and spuds all around," Storm requested.

"Sure. Steaks for all of you. Rare for you, Captain, same for Smoky and J.R., medium for Ty, burnt almost black for Jim and Charlie. How about you, Chuck? How do you want yours cooked?"

"Medium'll do just fine," Chuck said.

"And I'll have mine well done, but not burnt," Eddie added.

"Fine. I'll put in the order, then bring your beers."

While they waited for their meals to arrive, the Rangers discussed, yet again, everything they

312

had learned about the Ghost Riders. Every one of them, even Charlie, agreed they would have to get more information on the gang, or a lucky break, to find them before they struck yet again.

They had finished their dinner, and were working on final drinks when Teddy Mahoney stepped onto the saloon's small dance floor. The bartender motioned for quiet. He nodded to Spike Freulich, the derby-hatted piano player, to pause in his pounding on the ivories.

"Gentlemen, as always, the Silver Star Saloon prides itself on its entertainment," Mahoney announced. "Our latest singer is certainly not going to disappoint. She comes to us all the way from Omaha, Nebraska. I promised you a chance to hear her, briefly. Without further ado, I give you . . . Miss Lacey Burns!"

The room erupted in applause when the curtain parted and Lacey Burns stepped onto the floor. She was blonde and petite, with wide eyes of such a deep blue they appeared almost violet. Unlike most saloon entertainers, she was demurely dressed, in a high necked gown of blue silk. An enormous, feathered hat was perched on her head.

"Thank you for that wonderful greeting," she said. "For my first song, I'll be performing the old standard, 'Buffalo Gals'."

With that, she launched into a lively rendition of the song. Her voice was amazingly powerful, especially coming from one so tiny. It filled the room, reverberating from the rafters, shaking the chimneys of the coal oil lamps. When she concluded, the audience burst into raucous applause, stamping and whistling their approval. Her second number was a bawdy tune, "Down Behind the Old Corral", which she stated she'd written herself. From the reaction the song got, it was certainly appreciated by the patrons of the Silver Star.

"Why, thank you kindly," Lacey said. "Now, for a change of pace, I'm going to sing 'The Streets of Laredo'."

That powerful voice changed completely when she began to sing "The Cowboy's Lament", more popularly known as "The Streets of Laredo", the tragic story of a young cowboy who lay shot and dying. Lacey's voice was now soft and mournful, in some verses of the song barely above a whisper. By the time the song concluded, there wasn't a dry eye in the house. Even the battle scarred and toughened Rangers were wiping tears from the corners of their eyes.

"Thank you again, gentlemen," Lacey said. "If you'd like to hear more, come back this evening. The show starts at eight."

"You reckon we can come back, Chuck?" Eddie asked.

"I dunno. That's up to Cap'n Storm, I'd imagine," Chuck answered. "He'll probably want us to stick close to Headquarters, rather'n out gettin' drunk."

"That'll depend on what we find when we get back there," Storm said. "It you don't have to head out tonight, I'd have no problem with any of you comin' back for the show. But no gettin' drunk, and back in the barracks by midnight."

"Um, Cap'n, that might not be a problem," Jim said. "Yonder comes Paul Ramsey from the telegraph office. And he looks mighty anxious about somethin'."

The Western Union telegrapher rushed up to the Rangers' table.

"Captain Storm. I'm sorry to bother you durin' your dinner, but you said if I received any replies to your wires to bring them right over," he said.

"Don't trouble yourself about that, Paul," Storm answered. "You're doin' just what I asked. I take it you received a response."

"Not exactly," Ramsey answered. "Here. You'd better take a look for yourself."

He thrust a yellow flimsy into Storm's hand. The captain read it, his expression darkening. He crumpled the paper, with a curse.

"What's that say, Cap'n?" J.R. asked.

"The Ghost Riders struck again. They attacked Millsap the night before last," Storm answered. "It appears they tore up some of the T & P's tracks, and ripped down the telegraph lines

315

besides. That's why it took so long for word to get through."

"How?" Smoky said. "They couldn't have made that good a time, after ridin' out of San Leanna. That's close to two hundred miles. Even ridin' hard, day and night, it'd be impossible."

"They could if they took a train," Jim answered. "That's the only way they could've done it. I'd imagine, once they left San Leanna, they broke up into groups of two or three men, then scattered, and either picked up trains at different stations, or took several different trains. That's how they were able to disappear so quick, and completely. Then, they met up again in Millsap, rode out of town a short way to dress in those white robes, and came back and raided the town."

"But that makes no sense," Ty said. "Millsap's the western terminus for the Texas and Pacific, at least until they extend their tracks farther west. There's a depot, and train crews, and telegraph wires. It's a decent sized town. They took an awful chance."

"Not such an awful one, if you think about it," Jim said. "You practically answered your own question, Ty. Like you said, it's the end of the Texas and Pacific's main line. That means there'd be no chance of any organized pursuit by rail. And it's a railroad town. That means there's not a lot of horsemen livin' there. It'd be tough to round up any kind of posse, at least one that had much of a chance to find that outfit. No, once the Ghost Riders got out of town, it'd be real easy for 'em to just disappear into the brush."

"Which means you boys are gonna do exactly what they did, Jim," Storm said. "You're gonna catch a ride on the railroad. C'mon. You men get your horses, and get your gear together. Take plenty of extra shells from the Headquarters armory. Spare guns, too, if you feel the need. Tell Doke I said to give you whatever you want. I'm headin' over to the railroad station. By the time you catch up to me, there'll be a train waitin' for you."

As Storm had promised, by the time the Rangers reached the Texas and Pacific depot, not only was there a train waiting, the railroad had made up a special, just for the lawmen's run to Millsap. With the destruction the Ghost Riders had done to the Texas and Pacific's town of Millsap, the captain had no trouble convincing the station agent to provide the Rangers with a fast train, which would highball north all the way to Fort Worth, then switch to the westbound tracks for Millsap. The fireman had already built up steam in the locomotive, which sat idling, smoke puffing lazily from its stack. Behind that was a single coach, and a cattle car.

"Men, load up your horses, and we'll have you roll right out," Phil Fitzsimmons, the station agent said, when they rode up onto the platform. "I've got Mack Taylor on the engine, and Perry Montalvo's your fireman. Slim Carter's your brakeman. They're three of the best we've got. Old Number 10's one of the best engines on this branch, too. She's old, but reliable, and fast. You should pull into Millsap right around eight tonight."

"Appreciate that, Phil," Jim answered. "Those Ghost Riders have been ten steps ahead of us for far too long now. It's about time we got ahead of them, for a change."

"I think just about everyone in Texas would second that, Jim," Fitzsimmons answered.

"Let's get these broncs on board," Jim ordered. The horses were led into the cattle car, saddles and bridles left in place, their reins tied loosely to the slats, so they could still reach the hay set against the sides. Once they were settled, munching on the hay, the door was slid shut and latched. The Rangers headed for the passenger coach.

"Men, good luck," Storm said, just before they boarded. "If I get any more word, I'll wire you in Millsap. Jim, you make certain to keep in touch, so I know what's goin' on."

"I'll do that, Cap'n," Jim said. "If the telegraph lines are back up, that is. We'd better get movin'."

Jim was the last man to climb the steps into the

coach. He settled in a back seat, just as the train, with the clanking of couplers, the hissing of released steam, the clanging of the locomotive's bell, and a harsh blast from its whistle, lurched into motion. Except for brief stops for water and wood, the special would roll unhindered from Austin clear through to Millsap. Fitzsimmons had telegraphed up the line, so all switches would be set for the Rangers' train to roll right through them, without stopping. All other traffic on the line would be halted, shunted onto sidings, until the special passed.

As Montalvo, the fireman, furiously tossed wood into the firebox's hungry maw, building up steam, Taylor pulled back on the throttle, opening it fully. Soon, the train was racing along at nearly forty miles per hour. In the coach, the Rangers, knowing they might not have another chance for a good rest for quite some time, leaned back in their seats, stretched out their legs, and tilted their Stetsons over their eyes. Despite their anxiousness to reach Millsap, fearing they would find yet another scene of death and destruction, they allowed the rocking of the coach and clacking of the wheels over the rails to lull them to sleep, with each man hoping his next sleep wouldn't be his last, and permanent, one.

The train reached Millsap shortly ahead of schedule, just before eight o'clock. With the tracks being torn up for a quarter of a mile from town, it was forced to stop before reaching the depot itself. Even with dusk fast approaching, a full crew was hard at work, trying to repair the damage.

"Sorry, Rangers, but this is as far as we can go," Carter, the brakeman, said, once the train rolled to a stop and they descended from the coach. "I'm afraid you'll have to jump your horses outta the car."

"That's all right, Slim," Jim assured him. "They've done it before. C'mon, men, let's get 'em offa there."

The horses were quickly unloaded, the Rangers soon in their saddles. The men of the track crew paused from their work, just briefly, to glance up at the riders, whose faces were set in grim determination. The rays of the setting sun glittered off the silver star in silver circle badges Jim, Smoky, J.R., Charlie, and Ty wore pinned to their chests.

It only took a few moments to reach town. As in all the other settlements the Ghost Riders had attacked, they had left behind a scene of utter devastation. The railroad station was a pile of smoldering rubble, most of the rest of town in ruin.

"Reckon there's anyone who can tell us which way those hombres went, after they left here, Jim?" Smoky asked.

"I dunno," Jim said. "Mebbe there."

He indicated one of the few buildings still standing, a stone structure. Its walls were smoke and soot streaked, but still standing. Light shone through its shattered front windows.

"Let's go find out." He turned Sizzle toward the building. Hearing the riders approaching, a harried-looking man came outside, holding a sawed-off shotgun.

"What're you men lookin' for?" he curtly demanded.

"We're Texas Rangers," Jim answered. "I'm Lieutenant Jim Blawcyzk, and these are my pardners. We're on the trail of the renegades who did this. You have any idea which way they headed?"

"Sorry, Ranger, for bein' so rude," the man answered. "It's just that, after what happened, everyone's on edge. I'm certain you can understand that."

"Of course," Jim said.

"I'm Harry Sloane, the T & P's freight agent here," the man continued. "I'm lucky to still be alive. I was usin' the privy when those raiders struck. I ain't ashamed to admit I hid in there until they were gone. Besides, with what they did, I needed to stay in there, if you get my meanin'. They killed sixteen people. And you can see how they just about destroyed this town. Anyway, I can tell you they headed west outta here, but that's all. Wish I could be more help."

"That's plenty," Jim assured him. "It tells us which way to ride. Gracias. Reckon we'd better get movin'. They've already got a good jump on us."

"No problem at all, Ranger. Good luck," Sloane said. As he did, thunder rumbled in the distance. Smoky cursed.

"Jim, I don't reckon we're goin' anywhere tonight, unless it's to find a place to hole up and stay dry. Look at those clouds buildin' up on the western horizon. There's gonna be one whopper of a storm, and we'll be ridin' right into it." He cursed again. "Those Ghost Riders seem to catch all the breaks."

"And if it's stormin', that most likely means they're gonna hit someplace again tonight," J.R. added. "But Smoke's right, Jim. We can't trail 'em in that storm. We'll just have to ride it out here, and start again fresh in the mornin'."

"I hate to admit it, but you're right," Jim said. "Sloane, is there someplace we can put up our horses for the night, and roll out our blankets?"

Sloane rubbed his jaw before replying.

"Hmm. Lemme think. Let's see. There's a shed still standin' behind what's left of the depot. You can put your horses there. And you can sleep inside my office here. It'll be crowded, and it smells of smoke. It nearly burned along with the rest of the town, but Floyd Shelby, my assistant, managed to put out the flames . . . just before he got shot in the back."

"Then that's what we'll do," Jim answered. "C'mon, let's get the horses put up, before the storm hits."

"I'll have stew heatin' up when you get back," Sloane called, as they turned their horses. "It ain't much, but it'll fill your bellies."

"We appreciate that," Jim said. "See you in a few minutes."

Once the horses were unsaddled, rubbed down, and given hay and water, the Rangers shouldered their saddlebags and, carrying their rifles and bedrolls, returned to the freight office. The storm hit in full fury, wind whistling through the broken windows, causing the flame in the coal oil lamp to flicker and cast eerie shadows. Lightning flashed blindingly, while thunder cracked and rumbled.

"Reckon that means we won't be able to talk with folks tonight," Jim muttered. "They'll all be takin' shelter."

"No one'd be able to tell you much more than I already did, Ranger," Sloane said. "You boys might as well make the best of it. I've got some good sippin' whiskey to go along with this here stew. It'll warm your bellies just fine."

Realizing they had no choice, knowing the fickle Texas weather had stymied their plans yet again, the Rangers ate a quick supper, then spread out their blankets and slid under them. Soon, their snores accompanied the fading rumble of the thunder, as the storm blew itself out.

The next morning dawned bright and clear. Jim and his partners took a short time to question some of the surviving residents of Millsap. As Sloane had said, no one could provide any more information. The raiders were dressed in white robes, wore white masks and hats, and rode white or light-colored horses. After raiding the town, they had headed west, and disappeared into the night. That was all anyone knew.

"I reckon we'll just head in a westerly direction, and hope we can come up with some sign of those hombres," Jim said, as he gave Sizzle a peppermint and a pat on the shoulder. "Seems like the only thing we can do. Mebbe that storm last night didn't wipe out all their sign."

"Hold on a minute, Jim," Smoky said. "There's a rider, comin' hard."

He pointed down the street, where a rider was whipping his exhausted horse, trying to get the last bit of speed out of the worn-out animal. He swerved his horse and slid the lathered bay to a halt when he spotted the Rangers. The rider had a bullet hole in the side of his shirt, which was streaked with blood. Another bullet burn marked the left side of his neck. His horse stood quivering, spraddle-legged, and head hanging low.

"You . . . you're Rangers?" he gasped.

"We sure are," Jim answered.

"Boy howdy, am I ever glad to see you," the man answered. "The Ghost Riders hit Graham last night."

"The Ghost Riders? Are you certain?" Jim asked.

"As certain as you're standin' there," the man replied.

"All right. Get yourself patched up, Mister, and your horse taken care of," Jim answered. "Men, let's go."

He swung onto Sizzle's back, dug his bootheels into the big paint's ribs, and sent him leaping forward in a dead run.

It was almost forty-eight miles from Millsap to Graham. That would ordinarily be a close to two day trip for most riders, traveling at a steady pace. The Rangers' horses were far superior mounts than most, used to covering long distances at a brutal pace, with little food and water, circumstances which would kill most horses. In addition, Chuck and Eddie were also well mounted, on compact cowponies with plenty of mustang blood. Except for brief stops to allow the horses a breather, a chance to snatch some grass and a short drink, while their riders gulped down jerky and hardtack, washed down with swallows of tepid water from their canteens, Jim maintained a ground-covering lope for most of the day. A little more than eight hours after leaving Millsap, they rode into Graham.

Like every other ill-fated settlement to which the Ghost Riders had paid a visit, most of Graham lay in ruins. Jim stopped at the first place there was any sign of life, the blacksmith shop. The town blacksmith, who was banging an iron hinge on his anvil, attempting to straighten it, looked up from his work and set aside his hammer.

"If you're more of that Ghost Rider outfit, comin' back to get what little you might've missed, you're wastin' your time," he said. "They didn't leave nothin'."

"Mister, we're Rangers, on the trail of the men who did this," Jim said. "We just rode in from Millsap. That bunch hit there, before raidin' your town."

"Oh. Sorry, Rangers. Didn't notice your badges, with the sweat in my eyes," the blacksmith apologized. "I'm Jace Harper."

"Lieutenant Jim Blawcyzk. Don't trouble yourself about that," Jim said. "Which way'd those hombres head?"

"Almost due north," Harper answered. "They took the Olney road. I'd wager my life savin's they hit there next . . . if I had any left. The Ghost Riders got what little of those I had when they robbed the bank."

"I sure wouldn't take that bet," Jim said. "How long ago was that?"

"I don't rightly know," the blacksmith answered. "Sometime before midnight. It's less'n twenty miles from here to Olney. If they rode hard enough, they could've attacked there before dawn this mornin'."

"Much obliged," Jim said. "Boys, we'll grab some chuck real quick, and give the horses a rest. Thirty minutes. Jace, is there any place we can find some grub?"

Harper wiped his brow before answering.

"I'm afraid not. They burned down both the café and the saloon, and killed the owners. Same goes for the mercantile. I've got some mutton and spuds you're welcome to share, if you'd like. Got some grain for your mounts, too, if you want some. Corral's out back. Put 'em away, feed 'em, and I'll meet you back here."

"Gracias. We'll take you up on that," Jim said. He and the others dismounted. The rest of the men were introduced, then led the horses around back. Chuck stopped, picked up his horse's left hind leg, and cursed.

"Somethin' wrong, Chuck?" Jim asked.

"There sure is. I felt Samson miss a stride or two a mile back. He straightened right out, so I didn't pay it any more mind. But look. He's got a deep gash just over his hock. It's still bleedin', and the leg's startin' to swell. He won't be able to go any farther. And I'll bet there's not a decent mount left in this town. Not after the Ghost Riders raided it."

"We'll come up with a horse for you," Jim said. "Lemme ask Jace if he knows where to find one."

"Okay, Jim. I'll be tendin' to Samson in the meantime," Chuck said.

"C'mon, Siz. Reckon you can wait a few minutes for your oats," Jim said. "We've gotta see a man about a horse."

Sizzle snorted indignantly, and nipped at Jim's right ear.

"Not for me, you crazy cayuse," Jim said. "And yes, I know you're a horse. We need one for Chuck." He went back to the shop. Several other men, having seen the Rangers' arrival, were gathered in front of the shop.

"Somethin' wrong, Jim?" Harper asked.

"Yeah, and I sure hope you can help us out," Jim answered. "Chuck's horse injured his left hind leg. He can't be ridden, not without cripplin' him up permanently, and he won't make it far in any event. We have to leave him here for doctorin' and rest. That also means Chuck's gotta have a replacement mount. Any idea where he can find one? And is there a veterinarian in this town?"

"I'm the closest thing to a vet this town has," Harper answered. "You can leave that bronc with me. I'll fix him up, and Chuck can come back for his horse first chance he gets."

"Ranger, I'm Gordy King, owner of the saddle and harness shop," one of the men said. "I've got a horse your man can have. He's a bay gelding, with lots of speed, and plenty of bottom. He'll do. You want me to fetch him?"

"I'd be grateful," Jim said. "How much do you want for him?"

"Not one thin dime," King said. "Consider it a loan. When your man comes back for his horse, he can just return mine. Think of it as my bit in helpin' round up those Ghost Riders."

"Much obliged," Jim said. "Sure, bring him around."

"I'll be right back with him," King said.

"Take him around to Jace's corral," Jim said. "We'll be back there, carin' for our mounts."

Jim led Sizzle back to the corral and brought him inside.

"Any luck, Jim?" Chuck asked.

"Seems so," Jim answered. "There's an hombre gonna loan you his saddle horse. We'll have a look at it, and if it's any kind of a halfway decent animal, we'll take him up on his offer. How bad's Samson's leg?"

"The cut's pretty deep, but I think he'll be okay, with bandagin' and rest," Chuck said.

"That's good. Jace says he doubles as the town vet, and he'll look after your horse."

Jim gave Sizzle a peppermint, poured a good measure of oats into a bucket, and stripped the gear from him. While the horse ate, he brushed dirt and sweat from his hide. After a few minutes, Gordy King appeared.

"Here's your horse, Ranger," he called.

King was leading a blocky, heavily muscled bay gelding.

"Go ahead, Chuck. Look him over," Jim said.

"All right." Chuck went over to the saddle shop owner.

"This here's Cooper," King said. "He'll treat you right, and give you everythin' you ask of him and then some, long as you treat *him* right. He's got a real light mouth, so don't you be jerkin' hard on the reins."

"He's a fine lookin' bronc," Chuck said. "Easy, Cooper." He ran a hand over the horse's neck, then lifted his right front leg to examine the hoof. He continued around the horse, looking for injuries or flaws.

"Well. What do you think, Ranger?"

"He's a good one," Chuck said. "Seems real sturdy. Are you certain you don't want to sell him? I'd hate to see you lose what he's worth, if somethin' should happen to him."

"I'll take that chance," King said. "You sure can't ride a hurt mount, chasin' after the Ghost Riders."

"Then I'm obliged," Chuck said. "As long as

you agree, if anythin' does happen to Cooper, to take Samson in his place."

"We've got a deal, Ranger," King said. He held out his hand, which Chuck readily took. King passed Cooper's lead rope to Chuck.

"You do me proud, Coop," he told the horse. "Help this here Ranger bring back some of those Ghost Riders' scalps."

Once the horses were cared for, the Rangers went back inside the blacksmith shop. Harper had already set out plates of steaming mutton and boiled potatoes, as well as a pot of coffee. The men eagerly tucked into the hot meal.

"Jim," Smoky said, as they ate. "Looks like I might've been right, when I hazarded a guess that the Ghost Riders would start makin' a run for it. It sure appears like they are. I figure, after leavin' Olney, if that's indeed where they did ride next, they struck out northwest, headin' for Ike Stonefield's old stompin' grounds. Even if Ike ain't leadin' the group, he's convinced whoever is that's the perfect hideout. There's plenty of canyons and river breaks to hole up in, and it ain't all that far out of Texas from that territory. That's where I'd head if I were leadin' that outfit."

"I've gotta agree with you. That's a good theory," Jim answered. "It sure looks like they're headed that way. They seem to be bypassin' any large towns, which only makes sense. They rode right past Mineral Wells, and if they did head for Olney, they'll also skip over Wichita Falls. They've probably realized we're on their trail by now. I'd bet my hat they hit a few more small settlements, then make a beeline for Briscoe County."

"I'd guess they won't even hit any more towns, Jim," J.R. said. "There ain't really many, in fact none than I can recollect, between Olney and Quitaque, if they take the shortest route. It's wide open country, still pretty unsettled, and real rugged in a lot of spots. I believe they've already made their move. Think on this. They raided here in Graham, and mebbe over to Olney, last night, despite the fact it wasn't stormin'. In fact, it was a clear night, with a nearly full moon. That storm which rolled through Millsap would've come through here a few hours before the raid happened. That's not how they've operated, at least up until now. They might be thinkin' we're gettin' closer to findin' 'em, and will soon have 'em on the run. If they do figure we are after 'em, and mebbe not all that far behind, they'll most likely hit some ranches along the way, but mostly keep movin', hopin' they can outrun us to the Caprock canyonlands. Once there, they'll plan on givin' us the slip, or mebbe ambushin' us, which'd be real easy in those badlands. Then, once they think we've given up on 'em, or we're all lyin' dead, with their bullets in us, they'll light out for New Mexico, or the Territories."

"I sure wouldn't bet against your theory, either, J.R.," Jim answered. "Well, let's finish up our chuck, and hit the trail again. We're wastin' daylight, sittin' here while those renegades are still ahead of us."

The Rangers quickly finished their meal.

"Jace, thanks for the grub. It was sure tasty," Jim said. The others added their agreement.

"Anytime, Ranger," Harper answered. "And good luck, to all of you. *Vaya con Dios*."

Forty minutes after riding into Graham, the Rangers were in the saddle once more. They kept the horses at a walk for half a mile to warm up, then once again put them into their tireless, mile eating lope.

When the Rangers reached Olney, they found it in the same condition every other town hit by the Ghost Riders had been left. The majority of the buildings were in ruins, piles of still smoldering rubble. Ten citizens were dead, many more wounded. They stayed in town only long enough to give their horses a brief rest, ask a few questions, and determine that the outlaws, eighteen in number as could best be guessed, had indeed headed out of town to the northwest. A few men had managed to organize a brief pursuit, but had lost the raiders in the few low hills, west of town.

"Seems like you're right, Smoke. You too, J.R.," Jim said, as they tightened their cinches. "Looks like those hombres are gonna ride for Quitaque."

"Let's hope we catch up to 'em first," Ty said.

"We're gonna do our darndest. Bet your hat on that," Jim said. He gave Sizzle a peppermint, then swung into his saddle. "Let's get movin'."

With the thundering of hooves and a cloud of dust, the Rangers galloped out of Olney, each with a fervent prayer on his lips they would track down the Ghost Riders before they made good their escape.

The hundred and fifty miles between Olney and Quitaque was mostly wide open, level to gently rolling plains, except for grass sparsely covered with vegetation, interspersed with a few low mesas, occasionally cut by canyons and arroyos. Dependable sources of water were hard to find, most of those being small seeps or shallow creeks, the majority of which went dry by mid-summer. The Rangers pushed their horses to the limit, certain now they were on the trail of the Ghost Riders. The remains of several ranches they came across confirmed this. They had all been completely destroyed, with no signs of life. Every building had been burned, all the live-stock run off, and every man, woman, and child killed. The outlaws had made certain continued pursuit would be difficult. The carcasses of a number of light-colored horses, which had been run until they broke down, then shot and left at the ranches, made it plain they had obtained fresh mounts, while their pursuers would have to rely on their tiring animals. Despite their anxiousness to catch up with their quarry, knowing every delay meant the Ghost Riders got that much farther ahead of them, Jim and his partners did take the time to bury the dead, and say a brief prayer over their graves.

Two days out of Olney, Jim pulled Sizzle to a halt.

"Look up there," he said, pointing to a flock of large black birds, circling and wheeling in the sky, slowly descending.

"Buzzards," Smoky said, with a curse. "Somethin's dead up ahead, that's for certain."

"More likely someone," Jim answered. "Guess we'd better find out." He kicked Sizzle into a lope. A few minutes later, he and his partners pushed through a thin screen of brush, which surrounded a small waterhole. Several buzzards, disturbed from their feast of the corpse they'd been working on, squawked a protest, as they slowly flapped their wings and rose into the sky.

"It *is* a someone," Smoky said, "or, more properly, what's left of a someone."

The dead man was lying face down. He had

been stripped naked, and two bullet holes were apparent, in the middle of his back. Chunks of his flesh were missing, where the buzzards had ripped it away.

"Looks like some cowboy ran across our men," J.R. said. "Worse luck for him."

"Let's see," Jim said. "Gimme a hand, Charlie."

"All right, Pa."

Jim and Charlie dismounted, then rolled the corpse onto its back. The dead man still held a piece of white cloth clutched in his hand. Most of his face was gone, blown off by a close range shotgun blast.

The McIlroy brothers leaned over in their saddles and vomited at the gruesome sight.

"This hombre wasn't any cowboy," Jim said. He picked up a blood-spattered white hat which was lying alongside the corpse. "Appears to me he was one of the outfit. Looks like they must've had a fallin' out."

"There's no way of identifyin' him. Whoever killed him made certain of it. Not with his face blown away like that," Smoky said.

"Well, we know for certain he ain't Cannon," Charlie answered.

"How's that, Charlie?" J.R. asked.

"There's no scar on his belly, or his . . . genitals. That means he's still ridin' with the bunch. And that means he's still mine."

This time, in deference to his father, Charlie

caught himself before uttering the word he really wanted to use.

"Nothin' more we can learn here," Jim said. "I'm surprised there's still this much left of him. The buzzards and coyotes must've been workin' on somethin' else, before they found this hombre. We'll leave him for them. Let's go."

He and Charlie remounted. The Rangers resumed their pursuit.

"You reckon we've got any chance at all of catchin' up to those hombres before they disappear into the Caprock, Jim?" Smoky asked, as they neared Quitaque, around one in the afternoon. It was four days after they had ridden out of Olney.

"I doubt it," Jim answered. "The canyonlands are only about a half a day's ride from here. Those renegades are still at least four hours ahead of us. They might already be in there. But it don't matter none. We'll flush 'em outta there. Bet a hat on it."

"You reckon we should head into town, and see if they came through there?" J.R. asked. "Mebbe we could pick up some fresh horses, too."

"I don't want to take the time," Jim answered. "I don't think they'd hit Quitaque. Too many people know about 'em now, and it's too close to Ike Stonefield's home territory. They wouldn't want to rile up folks here. Besides, they're not even attemptin' to hide their trail, at this point. They've got to realize someone's comin' after 'em. They've probably known that would happen ever since they hit San Leanna. Whoever's in charge of this bunch is a right smart hombre. He'd have found out, somehow, that it was a couple of Rangers who killed his men. He's probably even learned it was me'n Smoke. He's deliberately tryin' to lead us right into a trap, is my guess. No, I figure they'll ride straight for the canyons, hole up there for awhile, hopin' to either give us the slip, or bushwhack us. After they're certain we're taken care of, I believe they'll attack Stonefield's family's place, then make a run for the Territories, or mebbe New Mexico."

"My money'd be on the Territories," Chuck said. "That's been a cesspool of robbers, killers, and desperadoes of all stripes for years. Seems like almost every bad man in the Southwest ends up there, sooner or later. The Indian police and U.S. Marshals do the best they can, tryin' to bring in as many of those hombres as they can, but there's not enough of 'em, and way too many outlaws."

"Boy howdy, you've got that right," Charlie agreed.

Jim pulled Sizzle down to a walk. Even his seemingly tireless paint was showing the effects of the hard pursuit. His flanks were gaunt, his ribs showing, and his sorrel and white coat, which ordinarily shined like a newly minted copper penny, was dull, streaked with dirt, salt, and dried sweat.

"Ease up, boys," he ordered. "We can't make the canyons before dark, in any event. We'll take it slow for the remainder of today, to give the horses a break, and make camp for the night just inside the Caprock. That'll give all of us, and the horses, a decent rest. Which we'll need, because after tonight there'll be no more rest until we come up with those Ghost Riders."

"Or until they put bullets in us," Ty muttered.

"That could happen," Jim admitted. "We'll just have to make certain it doesn't."

The Rangers reached the Caprock canyonlands, an expanse of vividly colored buttes, arroyos, eroded hills, and deep canyons, an hour before sundown. They stopped at a mound of fresh horse droppings. Jim dismounted, picked up one of the "road apples", and crumbled it between his fingers.

"They're still about three hours ahead of us," he said. "They've probably already holed up for the night. And I've got a hunch they aren't goin' much farther, not until they make sure we aren't still after 'em."

"Which means they'll either try'n hide their tracks, and bush up in one of these canyons until we give up searchin' for 'em, or they're gonna arrange a nice drygulchin' for us," J.R. said. "My money's on the drygulchin'. They're a bloodthirsty bunch, worse'n any Comanches or Kiowas I've ever fought. Stonefield undoubtedly knows these rocks like the back of his hand, and we don't. They could be waitin' for us just about anywhere in this maze, and would put bullets in us before we even knew what hit us."

"So we'll need to be extra cautious, from here on in," Jim said. "We'll ride a bit more, until we find a good spot to stop for the night."

He lifted his reins, clucked to Sizzle, and put him into a walk once again. A few minutes later, they spied a lone rider. He was mounted on a palomino gelding and led a gray burro, which was laden with packs, an easel with stand, and canvasses. He had stopped next to a small spring, and was preparing to dismount. He looked up at the Rangers' approach.

"Howdy, men," he called out. "I was just fixin' to spend the night here. You plannin' on doin' the same? You're welcome, if you'd like. I could use some company. It's been quite a spell since I've had another human to talk with."

"Yeah, we are," Jim answered. "Long as you don't mind sharin', since you got here first."

"Not at all," the rider answered. "The name's Andy Thomas, out of Carthage, Missouri." He swung out of his saddle.

Thomas was a tall, dark haired man, who

smiled readily. A flop-brimmed hat covered his thick hair. He wore a Remington .44 on his right hip.

"Jim Blawcyzk, Texas Rangers, and my pardners. Smoky McCue, J.R. Huggins, my son Charlie, Ty Tremblay, and these last two hombres are brothers, Chuck and Eddie McIlroy. Appreciate you're sharin' the camp. Let's get outta these saddles, men."

"Pleased to make your acquaintances," Thomas said, as the Rangers nodded to him. He waved at the burro. "In case you haven't already figured it out, I'm an artist. At the moment, I'm on an extended journey through Texas, trying to capture her on canvas."

"Speakin' of capture, we're after a real bad bunch," Jim said. "You happen to see anythin' of a band of about a dozen and a half men, most of 'em probably mounted on light-colored broncs, all of 'em wearin' white hats?"

"I did see those men, at least it sounds like them," Thomas answered. "About three hours ago. I was up on a rimrock, workin' on a painting of the canyon below, when they rode through."

"You're lucky they didn't spot you," Smoky said. "You'd most likely be dead if they had. Those were the Ghost Riders you saw."

"I've heard about them. When I saw them, I had a gut feelin' they weren't men to tangle with," Thomas answered. "So I faded back into the scrub before they saw me, and made certain they were well past before I showed myself again. I sure didn't want to be skylined, and get myself shot fulla holes."

"Which way were they headed?" Jim asked.

"I can't be certain," Thomas answered. "These canyons are a real maze, twistin' and turnin' back on each other. I think they were headed toward the northwest, but that's just a guess on my part."

"Jim, I've ridden after men in here a time or two," J.R. said. "A man could hide in these canyons for weeks. Water's real scarce, though. I'd wager they're headed for Gyp Springs. That's one of the few reliable sources of water in here. I'm bettin' they rode there, stocked up on water, then rode back into the canyons, figurin' we'd have to show up at Gyp Springs, sooner or later, for water. They'll be lyin' in wait for us, ready to drygulch us the minute we get there."

"I've gotta go along with J.R.," Smoky said. "That makes sense. They have to be figurin' they can gun down all of us real easy there, then ride away, with no one left to keep after 'em. By the time our bodies are discovered, if they ever are, those hombres'll be long gone from Texas."

"I'm not gonna argue that point, no, sir," Jim agreed. "We'll spend the night here, then start out for Gyp Springs first thing in the mornin'. Thanks, Andy. You might just have given us the lead we needed to find that outfit . . . and just mebbe, you saved our lives."

"Glad to be able to help, Ranger," Thomas answered. "I'd sure like to be able to come along with you, but I'm afraid I'm not very good with a gun. I wear this pistol for protection from varmints; however, I'm not much of a fighter. The only fast drawin' I've ever done is with a paint-brush, not a six-gun. I've also got a wife waitin' for me, back home in Missouri. Dina would get some upset if I came back to her full of holes, or in a pine box. She'd never let me hear the end of it."

"That's all right, Andy," Jim assured him, laughing. "Me, Smoky, J.R., and Charlie have wives of our own, so we know exactly what you mean. And please, call us by our names. You try'n call each of us 'Ranger' and it'll get mighty confusin'."

"Sure, Jim."

"There, that's better. And we're the ones paid to take chances runnin' down renegades, not folks like yourself. Now, soon as we get the horses cared for, we'll make supper."

"We gonna have a campfire, Jim?" Ty asked. "It might give us away to those outlaws."

"I'd ordinarily agree with you, Ty," Jim answered. "But from what Andy here's told us, those hombres are quite a few miles away. Even if they did double back, they probably have a good idea exactly where we are. I don't think a fire will make any difference. We'll post a guard tonight, just to be safe, but I don't reckon we'll have any trouble."

The horses were allowed to drink, then untacked, groomed, and picketed to graze on the tough grama grass surrounding the spring. Sizzle, as usual, was just turned loose. The big paint would not stray far from Jim's side. Andy's burro was also unloaded and curried. Once the mounts were settled, the men turned their attention to their own needs. Shortly, bacon was frying in the pan, beans heating, biscuits rising and coffee boiling.

"Jim," Andy said, as he turned the bacon, "if you wouldn't mind, I'd be plumb pleased to draw you and your men."

"I'd be glad to let you do just that, Andy. I'm sure the rest of the men would too," Jim said. "If we had the time. But, we've gotta be on our way at first light. We've come too far to let the men we're after slip away now. I'm not gonna tell you everythin' they've done, but they're responsible for wholesale murder, robbery, and more. We'll be leavin' at sunup."

"You misunderstood me, Jim," Andy replied. "I haven't had the chance to do a paintin' of cowboys around the campfire at night. I want to paint you men while you're havin' your supper. Besides, this painting will be even better than

344

that. It's probably the only opportunity I'll have to capture a company of Texas Rangers on canvas. If you'll pardon my usin' the word 'capture'."

"In that case, of course," Jim said. "You go ahead and ask the rest of the men. I doubt any of 'em'll turn you down."

"Much obliged, Jim."

All the men were ravenously hungry after their long, hard ride. With the knowledge that, hopefully, their desperate pursuit of the Ghost Riders would soon be over, they downed heaping helpings of their meal. Andy worked on his painting in between bites of his supper. He explained that he would get the basics down that night, then, as the oils dried, fill in the details later.

"That bright yella shirt you're wearin', along with that blue bandanna, is sure gonna stick out in this paintin', Jim," he noted, with a chuckle.

"My pa loves his bright shirts," Charlie said. "He's always bein' kidded about 'em by the rest of us."

"Yeah, Jim sure don't have much fashion sense," Smoky added, laughing.

"That's true enough," J.R. said. "But don't forget, many's the time we've been plumb grateful Jim likes those gaudy shirts. They make a nice, bright target for anyone tryin' to plug us. The bad guys just naturally aim for Jim first."

"Y'all are just jealous, because you can't wear shirts like these, and look good in 'em," Jim said.

"Nor would we want to, pa," Charlie answered. "Besides, you ain't the only good target this time. Eddie, that white shirt and bright red neckerchief you're wearin' are gonna shine like a beacon against these red rocks. You'n my pa are gonna catch the first bullets."

"Eddie, don't let 'em get to you," Jim said. "They'll all be lyin' stretched out in the grass, full of lead and dead as doornails, while me'n you are still fightin'. Those outlaws ain't gonna want to put holes in our nice shirts."

"I'd just as soon none of us catch any bullets," Ty said.

"I think we can all agree on that," Chuck answered.

While they ate, Jim set a schedule for the night guards. After supper, the men lingered over final cups of coffee. Smoky, Eddie, and Chuck had last cigarettes. The horses were checked one last time. J.R. had the first watch, so he took up a position just below the spring. The others rolled out their bedrolls, pulled off their boots, removed their hats and gunbelts, and slid under their blankets. Charlie and Ty, being close in age to the McIlroys, had formed a quick friendship with the two young brothers. They had made their beds on one side of the fire, Jim and Smoky on the other. Andy was still working on his painting when everyone, except for J.R., had drifted off to sleep.

The next morning dawned as did almost every summer morning in Texas, already hot and humid, with no hint of a breeze to provide relief from the oppressive heat. The Rangers took care of necessary business, washed up, and ate a quick breakfast. They bade farewell to Andy, who would remain at the camp for a few more hours, putting the finishing touches on his painting of the Rangers and allowing it to dry, before moving on.

"Good luck to all of you," Andy said, "and thank you again for allowing me to paint you."

"Thanks, Andy," Jim answered. "It's a fine picture. I hope you'll get a good price for it."

"It's a fine picture, except for your ugly mug right smack in the middle of it, Jim," Smoky said. "Well, that and those shirts of yours and Eddie's."

"Those shirts provide just the color this painting needs," Andy said. "Since it's a nighttime portrait and all."

"So there, Smoke," Jim added. "That's why it'll fetch a whole heap of *dinero*."

"I may not sell this one," Andy said. "I just might keep this one for myself. It'll hang in my studio."

"With luck, mebbe we'll run into you again,

once all this is over," J.R. said. He tugged on his cinch, then gave a yell of pain.

"J.R. What happened?" Jim asked.

"Monte. This doggone cayuse twisted and caught my hand in the cinch, right behind the buckle," J.R. answered. "Boy howdy, that hurts."

"You gonna be able to use that hand?" Jim asked.

"I'll manage," J.R. said. "And I can shoot with my left, if I have to. Let's just get."

"All right. Andy, we've got to be goin'," Jim said. "You keep a sharp eye out, just in case those men get past us, and ride back this way. If you do see 'em, I'd appreciate it if you got to the nearest town, and wired Ranger Headquarters in Austin, since that'll most likely mean we're dead."

"I'll do that," Andy assured him.

"Bueno. Let's go, men."

The Rangers mounted up and rode away from the campsite, leaving Andy staring at their backs, and silently praying the painting he had just completed would not be the last picture ever done of them, still alive.

Late that morning, the Rangers were nearing Gyp Springs. They were riding between the towering red rock walls of one of the innumerable canyons in this section of the Caprock. The tracks left by the Ghost Riders' horses were still plain to see. More and more, it was becoming apparent they were hoping to lure Jim and his partners into a deadly trap.

"We're still on their trail, all right. There's the prints of that horse which throws out his left front hoof, like Jorgenson, the blacksmith back in Brady, told us. How much longer do you figure it is until we reach Gyp Springs, J.R.?" Jim asked.

"About three more miles," J.R. answered. "We should be there in an hour or so."

"Bueno. Let's stop, and give the horses a chance to blow. We'll take ten minutes."

Jim waved the men to a stop. Smoky pulled the makings from his pocket and began rolling a quirly. The others all lifted their canteens from their saddlehorns, to take a short drink. Cooper, Chuck's borrowed mount, reversed direction when Chuck loosened his grip on the reins. Just as he did, a rifle shot cracked. Chuck screamed in pain and toppled from his horse. He landed on his back, then rolled onto his side, his hands clamped to his gut. He curled up and lay writhing in agony, moaning softly.

"Chuck's hit!" Eddie hollered. J.R. reached across his body with his good left hand to pull his six-gun from its holster, peering back down canyon as he did. Smoky pulled Midnight around and lifted his Winchester from the saddle boot. He pointed the rifle down the canyon, as he and J.R. scanned the rocks and cliffs for any sign of the hidden drygulcher. Charlie and Ty also pulled out their rifles, waiting in anticipation for the next shot.

Eddie had jumped from his saddle and was kneeling alongside his stricken brother. Jim dismounted and also hunkered alongside the wounded man.

"How bad is it, Chuck?" he asked.

"It's . . . pretty bad," Chuck answered, his breathing labored. "I'm gut-shot. Took that . . . bullet . . . right in . . . my . . . belly."

"Lemme take a look at it, son," Jim said. "Eddie, you hold him down if you have to, while I examine that wound."

"Sure. Sure, Jim," Eddie stammered, clearly shaken at the sudden shot which had downed his brother, without any warning.

Jim rolled Chuck onto his back. The bullet had struck in the left side of his belly, down low.

"It's . . . it's real bad, ain't it, Jim?" Chuck said.

"I'm not gonna try'n sugarcoat it, Chuck," Jim answered. "Yeah, it's bad."

"My brother's gonna die, ain't he?" Eddie cried. "He's gut-shot. A man can't live with a bullet in his guts."

"That's not necessarily true," Jim said. "I've known men who've survived bein' gut-shot. In fact, I'm one of 'em. And Chuck's caught a bit of luck. The slug hit him down low, so it just might've missed all the vital organs. But we've got to get your brother to a doctor real fast, if he's gonna have any chance at all."

"I'll do anythin' I have to, if it means savin' Chuck's life," Eddie answered.

"Good," Jim said. "Go over to my horse. There's some clean scraps of cloth I keep in there for bandages. There's also a spare neckerchief. Get that too. And a flask of whiskey."

"All right." Eddie hurried for Jim's horse.

"Chuck, I can't promise you that you're gonna be all right," Jim said, "but if Eddie can get you to a doc, you might have a fightin' chance."

"How's Chuck doin'?" Smoky called.

"He's hit bad," Jim answered. "The bullet's still in him. I'm gonna patch him up best I can, then Chuck's gonna try'n get him to a doctor."

Eddie came back, with the bandages, neckerchief, and whiskey.

"Here you go, Jim."

"Thanks, Eddie. Now, help me sit your brother up. I've gotta get his shirt off so I can bandage that hole, to slow the bleedin' as much as possible."

"Okay."

Eddie slid his hands under Chuck's shoulders and lifted him to a sitting position. Jim unbuttoned the wounded man's shirt and slid it off.

"Chuck, this is gonna hurt somethin' awful, but it can't be helped," Jim said, as he uncorked the flask. "I've gotta pour some of this whiskey into that bullet hole, to keep it from festerin'."

Chuck nodded.

"I understand, Jim."

"Good." Jim poured some of the raw whiskey into the wound. Chuck screamed, jerking in pain.

"That was the worst of it," Jim assured him. "Now, I'm gonna pad that wound with these bandages, then tie 'em in place. After that, we'll try'n get you back on your horse. You think you'll be able to ride?"

"I'll give it a shot," Chuck said, then winced. "Ouch. That's not what I meant."

"Don't fret about it. I'm always makin' bad jokes. Of course, I don't usually have a bullet in my belly when I do . . . although plenty of men have threatened to do just that, if I told one more joke," Jim said. He folded the cloths into a thick pad, then placed them over the blood-oozing hole in Chuck's belly. He tied the neckerchief around the young Ranger's middle to hold the bandages in place. That done, he put Chuck's shirt back on, buttoning it tight.

"Chuck, keep your hand pressed against those bandages, as hard as you can," Jim ordered. "The pressure'll help slow the bleedin'."

"Sure. Sure, Jim."

"Eddie, I think it'd be better if Chuck rode with you, rather'n try'n to stick to a horse by himself," Jim said. "Will your bronc carry double?"

"Yeah, he will," Eddie answered. "Scotty's carried the two of us, lots of times."

"Good," Jim said. "Help me get your brother on his feet. We'll get him over to your horse. Once we do, you mount up, and I'll help get him up behind you."

"Okay, Jim." Chuck was helped to his feet, then walked over to where Eddie's gray stood waiting.

"Okay, Eddie," Jim said. "Get on your horse, and I'll get Chuck on soon as you're settled."

"Sure."

Eddie climbed into his saddle. Once he was mounted, Jim helped boost Chuck onto Scotty's rump. Chuck grabbed his brother's right shoulder for support. While Jim pushed Chuck onto the horse's rump, Eddie placed his left hand against Chuck's left side, to shove him onto the middle of Scotty's back.

"You both all set?" Jim asked.

"I reckon," Chuck said. "My belly . . . hurts like the . . . blazes, though."

"I'd imagine it does," Jim answered. "You hang on tight to your brother, you hear? And keep pressin' against that bullet hole. We don't want the ride joltin' any of your guts through that hole. It's not as likely to happen as, say, from a knife wound, but it's still a possibility."

"Okay, Jim."

"Eddie, Quitaque's the nearest town. It's about an hour south of here," Jim said. "You just follow

353

the trail we rode in on, and turn south at the junction. You recollect that turn, don't you?"

"Yeah, I do."

"Good. There's gotta be a doctor in Quitaque. We've just gotta hope he's in, and not out tendin' to a patient on a ranch somewhere. Right now, time is Chuck's biggest enemy. You've got to get him to that doc as quick as possible. In fact, you'd better take Cooper, too. That way if your bronc gives out you'll have a spare."

"As long as Chuck can manage to get on another horse," Eddie said.

"Don't worry about that, unless it has to be done," Jim said. He took Cooper's lead rope, snapped it to his bridle, and handed the other end to Eddie.

"Jim, make sure you get the men who done this to my brother," Eddie pleaded.

"You can bet your hat on it. Now ride, son. And may God ride with you," Jim said.

Eddie jabbed his spurs into Scotty's side, putting the gray into a gallop. Jim stared after the brothers, until they were out of sight. Smoky and J.R. rode up to him.

"You think the kid's gonna make it, Jim?" Smoky asked.

"*Quien sabe?*" Jim shrugged his shoulders. "I sure hope so. Any sign of that drygulcher?"

"Not a one," Smoky answered. "There was that one shot, and that was it."

"Well, now we know for certain the Ghost Riders are here," J.R. said. "And we also know what their plans for us are. They're gonna try'n hide up in the rocks, and pick us off one at a time."

"They might try it, but they'll have a heckuva fight on their hands," Jim said. "C'mon, let's see if we can find any sign of where that bushwhacker was perched. Mebbe we can run him down before he gets far. If not, we'll find him with the rest of his outfit. And when we do, he'll be sorry he ever shot that kid. Bet your hats on it."

Smoky looked at the smudge of dust which marked where Eddie and his brother rode deeper into the canyons. He gave a grim chuckle.

"What is it, Smoke?" Jim asked. "Somethin' funny?"

"Not really," Smoky answered. "It just occurred to me, after all the ribbin' we gave you and Eddie about your bright shirts, it wasn't either of you who took that bullet. It was Chuck, who was wearin' a dull blue shirt."

"Don't matter none," Jim said. "Shootin' Chuck is just one more thing the Ghost Riders have gotta pay for."

# 14

It was slightly less than an hour later when Eddie raced into Quitaque. Chuck was still seated behind him, leaning against him, his arms wrapped around his brother's waist. He was drifting in and out of consciousness, his head lolling. Chuck slowed his horse and yelled at the first person he saw, a plump, gray-haired woman of about fifty.

"Where's the doc's office? I've got a badly wounded man here!"

The woman's eyes widened.

"It's at the other end of town, a white house with black shutters, and a picket fence around it. There's a sign out front. You can't miss it."

"Thanks, ma'am," Chuck answered, putting Scotty into a gallop once again. A moment later, he was sliding the exhausted gray to a stop in front of the doctor's house. "Dr. Keith Souter, Physician," was painted on a sign, which hung on chains attached to the front porch roof.

"You're gonna be all right now, Chuck," Eddie said. "We're at the doc's." He dismounted, then grabbed Chuck as he slid from Scotty's rump. He carried him onto the porch and kicked open the front door, entering what was apparently the doctor's waiting room. Several chairs, none occupied, were arranged along one wall.

"Doc! Where are you?" Eddie shouted. "I've got my brother here. He's hurt, real bad."

A gray haired man in his early sixties parted the curtains which covered the doorway at the opposite side of the room. He was slightly less than six feet tall, with silver-gray hair, receding in the front, and a goatee of the same hue. He was wiping his hands on a towel.

"Take it easy, son. I'm right here," he said, his voice quiet and calming. "Bring your brother right in." He held the curtains open. "Right this way. We'll go into that room, straight ahead. Lay him on the table there. You say he's badly hurt. What happened to him?"

"He got shot, shot in his belly, Doc. You've gotta help him," Eddie pleaded.

"Of course. Let me take a look at him, and I'll see what I can do," Souter said. "Lie him down, and help me get him undressed."

"Sure, Doc."

Chuck was placed on the indicated table. He moaned, and his eyes flickered open.

"Son, can you hear me? I'm Doctor Souter, and I'm going to try and help you get well. What's your name?"

Chuck's only response was an unintelligible mumble.

"His name's Chuck, Doc," Eddie said. "Chuck

McIlroy. He's my older brother. My name's Eddie."

"Very well. Let's get his clothes off, so I can see exactly how serious his wound is," Souter answered.

Chuck's clothes were removed. Souter tsked softly when he saw the bandages tied around his middle. They were soaked through with blood.

"Your brother's lost an awful lot of blood," Souter noted, as he began to remove the bandages. "You said he got shot. About how long ago did that happen?"

"I dunno for certain," Eddie answered. "About an hour ago, I guess. Back in the Caprock canyons. Me'n Chuck are Texas Rangers. We were ridin' with some other Rangers, lookin' for the Ghost Riders, when we got ambushed, and Chuck got hit."

"You can tell me all that later, son," Souter said. "Right now, the important thing is to start operating on your brother, and that has to be done immediately. If more than an hour goes past without treatment starting for a man shot in the abdomen, it's virtually impossible to save him. And I'll need your help, if you're willing."

"Eddie always did talk . . . too much," Chuck murmured.

"You're awake again. That's good, son," Souter said. "You just try'n rest. I know you're in great pain. I need to get the bullet out of you, as quickly as possible. I hope your brother will help me with that."

"Of course I'm willin' to help, Doc. I'll do anythin' to save Chuck. He's the only kin I've got left. The Ghost Riders killed our ma and pa."

"I see," Souter said. "Well, let me look at what we have here. The bullet hit your brother low, and on the left side of his abdomen. That's one thing in our favor. It clearly missed the abdominal aorta, or he would have bled to death within minutes. It won't have hit the liver, spleen, or any other vital organs, although it will have penetrated the intestines. That means there's a high risk of infection. Do you know if he was hit with a rifle bullet, or one from a pistol?"

"It was a rifle," Eddie answered.

"Then your brother was fortunate again. Since the bullet is still inside him, that means it must have been fired from some distance off, or it ricocheted before it hit him. He'll have less internal damage than from a shot fired from closer range. Let me get my instruments down, then I'll get to work."

Souter took several jars from a shelf, as well as scalpels, forceps, probes, and the rest of his instruments. He opened two wooden boxes, and removed a strange looking apparatus from each. He placed the instruments in a basin, opened one of the jars, and poured its contents over the instruments.

"Eddie, this is carbolic solution," he explained. "It sterilizes everything I use it on, to help prevent infection. You'll need to wash your hands in it, if you are indeed going to assist me."

"Of course, Doc." He and Souter washed their hands, then wiped them on a carbolic soaked towel.

"Eddie, I'm going to explain to your brother what I'm about to do," Souter said. "Chuck, can you hear me?"

Chuck mumbled what could be taken for a "yes".

"Good," Souter said. "Son, now that I know you can hear me, I want to explain what I need to do. You appear to have been lucky, in that the bullet was fired from far off and had mostly spent its flight up, or there wasn't too much powder behind it. But your brother says it's been close to an hour that he's been riding with you, and, despite all of that improvised bandaging, the bullet is still inside you. In addition, you've lost a lot of blood. I have to open your belly to see what damage has been done, and I need to get that bullet out. If I don't, then you'll die."

"I'm . . . gonna . . . die?" Chuck mumbled.

"No. Not if I can help it." Souter held up one of the apparatuses. "However, I can't have you awake while I operate. I'm going to put you to sleep with some chloroform I'm going to give you from this little box. It's called a Chisholm inhaler. I'm going to put these tubes up your nose and drop the chloroform in. You'll be asleep through it all. Are you ready?"

"I reckon . . . Doc."

"Good. Then I'll get started."

Souter inserted the inhaler's tubes into Chuck's nostrils, then added the chloroform. The solution soon took effect, and Chuck was deeply sleeping.

"Eddie, I'm about to start operating," Souter said. He handed the youngster the other apparatus, which consisted of a cylinder, attached jar, nozzle, and a hand crank.

"This is a Lister spray," he explained. "It's filled with the same carbolic solution you and I just washed with. Your job will be to spray the carbolic over the operation site as I work. That will hopefully help prevent your brother from getting an infection, which in a belly wound is almost always fatal. I'll tell you when to spray, and when to stop. Do you understand?"

Eddie nodded.

"Good. Now, I'm about to make my incision. Aim the nozzle over the wound, then crank the handle to spray the solution."

"All right, Doc."

Eddie began to turn the Lister spray's crank. Once the wound and the skin around it were soaked, Souter made his incision, slicing through flesh and muscle, then into the intestines.

"Just keep spraying as I work," he told Eddie.

362

"We need to make certain to sterilize as much of the intestines as we possibly can. Once I find the bullet and remove it, you'll be able to stop. I'll be swabbing out blood as I work."

"Do you think he's got a chance?" Eddie asked.

"I believe so. The bullet penetrated the gut, of course, but I've seen men survive with worse damage. Ah, I think I've found where the bullet stopped. It's in the muscles at the back of his abdominal wall."

Souter picked up a pair of long forceps and inserted them into the incision in Chuck's belly.

"Got it." He pulled the forceps from inside the wounded man, then held them up for Eddie to inspect the slug.

"There it is. I'll save it, in case he wants to have it for a souvenir. Now to make certain there's no further damage, other than to the intestines. Then I can close your brother's belly back up."

Souter began cleansing Chuck's intestines with more carbolic solution.

"Here's more good news, Eddie," he said. "There's no damage to the ureters, those are the tubes that run from the kidneys to the bladder. I'm certain I don't need to tell you, if they had been damaged, that your brother would be in serious trouble."

"You mean he wouldn't need a pot to pee in, Doc," Eddie said. Souter groaned.

"Son, I'll chalk up what you just said to your bein' worried about your brother. Now, you see these loops of gut. The bullet put several holes through them. I'm going to repair those, using catgut and what's called a continuous Glover's suture. You just keep working that Lister spray. And no catgut jokes, please."

"All right, Doc."

Souter finished his work, cleaning the intestines with carbolic, suturing them where necessary. Finally, he closed up the incision in Chuck's abdomen with silk sutures.

"I'm all finished, Eddie," he said. "All I need to do now is take those bandages I have soaking in carbolic and cover the wound. Then, we'll transfer your brother to a bed. He should be awake shortly, but he'll be groggy. He'll need lots of bed rest, of course. He'll also only be allowed fluids for the next two days. After that he can have some soup, then a bland diet. He'll need at least a week to recoup. After that, if everything goes well, he'll be able to get out of bed, for short periods of time. I'm certain I don't need to tell you that's a very serious wound your brother has suffered. And if you hadn't gotten him here when you did, he would not have survived."

"I appreciate everythin' you've done, Doc," Eddie said. "I'll pay you whatever you ask."

"Let's not worry about that right now," Souter answered. "Our only concern is making certain your brother gets well. Now, help me get him into bed."

Chuck was carried to a back room, where he was carefully placed on a bed, then covered with a sheet and thin blanket.

"He's going to sleep for a while," Souter said. "All we can do now is wait, and pray. Eddie, I'm about to partake of a drink. Would you care to join me?"

"I could use one," Eddie said. "Some grub, too. Now that everythin's over, I realized how starved I am. I haven't eaten since this mornin'."

"I noticed your brother hadn't, either," Souter said. "There were very little contents in his intestines. That also helped contribute to his surviving long enough to reach help. Tell you what. I'm rather hunger, too. As long as there are no patients waiting for me, we'll have that drink, then go to the Curry House for steaks. Does that suit you?"

"That'll suit me just fine," Eddie said. "I'll have to take care of our horses first, though. If they hadn't given everythin' they had, I'd never have gotten Chuck here in time."

"Of course," Souter agreed. "The livery stable is right on the way to the restaurant. Well, come into my parlor, and we'll have that drink."

Eddie followed the physician into the parlor. Souter took two glasses and a bottle from the top of a sideboard.

"Son," he said. "This is *The Glenlivet*, the finest whiskey ever to come out of my beloved native land of Scotland. It's the nectar of the gods. You'll want to sip this slowly, and savor every drop."

"I knew that wasn't Texan in your voice, Doc," Eddie said. "I reckoned you were some kinda Yankee."

"No, I'm a Scotsman," Souter answered. He filled the glasses, then handed one to Eddie.

"Remember, sip it slowly," he said.

Eddie took a sip, then smiled.

"You're right, Doc. This is really fine whiskey."

"I'm glad you like it. We'll finish our drinks, then after you care for your horses and we have our meal, we'll come back and set up a bed next to your brother for you. By then, he should be coming around."

"One question first, Doc? How'd you know what to do for my brother? I've always heard a man who got gut-shot was a goner."

"That used to be the case, and still is, quite often," Souter explained. "However, medical science is advancing quite rapidly. There is a Doctor Goodfellow, who has been doing quite a bit of research on abdominal injuries, in particular gunshot wounds. I've been reading all of his papers. He's quite amazing. It's his procedures I used on your brother."

"Then I'm grateful to you, and that Doc Goodfellow," Eddie said.

"I'm just glad I was able to help," Souter answered. "And your brother still isn't out of danger, of course. But he does have a good chance to pull through. Now, let's go get our meals."

# 15

"Jim, how are we gonna handle these hombres?" Smoky asked. They were once again riding toward Gyp Springs. "We know they're layin' for us, but not for certain where. They'll be well hidden, watchin' our every move, and we have no idea when one of 'em'll take another pot shot at us. There's about eighteen of 'em, from what we've been told, and now only five of us."

"Yeah." Jim smiled. "I almost feel bad for those renegades, with the odds stacked against 'em like that. They don't stand a chance."

"I'm guessin' by the time we make Gyp Springs we'll have whittled 'em down a bit," J.R. said. "Since it seems they've got men waitin', to pick us off one by one, all we've gotta do is make sure we find those men, and get to 'em first. Simple enough."

"See, Smoke. And you were worried," Jim said.

"Not worried, just wonderin' what your plans were," Smoky answered.

"I know one thing for certain," Charlie said. "They might get me, but before they do, I'm gonna make sure that Emerson Cannon hombre's dead. He ain't ever gonna do to another woman what he did to my Mary Jane."

"You might want to . . . Charlie!" Whatever Ty started to say was cut short, as he shoved Charlie off of Splash, then grabbed his rifle and rolled out of his saddle. A bullet split the air where Charlie's chest had just been. Ty leveled his rifle, took hasty aim, and pulled the trigger. A man half-rose from a cluster of rocks, dropped his rifle, clutched his chest, and pitched to his face.

"Got him," Ty muttered.

"Thanks, pard," Charlie said. "Reckon you saved my hide. How'd you spot that bush-whacker?"

"I saw the sun flash off his rifle barrel," Ty answered.

"See, Smoke," Jim said. "Now they're down to seventeen. We're cuttin' the odds already."

"Yeah, but a fog seems to be rollin' in," Smoky said. "That'll make it even harder to find those hombres, especially if they're wearin' those white robes."

Indeed, the clear sky had clouded over, and mist was beginning to swirl through the canyons and draws.

"It's also gonna make us harder to spot," Jim said. "And I don't think they'll be wearin' those outfits. Their days as the Ghost Riders are done, whether or not we finish 'em off today. They know that. All they want to do is get us off their tails, then make it outta Texas."

"Jim, when we reach Gyp Springs, I'd recommend we scatter," J.R. suggested. "If we ride in as a bunch, we'll be sittin' ducks. But, if we scatter, a couple of us can draw their fire. With luck, that should bring the others out into the open, or at least where we can spot 'em."

"That's as good an idea as any," Jim agreed. "You and I'll ride on ahead. The rest of you, cover us. Once the shootin' starts, don't quit until every last one of those Ghost Riders is dead, or has given up, which I doubt'll happen. Let's check our weapons now."

The weapons were checked, six-guns' cylinders spun and rifles' actions tested. Satisfied they were as prepared as possible, the Rangers rode silently toward Gyp Springs.

A quarter mile before reaching their destination, Jim and J.R. put their horses into a lope, riding out ahead of the others. When they topped the rise overlooking Gyp Springs, two shots rang out. They grabbed their Winchesters and left their saddles, Jim rolling behind a low slope, J.R. diving behind a large boulder. More bullets searched them out. One hit just alongside Jim, throwing dirt into his face. Jim rolled again, aimed at a shadowy figure, and fired. The figure screeched, dropped his gun, threw up his hands, and toppled to his side.

Across the trail, J.R.'s rifle also cracked, and another Ghost Rider went down, with Ranger lead in his chest. Then, pounding hoofbeats sounded, along with the Rebel yell, as the rest of the Rangers rode into the fray. Ghost Riders seemed to appear from behind every rock. Ty yelled when a bullet sliced across his ribs, but his return shot downed the man who'd shot him, with a bullet in the stomach.

The fog had thickened even more, the visibility now almost down to zero, making it almost impossible to tell friend from foe. When a Ghost Rider popped up fifty feet in front of him, taking aim at Jim, Smoky put a bullet in his back. The man arched, then spun, still holding his rifle. Smoky put a finishing bullet into his belly. The outlaw doubled over, and fell to his face. Ty ran up to the man and rolled him onto his back, to make certain he was dead. He had a fading, puckered scar on his left cheek. "This must be the hombre Jorgenson back in Brady hit with those hot tongs," he muttered. A bullet whined past his right ear. Ty dove to his belly, hit the ground hard, and rolled behind a rock.

Charlie was dashing blindly from rock to rock, nothing else on his mind except finding Emerson Cannon, the man who had attempted to rape his wife, and nearly succeeded. One of the Ghost Riders ran past him, not seeing him in the pea-soup fog. Charlie shot him in the back, slamming him against a rock. The man slid to the ground. Charlie ran up to him and rolled him onto his back.

"It's not Cannon," he muttered. A bullet ripped past his ear, driving him to the dirt.

Jim had dropped into a shallow arroyo, where one of the Ghost Riders had Smoky pinned down.

"Drop that gun, Mister!" he ordered. The man turned, cursing. Jim recognized him as Ike Stonefield. Both fired as one, Stonefield's bullet going wide, Jim's plowing into the outlaw's chest. Stonefield turned a half circle, then fell, dead.

"Behind you, Jim!" Smoky shouted. Jim spun. He and Smoky fired at the same time. Their bullets buried themselves in a Ghost Rider's belly. The man jackknifed to the dirt. Jim ran up to him and rolled him over.

"Trent Barclay!" he exclaimed, when he recognized the man. "You were one of this bunch?"

"Not just one of 'em," Barclay choked out in a high-pitched, scratchy voice. "Me'n Ike were the leaders of the outfit. Surprised?"

"Yeah, I have to say I am," Jim answered.

Smoky had also reached the dying man.

"That's Trent Barclay," he exclaimed.

"It sure is," Jim said.

"Trent, how'd you get mixed up with this outfit?" Smoky asked.

"Simple. I was . . . Ike Stonefield's attorney. The whole family's, for that . . . matter. Ike convinced me it'd be . . . a whole lot more . . . lucrative becomin' an outlaw, and organizin' a gang with him, than bein' a . . . lawyer. We nearly . . . pulled it off . . . too."

Blood welled from Barclay's mouth. He shuddered, then went slack.

"I reckon we'd better see if the rest of the boys need help, Smoke," Jim said. "Let's go."

The firing was growing more sporadic now. Most of the Ghost Riders lay dead or dying. Charlie was still searching, desperately, for Emerson Cannon. He finally came upon him, at the base of a red rock cliff, sheltered by a large fallen boulder.

"Cannon!" he yelled. "It's been a long trail, but I've finally got you in my gunsights. You're gonna pay for what you did to my wife back in San Leanna."

Cannon leaned from behind the rock and fired. His bullet burned across the top of Charlie's right shoulder. Charlie's return shot took Cannon in the same shoulder, but lower. Cannon staggered from behind the sheltering boulder. Before he could aim and fire, Charlie shot him right in the groin. Blood gushed from a severed artery. Cannon stubbornly attempted to raise his pistol. Charlie shot him again, in the right side of his belly. When Cannon still refused to go down, Charlie put a finishing bullet in the middle of his chest. Cannon dropped for keeps.

"It's over, Charlie," Jim said from behind him. "We've got 'em all, except for mebbe one or two. It's time to go home."

"All right, Pa," Charlie said. Jim put his arm around Charlie's shoulders. Together they walked to where the other Rangers were waiting.

"You get Cannon?" Ty asked Charlie.

"I did," Charlie confirmed. "Shot him right where I said I would. Blew the bastard's balls clean off. Just too bad he died too quick."

The rattle of horseshoes on gravel shattered the silence. Two riders burst out of the brush, and galloped down the canyon.

"Let 'em go," Jim said. "Our horses are too done in for a long chase. Those hombres'll get caught, sooner or later."

Two shots rang out.

"What was that?" Smoky asked.

"I dunno," Jim said. "And I'm too tuckered out to care."

"Here comes your answer, I'd reckon," J.R. said, as a lone horseman came into view. He held a smoking pistol in his hand.

"Andy!" Jim shouted, as the rider drew near. "What in the blue blazes are you doin' here?"

"Are you missin' a couple of Ghost Riders?" Andy Thomas answered.

"Two of 'em made a run for it, yeah," Jim admitted.

"Well, not anymore you aren't," Andy said. "They're both lyin' dead, back yonder."

"You shot 'em both?" J.R. asked.

"I sure did," Andy answered. "Plumb center."

"But I thought you said you carried that gun only for protection from varmints," Jim said.

"I do. Both two- and four-legged varmints," Andy said. "Now, before you Rangers clean up your mess, I'm gonna paint this battlefield. No one'll ever be able to question what happened to the Ghost Riders. As you'd say, Jim, bet a hat on that!"

# 16

Jim telegraphed Captain Storm from Mineral Wells what had happened to the Ghost Riders. Storm would relay word to their wives the men were safe, and would soon return home, once they stopped at Headquarters and filed their reports. An overnight train ride from Fort Worth would have Jim and his men in Austin first thing the next morning. Jim gave Charlie permission to head straight to San Leanna, to be with Mary Jane. When Ty asked to go with Charlie, Jim also allowed him to head for home. He couldn't say no to a man determined to propose to his fiancée as soon as possible.

"So, Trent Barclay, one of the most prominent attorneys in all of Texas, was behind the Ghost Riders," Storm said, once Jim had concluded his report. "Hard to believe." He shook his head.

"Ike Stonefield wanted revenge, and Barclay wanted money," Jim said. "That's a bad combination. The bartender and saddle shop owner up to Brady told us the leader of the bunch had a reedy, wheezy soundin' voice, and rode like he was crippled. Those descriptions fit Barclay. When we talked with him before he died, his voice was real scratchy. And we checked his body before we hauled him into Quitaque. He'd apparently busted his right leg somewhere, and it hadn't healed right. Left that leg a bit shorter than his other. So that tied right in with their descriptions."

"Jim's right," J.R. said. "But they're out of business, for good."

"Sadly, there'll be more just like them. It's only a matter of time," Storm said.

"Yeah, Cap'n, but I don't think there'll ever be a bunch as bad as this one," Smoky said.

"I hope you're right, Smoky," Storm answered. "Jim, you say Chuck McIlroy's gonna be all right?"

"He sure is, Cap'n," Jim answered. "Doc Souter says he'll be able to head home in another couple of weeks. He and Eddie'll be walkin' in here, lookin' for an assignment, before you know it."

"That's good news," Storm said. "That finishes our business. Get on home, and get some rest. J.R., anytime you get bored bein' a professor again, you get in touch with me. The Rangers will always have a job for you."

"I'll do that, Cap'n."

"Good. Now all of you, get out of here."

"You don't need to say that twice," Jim answered, laughing. "C'mon, men, let's go."

"Charlie!" Mary Jane exclaimed, when he walked into her room at Doctor Watson's clinic. "I didn't think you'd get home until later."

"I talked my pa into lettin' me come straight home," Charlie answered. "They didn't need me in Austin anyway, just to file a report. Pa can handle that. Let me look at you."

"No. Let *me* look at *you,*" Mary Jane answered, smiling.

"You mean . . . you can see. Doc Watson didn't . . ."

"I wanted to surprise you," Mary Jane said. "Yes, I can see."

"Mary Jane . . ."

Charlie was at a loss for words.

"You don't have to say anything, Charlie," Mary Jane said. "Just hold me."

"Sure. Sure." Charlie laid down beside her, and took her in his arms.

"You're safe now," he said, then kissed her, gently.

Exhausted, Charlie had fallen asleep, still holding Mary Jane. Now, later, they were still lying side by side.

"Charlie," she said. "Doctor Watson says I'll be going home in a week or so. Once I'm feeling well enough, I want to rebuild the store. I want to open it again, and run it. I need to do that, Charlie."

"Are you certain that's what you want?" he asked.

"I am. I need something to do while you're riding all over the state, rangering," Mary Jane answered. "And I always enjoyed working in the store."

"What about raising a family? I thought you wanted kids."

"I do, Charlie. I want lots and lots of children. But I can still raise a family and run a business at the same time. Is that all right with you?"

"Anythin' that makes you happy makes me happy," Charlie answered. "If you want to rebuild the store, we'll rebuild the store. Just as soon as we can get the money raised, and you're strong enough."

"That will be sooner than you realize," Mary Jane said.

"So will be that family," Charlie answered. "In fact, let's start workin' on that, right now."

"Charlie!"

Mary Jane's protest was cut short, by Charlie crushing his lips to hers.


"Jim, you're home, I'm home, and we're all alone at last," Julia said. "Just me, you, and that nice, big bathtub."

"And Pal," Jim answered, when Charlie's collie whined insistently for attention.

"I can get rid of him," Julia said. She unbuttoned Jim's shirt and slipped it off his shoulders.

"Go on, Pal, get the shirt," she said, as she

opened the front door, and threw the shirt outside. Pal bounded after it, grabbing it and shaking it furiously, as he disappeared behind the barn.

"My shirt!" Jim exclaimed.

"Trust me cowboy, you won't need a shirt in the tub," Julia said. She took him by the hand. "Bet your hat on it."

# About the Author

Jim Griffin became enamored of the Texas Rangers from watching the TV series, Tales of the Texas Rangers, as a youngster. He grew to be an avid student and collector of Rangers' artifacts, memorabilia and other items. His collection is now housed in the Texas Ranger Hall of Fame and Museum in Waco.

His quest for authenticity in his writing has taken him to the famous Old West towns of Pecos, Deadwood, Cheyenne, Tombstone and numerous others. While Jim's books are fiction, he strives to keep them as accurate as possible within the realm of fiction.

A graduate of Southern Connecticut State University, Jim now divides his time between Branford, Connecticut and Keene, New Hampshire when he isn't travelling around the west.

A devoted and enthusiastic horseman, Jim bought his first horse when he was a junior in college. He has owned several American Paint horses. He is a member of the Connecticut Horse Council Volunteer Horse Patrol, an organization which assists the state park Rangers with patrolling parks and forests.

Jim's books are traditional Westerns in the

best sense of the term, portraying strong heroes with good character and moral values. Highly reminiscent of the pulp westerns of yesteryear, the heroes and villains are clearly separated.

Jim was initially inspired to write at the urging of friend and author James Reasoner. After the successful publication of his first book, *Trouble Rides the Texas Pacific*, published in 2005, Jim was encouraged to continue his writing.

Books are
produced in the
United States
using U.S.-based
materials

Books are printed
using a revolutionary
new process called
THINKtech™ that
lowers energy usage
by 70% and increases
overall quality

Books are
durable and
flexible
because of
Smyth-sewing

Paper is
sourced using
environmentally
responsible
foresting methods
and the
paper is acid-free

**Center Point Large Print**
600 Brooks Road / PO Box 1
Thorndike, ME 04986-0001 USA

**(207) 568-3717**

**US & Canada:**
**1 800 929-9108**
**www.centerpointlargeprint.com**